B.J. DANIELS

"Daniels is truly an expert
at Western romantic suspense."
—*RT Book Reviews* on *Atonement*

"Will keep readers on the edge of their chairs
from beginning to end."
—*Booklist* on *Forsaken*

"Action-packed and chock-full of suspense."
—*Under the Covers* on *Redemption*

"Fans of Western romantic suspense
will relish Daniels' tale of clandestine love
played out in a small town on the Great Plains."
—*Booklist* on *Unforgiven*

B.J. DANIELS

MERCY

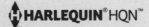
HARLEQUIN® HQN™

Recycling programs
for this product may
not exist in your area.

ISBN-13: 978-0-373-77895-9

Mercy

Copyright © 2014 by Barbara Heinlein

This edition published by arrangement with Harlequin Books S.A.

For questions and comments about the quality of this book, please contact us at CustomerService@Harlequin.com.

Printed in U.S.A.

www.Harlequin.com

I joke that this book tried to kill me. I realize now that the ones that really grab me are the ones that I struggle with and end up loving the most. This one grabbed me and wouldn't let go. So this book is dedicated to the man who saw me through it, even the three a.m. trip to the hospital with my first migraine.

To my husband, Parker, who takes good care of me so I can just write. I couldn't be more grateful for your loving support or the wonderful meals you cook me or the patience you have deadline after deadline. I couldn't do this without you. I love you.

CHAPTER ONE

SWEAT BEADED HIS forehead and upper lip. He tried to catch his breath, but it was impossible with the gag. It stuck to his dry tongue and cut into one corner of his mouth as he'd attempted to cry out for help. The blindfold kept him from knowing what time of day it was. He kicked, but his legs had tangled in the sweat-drenched sheets. His wrists, still bound to the headboard, were chafed raw, his aching arms numb where the restraints bit into his flesh.

He didn't know how long he'd been like this. The last thing he remembered was having sex and then asking the woman to leave. It had been a mistake picking her up at the bar and bringing her home in the first place.

After that, he must have fallen asleep. He'd awakened in a panic to find himself gagged, blindfolded and bound to the bed. That had to have been hours ago, but he had no concept of time.

He'd tried everything to free himself. But the way he was trussed up, nothing worked.

How long before someone would find him like this? At first all he could think about was the embarrassment. Now he prayed for anyone to stop by, knowing how remote a chance that would be. No one would even realize they hadn't seen him for days since he'd taken off for a short vacation.

Anxiety filled him, making him fear he was losing his mind. This wasn't happening. He couldn't seem to catch his breath. His chest rose and fell, faster and faster.

A sound made him stop struggling. He held his heaving breath. Had he only imagined someone in the room?

A floorboard creaked. She'd come back. Of course she had. She couldn't leave him like this. This was some kind of sick joke. Something straight out of a horror movie.

It had been his first night of vacation, so he'd thought, why not have a little fun? Maybe he should have been nicer once the fun was over. Too late to worry about that now, though. Once she cut his restraints, she would regret ever pulling this stunt on him.

He tried to remember her name. Something that started with a *C*. Candy. Cara. Catherine. Cassie. He tried to say Cassie around the gag. It came out unintelligible.

A thought suddenly struck him. It *was* her in the room, wasn't it? Who else? But now he wasn't so sure.

He felt someone move closer. He could hear breathing next to his bed. He thrashed against his bonds, moaning in both pain and terror.

A harsh whisper next to his ear silenced him. It was her all right. He remembered that voice. But at first he thought he'd heard her wrong. Then she repeated the same three words.

"Beg for mercy."

The gag muffled his screams as he felt the first slice of the knife.

CHAPTER TWO

I<small>T HAD SURPRISED</small> Laura Fuller when he'd called. Something odd in his voice. That and the fact that she hadn't heard from him in months. It made her anxious. As she stepped into the small restaurant off Pioneer Square in downtown Seattle, she stopped to scan the place. Maybe it was the cop in her, but she couldn't help feeling on guard as she spotted him.

He looked good. That thought made her smile to herself. Rourke Kincaid always looked good, all six foot four of him. He had classic dark looks that were almost as amazing as the rich depths of his eyes. If he wasn't usually so serious, he would have been sinfully gorgeous. Women always noticed him. He, on the other hand… Did he notice other women? Or was Laura's former partner just unaware of *her* as a woman?

As she let the door close behind her and moved in his direction, she thought he looked a little pale. The lines around those dark eyes a little more defined. She thought of the first time she'd seen him as she limped toward his table. She had detested the idea of working with someone who looked like him because she'd thought he wouldn't take the job seriously. She'd thought he was a womanizer, one of those men who had to have the attention of every woman around him. She couldn't have been more wrong.

Rourke, like her, had been interested in only his job. At least that was how it had been back then.

As Laura drew closer, she saw that all his attention was on the papers he had spread on the table. But when he saw her, he hurriedly tucked them back into the folder and set it on the chair next to him.

He'd brought some case he was working on. Of course that was why he'd called her. It was the only reason he had ever called her, except for the few times to see how she was doing after she'd gotten out of the hospital.

He rose now, hastily getting to his feet. His expression brightened, and he flashed her one of his disarming smiles. Even after bracing herself against it, her heart kicked into gear, all those old feelings rushing at her.

"Laura." He took both her hands in his large, warm ones and brushed a kiss across her cheek. She noticed then that he wasn't wearing his U.S. Marshals uniform. Maybe it was his day off. But then, Rourke never really took a day off, especially when he was deep in a case.

To a bystander, he probably looked relaxed in a pair of worn jeans, equally worn boots and a blue chambray button-up shirt, and yet she could tell he was anxious. His Stetson was on the seat with the folder he'd brought. You could take the cowboy out of Wyoming, but you couldn't take the cowboy out of him, she thought.

"How are you?" he asked, genuine concern in his voice. She knew then that he'd seen her limp, even though she'd tried so hard to hide how bad it was. Rourke missed little. It was what had made him such a good homicide detective and now criminal investigator.

"I'm fine," she said automatically. "How about you?"

"Me?" He seemed surprised by the question as he stepped around the table to pull out her chair. It was such a gentlemanly thing to do that she couldn't help but smile. A year ago he wouldn't have touched her chair. She wouldn't have let him because they'd been equals back then. But a lot had changed in a year, hadn't it?

She sat and watched him move back around to his own chair. "What's wrong?" she asked as she got a closer look at him.

He blinked. "Can't I ask my former Seattle P.D. partner to lunch without you thinking—"

"Rourke," she said with a shake of her head as he lowered himself into his chair.

He laughed, his dark gaze meeting hers as he stretched out his long legs. "I forget how well you know me." His look alone made her pulse purr just under her skin. How long had she been in love with this man? Too long.

"Tell me what I'm doing here besides having lunch?" she said, needing to clarify for herself what this meeting would cover. She knew what she'd hoped it was about, but clearly she'd been kidding herself.

"I'm sure you heard about what happened six months ago," he said, dropping his voice.

Law enforcement was a tight-knit community. Even if she was no longer one of the gang, she still heard things. Rourke had risen so quickly in his field that she knew there were some who'd enjoyed his fall from grace.

Six months ago he hadn't waited for backup even though he'd been ordered to do so. The bust had gone badly, a civilian was shot and almost died, and Rourke was reprimanded and pulled off active duty.

She picked up her napkin, unfolded it carefully and laid it across her lap before she spoke. "You have always followed your intuition. It's what made you such a good homicide detective. Now as a U.S. marshal, well, I would expect you to continue doing what you do best. I would still trust you with my life." When she looked up, she saw the shine of his eyes and felt a lump form in her throat. Was it possible he missed her as much as she'd missed him?

"You were the best partner I ever had," he said, emotion making his deep voice even deeper. "Sometimes I miss the Seattle P.D." His gaze narrowed as he studied her. "If I could go back to that night—"

"I've put that part of my life behind me." Laura couldn't find words to describe how much she missed it. But not for the reason Rourke Kincaid thought. Even if they could change what had happened that night a year ago, she doubted he would still be with the Seattle P.D. Even back then, she'd known he wouldn't stay in Homicide long. He was destined to greater things.

"Want a drink before we eat?" He didn't wait for an answer before signaling the waitress. "The usual?" he said to Laura with a grin. "Scotch on the rocks for my friend. Nothing for me."

"You're not joining me?" she asked as the waitress left. "I just assumed you were off duty."

"Off duty." He chuckled at that. "Today is my first day of my latest suspension. My boss suggested I take two weeks to reevaluate my career choices."

She reached across the table and touched his hand. "I'm sorry."

"He's probably right. I'm not sure I'm cut out for taking orders. Nor am I so sure I can still trust my instincts." He took a sip of his water and waited as the waitress returned to place the drink in front of her. "We should probably order. Two cheeseburgers and fries?" he asked, smiling at her again.

Laura nodded even though she didn't eat like that anymore. Couldn't. Being on the force, she had worked out all the time, kept active and could eat anything she wanted and did. Now…well, now things were different.

Once the waitress left again, he said, "Six months ago, I was put on cold cases down in the basement." He nodded. "I know. I was lucky they didn't send me packing."

"I'm sure you'll be back on fieldwork soon. Rourke, you're too good to leave you stuck away much longer. If you can just hang in—"

He shook his head. "Surprisingly that's not the problem. They've reinstated me for fieldwork. They want me back on the job."

Frowning, she said, "Then I guess I don't understand."

"I found something in an old case file. Something I want to chase."

This was the Rourke she knew so well. Once he got on the scent, he couldn't let up until he caught what he was chasing. Wasn't that why he'd ended up in the basement with the cold cases?

"I've been ordered to assist with an asset seizure on a drug case that any fool can handle."

She stared at him. "This is why you invited me to

lunch. You want me to talk you out of whatever it is you're thinking of doing?" She shook her head, seeing her error as she studied his face. "No, you want me to *encourage* you to chase it."

Laura couldn't help being touched that her opinion meant that much, while at the same time, it really wouldn't matter what she said. She was sure his mind was already made up. He just wanted that little push and from who better than his old partner?

Her gaze shifted to the file he'd placed on the seat of the chair next to him. What had he found that would make him risk his career over it? "So, let's see it."

"Maybe we should eat—"

Laura rolled her eyes. "You didn't get me down here for the burgers or the Scotch. Let's see what you've got."

He gave her a sheepish grin as he reached for the file folder. "I found something—some old photographs," he said with an excitement that would have been contagious when they'd worked together. He opened the folder and leaned toward her. She caught a whiff of his oh, so familiar aftershave. Her pulse thrummed. She loved seeing Rourke like this.

ROURKE FELT EVEN more anxious as he pulled out the photographs. He trusted Laura's judgment. Now he worried that she'd tell him he was wrong, that he'd lost his edge. That he was about to make yet another mistake. Only this one would cost him his career and for nothing.

He slid the photographs from the folder and reached into his jacket pocket for the magnifying glass he'd brought. The photos were all of a group of onlookers standing behind yellow crime-scene tape. As he started to hand over the shots, his eye went to the one face, a face he hadn't been able to forget from the first time he'd seen the young woman—and realized that he'd seen her somewhere before.

Laura took the three photographs and the magnifying glass. "What am I looking for?"

He didn't answer as he watched her scan one photo, then another until she had looked at all three.

She frowned and studied each again, more slowly this time. "These are from three different crime scenes."

He smiled. He'd been right to bring this to her. He just hoped she saw what he had—that *one* face in the crowd. What Laura might have lacked in polish as a homicide detective, she more than made up for in street sense and down-to-earth logic. She didn't jump to conclusions. She took in information, digested it, considered and then assessed the situation with almost a coldhearted clarity.

Rourke had always trusted her judgment because of it. Not that he'd been happy at first about being part-nered with a woman when he'd joined the Seattle P.D. Like a lot of other men, he'd been biased, believing that when the cards were down, even a good woman cop would be weaker than a man or may become emotional and be a liability.

He could laugh about that misconception now. Laura Fuller was tougher, more capable and less emotional in a tight spot than a lot of male cops he'd known. As he had in the past, he wondered now how she'd been raised. She'd never talked about growing up, but at first he'd suspected, because of how tough she was, that she might have been the only girl in a houseful of brothers.

She'd never seemed to want to talk about what she off-handedly called her boring childhood, but then she'd mentioned once that she had a sister. He'd gotten the impression that the sister was her only family and that they weren't close.

As inseparable as he and Laura had been in the past, he realized that he didn't really know her. His fault, since all his focus had been on his career for as far back as he could remember.

The waiting now, though, was killing him.

He started to say something when Laura hesitated on a corner of a photo where a dark-haired young woman stood just beyond the crime-scene tape. He watched Laura spread the three photos on the table, going from one to the next. He could feel the change in her. She'd seen it!

His relief was almost palpable. He couldn't help the surge of adrenaline that shot through him. If Laura saw it, then he had to be right. He was onto something.

"It's the same woman, isn't it?" he said, no longer able to contain himself.

As Laura studied the woman in the three photos, she unconsciously pushed a lock of her blond shoulder-length hair back behind one ear. He realized that she'd let her hair grow out since he'd last seen her and felt a wave of guilt. After she'd been shot and left the Seattle P.D., he'd checked on her often during the first few months. But since taking the job with the U.S. Marshals, he had gotten so busy he couldn't remember the last time he'd called her.

She handed back the magnifying glass. "Three different neighborhoods? Three different homicides?"

Rourke nodded.

"And these are the best shots you have of her?"

"Unfortunately. But she's the key to those three murders. I can feel it."

"She might just be a murder junkie. Probably has a scanner next to her bed and responds whenever she hears the call." Laura shrugged and pushed the photos back toward him. "Have you been able to identify her?"

"Not yet. I've hired a private investigator to canvass the neighborhoods where the murders were committed."

She raised a brow in surprise as she realized he had been working outside the U.S. Marshals Service and apparently for some time. "Aren't you taking this a little too personally?"

He'd already gone rogue, and now she knew it. "I just have a feeling about this one. I can't let it go." He looked down at the photos spread on the table, his eye going to the dark-haired woman. Her face had been haunting him for weeks. When he closed his eyes at night…

She shook her head. "What are you doing, Rourke?"

He could hear the skepticism in her voice. He wished now that he'd ordered a drink. He could use it. Laura thought he was looking for a lead where there wasn't one. Unfortunately, his boss thought the same thing.

He'd never been plagued with self-doubt when it came to his instincts. But after almost costing a man his life…

"Rourke, what am I really doing here?" Laura asked.

"I NEED YOUR HELP," Rourke said, leaning toward her conspiratorially. "I remembered that your background was psychology and criminology. Did I hear correctly that you're doing freelance profiling for the Seattle P.D.?"

Laura shouldn't have been surprised that he knew this, but she was. Just as she shouldn't have been disappointed that he'd asked her to dinner because he wanted her help on a case.

"I need to know about this woman and the kind of man who would be in her life," he said.

"Based on three photos?" she asked, thinking he must be kidding.

"This woman is the connection between the three different crime scenes, but I think there's more. I think she's working with a serial killer."

Laura leaned back in her chair in surprise. She studied him for a moment before she looked at the photographs again. She tried to imagine why this woman was at three separate crime scenes in three separate neighborhoods. It could be as simple as morbid curiosity. Or not.

Profiling was a science based on statistics compiled of criminals. Depending on the type of murder, she could paint a fairly accurate picture of the killer once she had all the information. Or, if Rourke was right about the woman, in this case, co-killer.

Of course, it was much more likely that this woman could be just as Laura had said before, someone with a scanner who lived such a dull life that going to crime scenes was her only source of entertainment.

Had it not been Rourke, she would have dismissed this without a thought. But she'd learned a long time ago to trust him. If he felt he had to chase this, even jeopardize his job to do so, then she had to take it seriously.

She motioned for the magnifying glass again. What was funny was that when she'd first noticed the woman, she'd thought she recognized her. Something about the woman's face… But when she studied the features, she decided the woman merely had one of those sweet, innocent-looking faces. That didn't make Laura hate her any less.

She knew it was crazy to be jealous of a woman in a crime-scene photo who was possibly involved in at least three murders. But she could see that no woman had ever captivated Rourke like this one had. He couldn't seem to keep his eyes off her in the photo.

Laura figured he'd be disappointed when he finally came face-to-face with her. That was if he could find her—and didn't get himself killed in the process.

Pushing the photos away, she was torn between laughter and tears when she thought how excited she'd been after Rourke's call. What a fool she'd been, taking forever to get dressed. She'd even put on a little makeup, not that Rourke had noticed. And while she was touched that he'd called her to help with this, she wanted him to see *her*. Not the former cop. Not the former homicide partner. For once, she just wanted him to look at her and see the *woman*.

"So, what are you planning to do?" she asked, already knowing the answer.

"Laura, I can't get these three cold cases out of my mind. I have no choice but to try to find this woman. I know you think I'm a fool to chase this."

She sighed, seeing *his* disappointment. He'd hoped she would jump on board just like in the old days when he'd bent the rules and she had gone along with it. But the last time she'd bent the rules, she was almost killed.

Her world, as she had known it, ended the day she was shot. She still had the scars, both inside and out.

Now, sitting here with him, she found herself battling a growing anger, more at herself than at him. Not that she thought it made any difference. Picking up her glass, she took a sip of her Scotch, hoping the alcohol would steady her.

"I've got two weeks," he said, oblivious to her mounting resentment. "Once I get this woman's name—"

"You're really going to risk throwing away your career for some questionable lead in some old cold cases?"

He waved a hand through the air. "You know the 'career' part is the least of it for me. Sure, I love what I do and have worked hard to get where I am, but what is the point if I can't chase a case that's gotten into my blood?"

Her blood was on fire now. She could feel it flush her cheeks as she took another drink. The Scotch was like throwing gasoline on a blaze. "You don't *care* about a career I would give my left leg for?" She let out a bark of a laugh, trying to keep her voice down when she was raging inside. "Oh, that's right—I *lost* my career because of my left leg. Shot in the line of duty. Bang. Career over and you…" She lifted her nearly empty Scotch glass, suddenly at a loss for words. Tears welled and spilled. She wiped furiously at them. She'd promised herself she wouldn't let him see how messed up she was or how deep her hurt ran.

Rourke looked shocked as he reached for her. "Laura, I'm so sorry."

She shook off the hand he placed on her arm. He motioned to the waitress to bring her another drink.

That was *all* she needed. Didn't he realize how close she was to telling him not only how she felt about the loss of her career but also how she felt about him?

"You're going to do it—jeopardize everything." Her chest ached with unshed tears. "Why would you do this?" Because of the woman in the photo. Something about that face had gotten to him.

Rourke looked distressed that he'd upset her, but also shocked. "I'm doing this because of you, Laura. I wanted to do this for you, and once I found the lead…"

She stared at him. *"What are you talking about?"*

"The third murder case? It was yours before you and I became partners."

"I wasn't on Homicide until—"

"No, you were still a street cop, but I saw your notes on this case in the original file. You were *there,* Laura. *You* took these photographs."

She shook her head, telling herself this couldn't be true, but an inkling of a memory fought to surface. Was that why she'd thought she recognized the woman in the crowd, because she'd taken her photo?

"I know it sounds crazy," Rourke continued, "but it's the reason I first got involved in this case. I saw your notes, and I wanted to solve it for *you.* Then, when I found the other two similar murders from the area and the same woman in all of the shots…"

All the fire in her blew out as if doused by a bucket of ice water. For a moment, she couldn't breathe. This was the Rourke she knew and loved. And wanting to solve this case because of her… Well, this was as romantic as Rourke Kincaid got. At least with her.

As the waitress arrived with their burgers, Rourke quickly pocketed the magnifying glass and slid the photos back into the folder, dropping it again on the seat next to him. The waitress exchanged her empty Scotch glass for a full one.

Laura picked it up, closed her eyes and took a gulp of the icy cold booze.

She couldn't believe this. He'd gotten involved in the case because of her. But it was the woman in the photograph who had him about to commit career suicide.

Even with her eyes closed, she could see the image of the dark-haired young woman with the angelic face standing behind the crime-scene tape. Rourke wouldn't be the only one haunted by the woman now.

CHAPTER THREE

ROURKE MENTALLY KICKED HIMSELF. What the hell had he been thinking, going to Laura about this?

Had he thought she might want to help him by living vicariously while he solved this one? He'd been more than insensitive, but then again, Laura had also changed. He'd never seen her in tears before—even the night she was shot.

Her wounds had been nearly fatal, but she'd recovered—all except for her left leg. Like him, though, she wasn't built for a desk job, so he was glad she had gotten into the profiling field. He thought she'd be damned good at it. Which was another reason he'd asked her to dinner.

He'd foolishly assumed, though, that the old Laura, the one who felt like an equal, would show up. This Laura… Well, she was more fragile. He should have realized that would be the case.

They ate their meals, him changing the subject to the weather. It didn't always rain in Seattle, but still, there wasn't that much to say.

"Is your food okay?" he asked, noticing that she'd barely touched hers. That wasn't like her either. One of the things he'd always loved about her when they were partners was that she liked to eat as much as he did. Seattle offered every kind of fare there was, and the two of them had consumed their share.

"I had to quit eating like I used to," she said, spearing a French fry and taking a small bite.

How had he not noticed that, along with the change in hairstyle, she'd also dropped the weight she'd gained after the shooting? Laura was an attractive woman, not classically beautiful, but striking. At five-eight, she looked strong, as if she'd been working out in spite of her leg. She'd been a blonde for as long as he'd known her, and yet her coloring seemed wrong for the pale shade, making him wonder what her natural color was. Something else he hadn't noticed until now.

"You look great," he said, again reminded of how little he really knew about his former partner, when she seemed to know him so well.

She smiled as if she knew he hadn't really looked at her until that moment.

"So, you're doing okay?" he asked, worried about her.

Laura was his age: thirty-six. It surprised him that she'd never married again. She'd apparently been married for a short time before he'd met her to a man named Mike Fuller. She never talked about it. Nor did she date much, seeming more interested in her career.

He wondered if there was a man in her life, now that, thanks to the shooting, she didn't have such a demanding career. In the old days, he might have asked. But a lot had changed since those days, and he didn't feel close enough to question her about her love life.

"I was glad when I heard you were finishing up your studies to be a profiler," he finally ventured. "Laura, I know you'll be a great one."

She shrugged, looking uncomfortable. "I started doing some studying on my own while I was laid up and realized it might be something I was good at." She met his gaze. "I can help you with this case, if you'll let me." She raised a hand before he could say he'd changed his mind and wasn't sure it was a good idea. "If I could talk you out of this, I would. But since we both know I can't…"

This was what he'd hoped she would say. If he hoped to solve these murder cases, he could use her help since all of the resources of the U.S. Marshals' office were off-limits during his suspension. While he thought profiling could be useful, he knew it was good old-fashioned investigative work that usually solved crimes. But he wanted Laura on his team.

The truth was that he needed her for more than profiling. Lately, he'd been second-guessing himself, no longer sure he should trust his own judgment. He needed Laura's analytical mind. "I—" But he didn't get a chance to finish whatever he was going to say.

His cell phone rang, and when he checked it, he said, "Sorry, I have to take this. It's the P.I. I hired." He stepped away, relieved for the call as he hurried outside. Laura seemed so fragile right now. Even though he needed her help, did he dare involve her in this?

Outside the café, it had begun to drizzle, the sky a dull gray wash as everything quickly became slick with rain. Seattle had a fairly high suicide rate. He'd never felt that internal darkness as much as he did now, standing under the awning of the restaurant.

"I found something," Edwin Sharp said without preamble. "I think it could be who you're looking for. A landlady identified the woman in the photo as Callie Westfield. She worked as a waitress at a café in the neighborhood. The owner of the café required her driver's license when she started work, so I was able to get a copy. Her full name is Caligrace Westfield. I ran her through the system. I couldn't find a residential address, but I do have an address where she is currently employed."

Rourke pulled out his notebook and pen.

"She's working as a waitress at the Branding Iron Café in Beartooth, Montana."

LAURA FELT SICK to her stomach as she left the restaurant. She'd been too upset to eat, but she'd forced herself to consume as much of her meal as she could. Rourke had felt bad enough, without her making him feel worse.

As astute as the man was when it came to solving crimes, he seldom saw what was right in front of his face. Rourke didn't have a clue when it came to her. He'd really believed that missing her old job in law enforcement was the reason she was upset. How could he not know that she'd been in love with him almost from the start?

"It's you, Rourke!" she had wanted to scream. "I miss *you!* I miss the damned force, but it's because I miss talking to you every day!" Even if it had been about only their latest cases. "I miss being *with* you." Days off used to be hell. She couldn't wait to get back to work. Back to Rourke.

Like him, she'd been on the fast track, moving quickly from a Seattle P.D. officer to Homicide. The sky had been the limit for both of them. They had been called the Dream Team. She could laugh about it now, but back then, she was sure everyone thought she and Rourke were sleeping together. They were that compatible. They could finish each other's sentences. They were that close. So no wonder they had worked so well together.

And they *were* good. Between the two of them, they solved cases. Their futures were so bright, they felt like rock stars, she thought bitterly.

Then that night in the alley… She'd gone in alone even though Rourke had told her to wait. He'd had one of the felons on the ground, restraining the man with cuffs. But she didn't want to wait. She'd felt a singing in her blood. A feeling that she was invincible. She'd gone down the alley not realizing the man was trapped at the end, hunkered down, shot full of drugs, a loaded gun in his hand and his finger on the trigger.

Reaching her car now, she climbed in, her leg aching from either the short walk to her parking spot—or the memory of that night and the impact of the bullet as it struck the bone.

Everyone told her that she was lucky to be alive. *Lucky.* Sick to her stomach now, heart aching and her mind racing, she didn't feel lucky at all. She felt scared.

Rourke thought he was chasing a serial killer and was now headed for some town in Montana called Beartooth. He had been quiet after his phone call, and she'd had to drag what little she could out of him. Clearly, he'd changed his mind about involving her, but she wasn't having any of that. She'd prove to him that he needed her help. She'd put her personal feelings aside and be the cop he needed her to be.

"So, what's her name?" she'd asked, hating that he'd wanted to close her out.

"This whole thing could blow up in my face. I shouldn't have involved you."

She'd given him a sideways look. "But you *did* involve me, and now you're stuck with me. I can tell that you have more than just her location. What's her name?"

He'd relented as she'd known he would. He wouldn't have brought her the photos if he hadn't really wanted her help—needed her help. It was that thought that had made the rest of the dinner bearable.

"Caligrace Westfield."

Her fingers trembled now as she put the key into the ignition. As far as she knew, she'd never heard the name before and yet…

She was anxious to get home, even though Rourke had wanted to put her in a taxi. She'd pointed out that she hadn't finished her second Scotch and was fine to drive. She was still shaken, blaming it on the fact that she'd gotten her hopes up that the dinner was going to be more than it was.

There was another reason she felt the need to get home quickly. She couldn't wait to get her hands on her files. From the time she'd started with the Seattle P.D., she had copied all of her notes on the cases she'd worked on and photocopied everything in the files, including making duplicate photos. She didn't care that it was against protocol. She liked to look at them, study them, see what she could have done differently. See what she might have missed.

If this cold case of Rourke's really was one she'd worked on—even as a street cop taking photos of the looky-loos behind the crime-scene tape—well, then she would have all the information in her files at home.

The engine turned over. Shifting into Drive, she pulled out without looking. A car horn blared. She slammed on her brakes. The driver of the vehicle swerved around her, barely missing her. Anywhere else but Seattle and the driver would have given her the finger.

Shaken, she looked back to see a second car. This driver had managed to stop in time. The driver impatiently motioned for her to go. She smiled a thank-you back at him and, her heart hammering, pulled out into traffic.

Fortunately, her apartment wasn't far from downtown Seattle. She navigated the half dozen blocks, concentrating on her driving, still upset from her near accident.

As she pulled into her parking garage and shut off the engine, she tried to calm down. But it was useless. Seeing Rourke again had stirred up a cauldron of emotions that now roiled inside her. Loving Rourke hurt and always had, but she'd thought she had learned to live with it.

Today she'd realized how wrong she was. She smacked the steering wheel with her palm, hating him and the spell some woman in a photo had cast on him. She couldn't let him jeopardize his career, not for some old cold case. Maybe especially for one he said he was doing for her. But even at that thought, she knew she couldn't stop him.

The parking garage seemed to close in around her. She *had* been getting better. Her psychiatrist had said during her last appointment that he was pleased with the progress she'd made.

"I still get scared sometimes," she'd admitted. "But I'm not so afraid when I leave my apartment now. I still check the backseat of my car. Not as often as I used to, though."

He'd nodded sagely. "It's wise to be aware of your surroundings, living in a city. You're getting out more, then?"

"I'm shopping for my own groceries again and going to lunch occasionally with friends." The last part wasn't exactly true. She'd never had a lot of friends. But, unlike some people, she didn't mind eating alone.

The doctor had studied her openly. "You seem better. Do you *feel* better?"

She had.

Now, though, she couldn't catch her breath. She listened for the sound of footfalls in the cool dimness of the garage, suddenly afraid she was no longer alone. Logically, she knew there probably wasn't anyone crouched in a dark corner of the garage, waiting for her. Just as she had known there probably wasn't a boogeyman hiding under her bed when she was a child.

But once a boogeyman crawled out from under your bed in the middle of the night... Well, from then on you knew that he could be waiting for you in any dark corner—or dark alley.

For a while, she'd thought her badge and gun were like a powerful shield that would protect her. She'd let herself believe that she'd conquered her fears, that nothing could ever hurt her again as long as Rourke was by her side. He'd made her feel powerful and immortal, when in truth, she was that little girl cowering in the corner of her bed as the boogeyman loomed over her.

Laura let out a sob as she searched the dark recesses of the garage, then hurriedly opened her door and fled to the elevator. She punched the up button, hammering at it, before she dared look behind her. There were street traffic sounds beyond the garage, but no closer, more ominous sounds of footfalls coming from the dark shadowed corners of the garage—at least none she could hear over the pounding of her heart.

She turned back to the elevator, leaning on the button again. She heard the elevator car groan from somewhere inside the building. Her every instinct told her to take the stairs. *Now!* But with her leg...

The elevator opened noisily, the yawning doors revealing no one inside. She practically threw herself in, hit the ninth-floor button and punched Close a half dozen times before the doors slowly closed.

The breath she'd been holding rushed from her. Tears burned her cheeks. She leaned against the elevator wall for support. She *wasn't* better.

CHAPTER FOUR

WITH NO TIME to spare, Rourke had flown into the Gallatin Valley near Bozeman, Montana, the next morning, rented an SUV and driven to Big Timber, following a map he'd printed out on the internet. Beartooth proved to be another twenty miles on two-lane blacktop toward snowcapped peaks, which, according to a sign beside the road, were the Crazy Mountains.

The town, if you could call it that, came as a shock even though he'd done a little research on it while waiting for his flight. Beartooth was what was left of a once-thriving mining town back in the late 1890s. All that had survived, other than some old stone buildings, was a café, post office and bar. Apparently, there had been a general store across from the café, but it had burned down last spring.

Thanks to the internet, he'd found a cabin to rent on the mountainside across the road from the café. He could see the cabin through the trees as he pulled into a spot in front of the café. He'd thought about stopping by the cabin first, but he was too anxious to see Caligrace Westfield.

The Branding Iron Café was easy to find, given how few businesses were left in Beartooth. As he climbed out of the SUV, he tried not to get his hopes up. The P.I. had told him that Caligrace Westfield had changed jobs and residences often over the past ten years. For all Rourke knew, she might have already moved on.

A bell tinkled over the door as he stepped into the café and was hit with the combined smells of cinnamon, bacon and coffee. He breathed in, his stomach growling, reminding him that he hadn't had much to eat. He'd been too anxious. Just as he was now. Anxious and nervous at the thought of finally seeing the woman face-to-face.

He took in his surroundings quickly. A variety of brightly colored quilts hung on the café's walls. He'd expected a more Western interior, given where the town was located—in the heart of ranching and farming communities.

There were only a half dozen tables arranged at the front of the café, with four booths along one side and a counter back by the kitchen with a half dozen stools. One large table at the front was full of ranchers he took for regulars.

"Sit wherever you like," a young woman called over her shoulder without looking in his direction.

He chose a table at the front of the café that gave him a view of the whole place. He could even see into the kitchen via the pass-through on the other side of the counter. A thin, pale man—in his fifties, he guessed—was busy cooking to the distant drone of a song on the radio.

The waitress who'd told him to seat himself stood at the pass-through, her back to him. Her long, curly dark hair was pulled into a knot of sorts at the nape of her neck. Loose strands hung at her temples.

Rourke waited impatiently for the woman to turn around, thinking about the latest information from the P.I. he'd hired. Edwin Sharp, a seasoned private investigator who used to be a cop, was in his sixties. Rourke had liked him the first time he'd met him. He needed someone he trusted, and since he couldn't do his own digging without making his situation with the marshals' office worse, he'd hired the man.

"I found *something*," Edwin had said cryptically when he'd called on Rourke's journey to Beartooth. "Your...mystery woman didn't exist until her seventeenth birthday, when she used a fake birth certificate to get her driver's license and a social-security card."

"How do you know the birth certificate is fake?"

"She wasn't born at the hospital on the certificate because it doesn't exist—never has."

"Is anything on the birth certificate real?"

"Doubtful."

"What about the address?"

"Well, that's where it gets interesting. The address is Westfield Manor."

Rourke frowned. "An old folks' home?"

The P.I. laughed. "I have no idea. But apparently, it is in Flat Rock, Montana, about four hours north of Beartooth, where she is now living."

"How soon can you get to Flat Rock?"

"I would have to fly." Edwin had told him he didn't like flying and charged extra if he had to.

"*Fly.* Call me when you know something."

Now Rourke waited, willing the woman in the café to turn so he could see her face. She looked about the right height. Maybe slimmer than he'd guessed Caligrace Westfield would be and in better shape. But then again, he was going by a police shot at a crime scene and that one face in the crowd.

She finally turned.

He caught his breath as he got his first good look at the woman who had haunted him for weeks.

FOR CALIGRACE—"CALLIE"—Westfield, it was just another day slinging hash at the Branding Iron Café in Beartooth. She moved through the restaurant with plates of food and pots of coffee. After a year here, she knew most everyone's story.

This morning the information came as it always did: in short psychic bursts. The young ranch hand at the first table was hungover and worried he might lose his job. The young mother who'd asked for a high chair was concerned because her husband didn't spend much time with her and the baby anymore. The old rancher was anxiously awaiting the results of his wife's biopsy.

Callie had experienced this phenomenon on some level from as far back as she could remember. Since she didn't want to know any of it, she thought of the constant influx of information as white noise. She'd learned the hard way that she couldn't take on everyone's troubles, so she tried to tune it out as best she could. That should have made it easier to live with, but it often didn't.

The café wasn't particularly busy this morning— just the usual crowd who couldn't resist Kate French's cinnamon rolls warm from the oven. The smell of cinnamon, frying bacon and fresh coffee filled the air. Callie had found all of it comforting over the past year.

She had just finished refilling cups with coffee at the large table at the front of the café where a group of older ranchers met each morning, when she got her first good look at the cowboy who'd come in. She'd felt him staring at her, but hadn't thought anything of it. She was used to men noticing her. This cowboy was different, though.

His look, as she approached his table, was speculative. Not as if he was wondering whether or not she would sleep with him if he asked her out. No, this was more of a rapt interest that sent a chill up her spine and made her hand holding the pot of coffee unsteady.

He was dressed like the others who came into the Branding Iron. Jeans, boots, Western shirt, all worn enough that he almost blended in. His tan Stetson rested on his sheepskin coat on the chair next to him. There was nothing about the tall, dark cowboy that should have set off warning bells since he looked like the real thing. But her instincts told her he wasn't just another cowhand.

"Coffee?" she asked as she reached his table.

"Thanks." His voice was deep, a rumble to it that seemed to reverberate in her chest, making her heart kick up another beat or two.

Her gaze rose of its own accord. The moment she met his dark eyes, she regretted it. They were nearly black. But it was the look in them. She'd found few people looked beyond the surface. This man peered into her as if searching for her soul.

Then he smiled at her, exposing a whole lot of perfect, white teeth. The smile transported his dark chiseled face, making her suddenly aware of how magnificent he was. What surprised her more, though, was her reaction. Chemistry? It had been so long since she'd been attracted to a man, she couldn't be sure if it was desire or danger. Or maybe a little of both.

She had to suppress a shudder and quickly dropped

her gaze, fighting to keep the trembling out of her hand as she poured the coffee. Suddenly she realized that she wasn't getting a flash of information. Nothing. It was as if the room had fallen silent or she had gone deaf.

That shocked her so much that she wasn't even aware she was still pouring coffee into his cup until it splashed over onto the table.

"I'm so sorry," she cried, jerking back.

"No big deal," he said with a chuckle as he grabbed some napkins and began to mop up the worst of the spill. "Blame it on me. I distracted you." He gave her a reassuring smile that unnerved her even more.

The cowboy had the kind of good looks that broke hearts. A lock of his thick dark hair had fallen down on his forehead. He hadn't shaved for a day or two, making her even more aware of his rugged strong jaw. Everything about him said strong, capable and all man. Maybe the cowboy was just what he appeared to be. Maybe.

She didn't realize she'd been standing there staring at him until her boss, Kate, came over with a cloth to clean up the table. "I'll give you a few moments to look at the menu," Callie said and hurried off.

"Are you all right, Callie?" Kate asked when she caught up to her at the back of the café.

"I...I..." No one knew about her "gift." So there was no way to explain why this stranger had thrown her the way he had. The fact that she'd gotten absolutely nothing scared her. It had happened only a rare few times in her life. Reminded of those times, she shuddered at the memory.

"I guess I'm just clumsy this morning."

Kate laughed. "Uh-huh. Has nothing at all to do

with how handsome that cowboy is," she said in a con-spiratorial whisper.

Callie gave her a sheepish grin as if that was all it was. "Would you mind taking his order?"

Kate gave her a sympathetic look as if she'd been there herself. "Sure," she said before turning to head for the man's table. Callie could feel the cowboy's gaze burning into her flesh, even before she looked in his direction. He smiled, then looked down at his menu as Kate approached.

The whole encounter had taken only a few min-utes, and yet the memory of his searching gaze lin-gered, leaving her off balance. She just prayed her worst nightmare wasn't happening all over again.

Just then, all heads in the café turned as a large construction truck rolled into town and stopped across the street in front of the burned-out site of the former Beartooth General Store. Callie watched as another truck pulled in right behind it. More trucks, loaded with lumber and building materials, followed.

One of the regulars at the large table at the front said, "Hell's bells, it almost looks as if Beartooth has been invaded by an army."

"They must be lost," one of the ranchers joked. "Ei-ther that or Nettie Benton is going to rebuild the store."

"Not likely," Kate said as she stared across the street at the activity. "She sold that property to marry the sheriff."

"Well, something's coming up over there," a rancher noted. "But who in his right mind would invest in Beartooth? One good wind and the whole town could disappear overnight."

As Callie looked around the café, she saw that everyone was watching the men unloading building materials across the street.

Everyone but the cowboy at the table in the corner. He was looking at *her*.

ROURKE COULDN'T TAKE his eyes off Caligrace "Callie" Westfield. The blurry police photos hadn't captured her beauty. She looked angelic, from the wide brown eyes to the freckles that bridged her nose and highlighted the tops of her cheeks.

Not only did she look like an angel, she also had an innocence about her that was almost palpable. She wore jeans, an apron over a turquoise T-shirt and a pair of sneakers. As he noticed earlier, she was slimmer than she'd appeared in the photographs, more athletic and in better shape. Rourke estimated that she stood about five and a half feet tall.

He knew looks could be deceiving. Ted Bundy proved that. But he was still having a hard time believing this woman was a serial killer—or even intimately involved with one.

As the owner, a pretty brunette he'd heard called Kate, took his breakfast order, Rourke told himself that he'd been right to question his judgment about coming here. This case had gotten to him. Or maybe Laura was right and Caligrace Westfield had gotten to him from a few grainy snapshots. But right now, he was more than intrigued by the woman.

He hadn't anticipated his reaction to her—or hers to him, now that he thought about it. For a moment when their eyes had met, he'd thought she recognized him. It was more than possible since he'd been the lead detective on several homicide cases that had gotten him on the nightly news before he'd left the Seattle P.D.

Seeing her in the flesh made him even more curious about her. According to her history, the longest she'd ever worked in one place was here in Beartooth. His P.I. said she lived upstairs in an apartment over the café. Like the other buildings in town, it had been constructed of stone, stood two stories and appeared to be one of the original businesses in town.

The fact that Callie had moved so many times in the past seemed to indicate that she was running from something. He'd thought he had a pretty good idea from what when he'd left Seattle.

Now he wasn't so sure. But he'd gotten this far. He wasn't ready to give up yet. He could feel the clock ticking, though. He was already a couple of days into his two weeks. He needed something concrete—and quickly.

IT TOOK LAURA FULLER all night before she found the homicide case. While she'd kept copies of all of hers, she hadn't filed them in any order once she'd moved on to others. So she'd had dozens of boxes to go through. Now spread out on the floor, the papers made her apartment look as if a bomb had gone off. Good thing she didn't have friends who stopped by unannounced.

Her head hurt, her fear growing with each file she set aside as she worked her way through a history of the career she had loved.

When she found it, her fingers froze an instant before they began to tremble. She moved from the floor to the table. Sitting down, she took a breath and then opened the file folder.

On the surface, it was like any other case.

This one had been before she was made a homicide detective. She'd been assigned to crowd control and hadn't known any more details than those looky-loos who'd stood gawking behind the crime-scene tape.

Later she got to go door-to-door, asking if anyone had seen or heard anything suspicious. It was always the same. Little old ladies would remember some strange man they'd noticed, but gave vague details or such good details that finding him had only taken her to the local grocery, where he turned out to be the young man who delivered her groceries every week.

Dead ends, all of them.

No wonder she hadn't remembered the case. While her notes had been in the file with her name on them, it hadn't been her case. She could see why Rourke had wanted to solve it for her, though. She had worked tirelessly on her own time, trying to track down a witness to the murder.

Amusing, she thought as she read her notes. She hadn't known anything about the murder victim except that he was a single male, drove the local bus and lived in an old run-down apartment house. No wonder the case had gone cold. She'd put more time into it than anyone else and had gotten nothing. No witnesses. Or at least no one who would talk.

When she'd made Homicide, she'd put it all behind her and wouldn't have remembered the case at all if not for Rourke. The other two murders that he'd found weren't in her jurisdiction.

Dumping the photocopied contents of the file onto her table, she sorted through her notes, the reports and the two short newspaper clippings she'd put into the file about the case. She couldn't help but smile to herself at how much she'd been into all this. She'd wanted desperately to learn, to be the best, to go the furthest.

Ironic that this case would be the one Rourke would stumble across and decide he had to solve. As she reached the bottom of the paperwork, she saw the corner of a photograph and pulled it out.

A shockwave rattled through her. She'd remembered taking photos of the crowd gathered behind the crime-scene tape, but she'd thought she had put them all in the original file at the department. And yet here were more photos. At first they appeared to be identical to the ones Rourke had shown her.

But the closer she looked, she saw that these weren't duplicates. In fact, there were four photographs instead of three, and several were shot from different angles than the ones Rourke had shown her.

She felt sick. Why had she kept these and not put them in the police file? What had she been thinking?

Shaken, Laura stared at the shots she'd taken. There had to be something about them that had made her do this. But she could find nothing in them that would warrant her basically stealing them from the department.

She quickly looked for the young woman she'd spotted in the photos Rourke had shown her. With a start, she saw her. The woman was looking right at the camera in all *four* of these shots. Right at Laura.

A chill ran the length of her spine. She hugged herself as she stared at one of the photos and the odd expression on the woman's face, suddenly filled with a

horrible premonition. The woman almost looked as
if she—

Her cell phone rang, making her jump.

Let it be Rourke.

CHAPTER FIVE

IT WASN'T ROURKE CALLING. The woman's voice was old and weak, almost a whisper. "Laura?"

Laura glanced at the clock. It was after midnight. She swallowed back the lump that rose in her throat. "Mother?"

"No, honey, it's her neighbor Ruthie. You don't know me. Your mother gave me your number and asked me to call you. I'm sorry it's so late." When Laura said nothing, she continued, "She's real sick, honey. She... she says she's dying."

Laura was surprised. Not that her mother might be dying, since she'd often complained of being unwell. No, Laura just hadn't expected anyone to notify her. Most of the time, she felt as if her mother had already died. Hadn't she once told Rourke that her mother was deceased?

"Thank you for letting me know," she said, wishing her mother hadn't given some stranger her number. Why couldn't she have done them both a favor and just died quietly in her sleep?

Laura recoiled at her uncharitable thoughts. A stranger would think she was a horrible person. A stranger, though, wouldn't know her mother.

"She wants to see you," the neighbor said. "Your mother says there's something she has to tell *you*.

Something you need to know and that it is very important."

For a moment, she tried to imagine anything her mother could tell her that would be of any interest to her. To apologize for what she'd done and hadn't done as a mother? Too late for that.

But even as Laura thought it, she knew there were things that her mother *could* tell her, things she didn't want to hear.

"She said it has something to do with when you were twelve."

Laura felt her blood run cold. The last thing she wanted was to relive her childhood. It had been bad enough the first time. She definitely had no desire to talk about the year she'd turned twelve.

"I hope that makes sense to you," Ruthie said. "She didn't elaborate. The truth is, I hardly know your mother. I was surprised when she called to ask for my help. She's always stayed to herself, making it clear she didn't want to…socialize with any of her neighbors." Silence. "She really is very upset about this, afraid she was going to die before she speaks with you."

Her mother had secrets she needed to get off her chest before she died? Laura thought of blanks in her memory, the black holes of time she couldn't recall. But when she thought of her childhood, she couldn't have been more grateful for those lost memories. Why open up old wounds?

Even as she thought it, though, she knew there were questions, things she was unclear about, vague shadows of memories that often woke her in the night and made her anxious and afraid. Did she really want to know, though? Weren't the memories she did have horrible enough?

"Can I tell her that you're on your way here?" the neighbor asked, almost pleading.

Laura closed her eyes. She could hear the shock and disapproval in the woman's voice. Ruthie couldn't imagine a daughter not wanting to see her mother before she died. But then again, Ruthie, in her wildest nightmares, couldn't imagine a mother like Laura's.

What was it that her psychiatrist kept telling her? *"You aren't going to get well until you face your past. You're a strong woman. Put whatever darkness there is behind you so you can move on with your life. Isn't that what you want?"*

Her mother had the key to a past that had been locked away for so long. Just the thought of possibly being able to put those awful years behind her and move on...

"Tell her I'm on my way." *And not to die until I get there,* she added silently, because she had a stop she had to make first.

P.I. EDWIN SHARP hated to fly—especially in a small plane in the middle of a thunderstorm. He stared at the dark clouds around the aircraft, wishing he'd driven. If Rourke Kincaid hadn't insisted on the urgency of this trip—and paid him triple his usual amount—he would be on solid ground right now.

The small plane found an air pocket and dropped into it, sending his stomach up into his throat. He'd been fighting airsickness since they'd crossed the Rockies. Now the prairie stretched below them in a patchwork of autumn colors. Edwin couldn't appreciate any of the breath-stealing views.

"You look a little green around the gills," Pete, his young pilot, said and laughed.

He wouldn't be laughing if Edwin lost his lunch. He'd chosen this pilot because he was Montana born and bred. "You know the area, then?" he'd inquired when he'd landed at the Missoula, Montana, airport.

"You bet."

"So you can fly me to Flat Rock?"

Pete had grinned. "I can fly you anywhere you want to go."

Ahead the clouds parted. Edwin didn't see a town, but the plane began to descend. "I don't see the airport."

The pilot let out a chuckle. "Look closer."

Closer was what appeared to be a harvested wheat field. "You aren't going to land there." But even as he said it, he saw the ragged wind sock and felt the plane hit another air pocket. The ground was coming up fast.

He braced himself as the plane skimmed over the top of the stubble field. The wheels hit the ground hard and the plane bounced up, then settled down on the so-called airstrip. For the moment, Edwin was just glad to be on the ground again.

"What time do you want to fly back?" Pete asked as he taxied the plane to the edge of some old buildings.

"I won't be flying back. I'll be renting a car and driving."

The pilot got a good laugh out of that. "You won't be renting a car—not in this town."

"What town? I don't see anything but a few abandoned buildings."

"That's Flat Rock, Montana. What there is of it. Shouldn't take you long to find out what you need to. We'll let the storm pass. Why don't we meet at the café when you're finished."

"There's a café?" He couldn't help sounding doubtful. The town—if it could really be called that—consisted of a couple of grain elevators and a row of old buildings on each side of a strip of pavement. The buildings he could see appeared to be boarded up.

"If you don't show up, I'll just assume you're planning to hitchhike back to Missoula."

Edwin waited while Pete secured the plane, and then the two of them walked toward Flat Rock. Even at a glance he could see that there were more empty buildings than occupied ones. He looked around for a large flat rock, wondering how the town had gotten its name.

"What's that over there?" he asked of a huge, vacant-looking three-story building in the distance. The stone structure had gaping holes where windows used to be and a forlorn look. Probably the tall dead weeds that had grown around it, he thought.

"It used to be a girls' home."

"Like an orphanage," Edwin said.

"More like a home for kids nobody wanted, troubled kids. Folks claim it is haunted now."

Edwin scoffed at that, but quit when he saw Pete's expression. "You believe in ghosts?"

"Let's just say you couldn't get me in that building after dark."

He found that amusing, given that Pete seemed to be a daredevil pilot who wasn't afraid of a thunderstorm or flying within feet of high mountain peaks. But give him an old empty building…

"I'll see you at the café. Don't leave without me."
Edwin set out down what he figured was the main
drag. As he passed what appeared to be a vacant school
building, he saw that someone had spray-painted the
words *Consolidation of Schools Sucks* on the front.
He wondered where the children were bused to now.
Apparently, another school that wasn't close since he
hadn't seen hide nor hair of another town from the
plane.

He passed more abandoned buildings and cursed his
luck. Other than a couple of pickups parked in front
of the Longhorn Café, the only other sign of life was
a small grocery/gas station at the end of the street.

A woman in her mid-forties stood behind the counter
as he pushed open the door. She eyed him over the
glasses perched on her nose. "Help you?" She made it
sound doubtful.

"I'm trying to get some information on a woman by
the name of Caligrace Westfield," he told the woman.

"Westfield?" she said, one finely drawn-in eyebrow
shooting up.

"Do you know the Westfields?" he asked hopefully.

She gave him an impatient look. "The only Westfield around here is the manor."

"The *manor?*" He couldn't believe that he'd hit pay
dirt.

"You didn't see it on the way into town?" she asked
incredulously. "Hardly anyone misses that big old eye-
sore."

He blinked. "Are you talking about that abandoned
girls' home?"

"Girls' home?" she scoffed. "Some locals called

it that, giving it a fancy name to cover up what a terrible place it was."

It couldn't be a coincidence that Caligrace Westfield shared the same name as the girls' home. "How long has it been closed?" he asked.

"Twenty-five years now. I remember because I was fifteen when it shut down." She shuddered. "I'll never forget the night they came to take those girls away."

"They?"

"The state. Loaded all those girls into a few vans and off they went. Just like that, they were gone and the place was closed."

"So it was state run?"

She shook her head. "It was privately owned by some big corporation from Michigan or some place. The state finally stepped in."

"So you don't know who would have the names of the girls who were there?"

"Names?" She scoffed at that. "Maybe first names. Most of them were dumped there in the middle of the night. Babies left on the doorstep. Older girls brought there in handcuffs from other towns. The sounds that came from that place at night…" She shuddered again. "Then one day the state shows up and takes the whole lot of them, never to be seen again."

Edwin told himself that the woman was probably exaggerating, and yet he felt a chill move up his spine as he remembered what Pete had said about it being haunted. "Where did they take them?"

"No one ever knew what became of them," she said, then looked around the empty room as if she thought someone might be listening, before leaning toward him conspiratorially. "I think they got rid of them. Some of those girls were the worst there was." She shook her head. "There's a whole lot of country around here where you could dispose of bodies that would never be found. And with at least one of them being a murderer…"

"I beg your pardon?"

She looked surprised that he didn't know what she was talking about. "That's why they finally shut the place down. The murder of the young man who worked there." She grimaced. "I heard it was brutal. Used a knife from the kitchen and cut him up bad."

WITHIN MINUTES OF the construction crews arriving, the Branding Iron Café was a madhouse. Callie tried to keep up with the tables, all the time aware of the cowboy. She was glad to see that he'd gotten his order and seemed to be more interested in eating than in studying her. And yet, she suspected he was just as aware of her as she was of him.

"What's going on?" one of the regulars asked her, surprising her for a moment. She'd thought he'd seen her staring at the stranger at the front table.

"You hear yet what's going on across the street?" The rancher was seated at a large table by the window where the bunch gathered each morning to discuss cattle prices, the weather and complain about the government over coffee.

"One came in to refill his Thermos with coffee and said they're rebuilding the store," Callie told him. She felt disoriented by the clatter of dishes, the roar of voices, the crush of bodies packed into the space. She was doing her best to tune out the flashes of information that kept coming from the construction workers who wandered in and out.

"So it's not Nettie Benton's doin'?" another rancher asked.

The Beartooth General Store, which had stood across from the café for more than a hundred years, had burned down last spring. There'd been all kinds of speculation about what owner Nettie Benton would do now.

"Doesn't take five truckloads of men to rebuild one general store," another commented as he looked toward the street where more men were unloading materials next to the old hotel.

Callie shrugged. "That's all I've heard." She moved on, refilling cups, leaving bills and clearing dishes as she went. She'd been as surprised as anyone when she'd overheard one of the construction crew talking about rebuilding the store.

For the year Callie had worked as a waitress at the café, Beartooth, Montana, had looked and acted like a near ghost town. It was one of the reasons she'd taken the job. She had loved that it was twenty miles from the nearest "real" town. She'd loved the isolation, the quiet and the remoteness of the small old mining town.

That the waitress job came with an apartment over the café made it perfect. Callie loved the feeling of being far from everything, as if living at the end of the earth. She'd settled in quickly, liking that people here didn't ask a lot of questions, and had swiftly fallen into the rhythm of this easygoing life.

Her days all blended together in a familiar pattern. Each morning like clockwork, a group of ranchers would come in and take the large table by the window, order the same thing and talk about the same topics. At lunchtime, cowboys often stopped in from the many ranches around the area.

By afternoon, the quilters would come for pie and coffee and a visit. Some nights they would all gather at the café and change out the quilts on the walls. Callie often came down to the café from her apartment to listen to their chatter. She and Kate agreed they couldn't sew a stitch, but they loved the patterns and colors and the enthusiasm of the quilters.

The rest of the evenings the café crowd could be large, depending on whatever "special" owner Kate French was serving that day. This was a community of women who cooked. They went all out for potlucks and made huge meals for the help at brandings, cattle drives and harvesting. So eating at the café a few nights a week seemed to be a treat for them.

It was comfortable, living over the café and mixing with the locals of this small ranching and farming community. Callie had found herself relaxing. She felt as if she'd escaped the trouble in Seattle. She'd even thought she might end up staying here.

Then this morning all that changed in more ways than one, she thought, as the cowboy finally got up. She just hoped he kept going and didn't come back. But as he paid his bill and turned to leave, he tipped his Stetson in her direction. She felt ice cold. Why hadn't she picked up even the slightest psychic peek as to who he was and what he wanted?

All her instincts told her that she had reason to be scared. It was as if an ill wind had blown into Beartooth, bringing not only change, but also a handsome cowboy with a look in his dark eyes that foretold trouble.

ROURKE WAS LEAVING the café when he realized with a start that he knew the big older man coming in. He ducked his head to hide his face beneath the brim of his Stetson, shocked to recognize Sheriff Frank Curry. He'd met the sheriff when he'd first started with the U.S. Marshals. It had been only in passing on a drug-seizure case, but Rourke remembered Frank. Who wouldn't? Sheriff Frank Curry was a large handsome man, about sixty, who looked like an old-timey sheriff, with a thick horseshoe-style mustache, a six-gun on his hip and a Stetson on his thick head of graying blond hair.

Pushing on out the door into the cool fall weather, Rourke hoped Frank hadn't recognized him. How would he explain what he was doing in Beartooth if the sheriff did? How also would he explain the fact that he didn't want anyone knowing he was with the U.S. Marshals' office?

He was almost to his SUV parked to the side of the café, telling himself that there was a good chance Frank Curry wouldn't remember him, when Frank's big voice boomed behind him. "Rourke, right?"

Rourke had no choice. He turned and smiled at the sheriff.

"Rourke… No, don't tell me," Frank Curry said as he approached, those keen blue eyes intent on him. "Just give me a moment." He ran two fingers down his mustache and then smiled. "Kincaid. U.S. Marshals' office." He frowned as he glanced at Rourke's

SUV, which lacked the logo that would identify him as a U.S. marshal. "What brings you to our little town of Beartooth, Montana?"

CHAPTER SIX

ROURKE STOOD OUTSIDE the Branding Iron with Sheriff Frank Curry, trying to decide how much he wanted to tell the man. If he hoped to keep his identity a secret, then he couldn't see any way around this other than to confide in Frank. "Can we talk about this somewhere…private?"

The sheriff nodded slowly. "There's my office in Big Timber."

"I was hoping for somewhere even more private than that."

Frank lifted a brow. "I ranch down the road a spell. If you'd like to follow me…"

"I'll do that," Rourke said. "I'd appreciate it if you wouldn't call my office in the meantime."

The older man looked a little concerned, but not overly. "I look forward to our chat."

On the drive to the sheriff's ranch, Rourke's cell phone rang. He checked it. Laura calling. He let it go to voice mail, feeling a little guilty. Had she already come up with a profile on his serial killer and possible co-killer? It was hard for him to think of the young waitress he'd met this morning as a co-killer, but he knew she could surprise him.

Right now he was more concerned about whether or not he should have brought Laura in on all this. His instincts told him she wasn't well enough. The wounded Laura seemed…fragile. He was afraid working on this case might… What? Push her over some edge he hadn't been aware even existed before seeing her yesterday? He hated the thought that she was that close to an edge that it should even be a concern.

But there was no doubt that she was different. Maybe working on this case would help her, he tried to tell himself. He knew the police department had required her to see a psychiatrist after the shooting. Standard protocol, he was pretty sure. She'd never mentioned it. Was she still seeing someone?

With a sigh, he knew he had bigger worries right now than Laura. He debated for a moment what to tell the sheriff, but his real concern was the P.I. he'd hired. Edwin should be in Flat Rock by now, and yet he hadn't called. That made Rourke nervous. He was counting on Edwin to come up with more information on Caligrace, something that would lead him to the person who'd committed the actual murders.

He'd done a little homework on women serial killers. Few worked alone. Most set up the victim while their so-called "co-killer" did the dirty work. It was the killer in the shadows he told himself he was looking for, although Callie, if he was right, was a part of it. He just didn't know what part yet.

True, the crime-scene photos hadn't done her justice, but still there was something about her in person… He'd been more than a little surprised when he'd gotten a good look at her. How was that possible, given how many times he'd studied the photos of her? Hell, he'd dreamed about that face for weeks.

He hadn't expected the freckles. Or those eyes so

full of intelligence. The woman was even more of a mystery now that he'd met her face-to-face. He couldn't help being fascinated by her. So few criminals were interesting. Their motives were often clichéd. Jealousy, greed, revenge. Serial killers had their own crazy reasons for killing.

Rourke was convinced that this woman was hiding something and that the something was a man. He couldn't wait to see the profile Laura was compiling for him. What kind of man would a woman like this find herself drawn to?

He realized the sheriff might be able to shed some light on Caligrace Westfield. Not that he would have gone to the sheriff for help if Frank Curry hadn't recognized him. Rourke had really hoped to make this a quick trip with as few people as possible knowing what he was doing in town.

As he drove out to the sheriff's ranch, he thought again of Callie's reaction to meeting *him*. From the moment she'd looked at him, she'd been...wary, as if she'd sensed he'd come looking for her. It was almost as if she'd tagged him as being a cop. Was it possible they'd crossed paths in Seattle? Perhaps at some other crime scene?

What if the three murders were just the tip of the iceberg? And maybe even more troubling, what if this woman knew more about him than he did her?

As EDWIN LEFT and walked down the deserted main drag of Flat Rock, he tried to make sense of what the woman at the gas-station-slash-convenience-store had told him. Westfield Manor had closed twenty-five years ago. Caligrace Westfield was thirty—at least

according to her fake birth certificate. Even if she'd
lied about her age, she couldn't have been one of the
bad girls from the place because she would have been
only a child.

But her last name and the address she'd given on
her driver's license were proof of a tie-in to the place,
weren't they?

"You're sure there aren't any Westfields around?
Maybe whoever started the home?" he'd asked before
leaving the woman at the store.

"There were no Westfields. The home was located
in the *west field* of Pauper's Acre. *That's* how it got
its name."

"So the manor part was supposed to be a joke?"

"A sick joke. It was always just called Westfield
when I was growing up. Then someone started calling it Westfield Manor and it caught on, the way bad
jokes do."

"You must have met some of the girls in school."

She'd looked appalled at even the idea. "They weren't
allowed to attend our school, and we weren't allowed
to go near the home. I'd see them occasionally playing outside or looking out one of the windows." She'd
hugged herself as she'd shivered. "They were scary. I
wasn't about to go near any of them."

"What about the people who worked there? Surely
some of them are still around."

She'd shaken her head. "No one around here was
insane enough to work there."

"Any idea who ran the place?"

"No, but I can tell you she was gone just minutes
before the raid on the place. I heard she set a fire to
burn any evidence of how badly she'd operated things.

If she hadn't escaped when she did, I'm sure she would have gone to jail."

Edwin had been so hopeful, but now he'd hit a dead end—and after that horrendous plane ride—but he couldn't bear the thought of flying back to Missoula without something for his client.

"Is there a newspaper in town? There must have been a story about—"

"No paper, no story. The town kept it hushed up and so did the state authorities. We were told not to talk about it. Everyone just wishes that old place would fall down, but the town can't afford to tear it down. Part of it burned the night they took the girls away, but all the fire managed to do was gut some of the lower floor. It was like even fire couldn't destroy it." She'd glanced toward the west field and the dark skeleton etched against the skyline and shuddered.

"COME ON IN and have a seat." The sheriff studied him as Rourke Kincaid stepped into his modest farmhouse. "I'll get us a cup of coffee." Rourke opened his mouth, no doubt to say he didn't need any more coffee, but Frank didn't give him a chance to speak as he hurried out to the kitchen.

He liked to give a man time to think. The U.S. marshal wanting to meet here instead of the sheriff's department told Frank a lot. He was curious, but he'd learned to take things slow, especially when dealing with people who had secrets. Rourke Kincaid, Frank was betting, had a secret that had brought him to Beartooth. The same one that had the man not wanting Frank to call the U.S. Marshals' office.

When Frank came back into the living room, he

found Rourke standing at the front window, looking out at the crows lined up on the telephone wire.

"Are you interested in crows?" he asked as he put down a mug of coffee on the small table between the chairs and handed the other to Rourke. "They're part of my family. I lost them for a while...." He couldn't put into words how desolate that had left him. "I'm so glad to have them back. Crows are fascinating birds. I've been studying them for years."

Rourke looked over at him as if a little surprised.

One of the crows closest to the house seemed to see Frank and let out a loud caw. Frank smiled and touched the window. "That's Uncle. I think he's the boss of the family. He has the most to say, anyway." He turned back to his chair, sitting down and picking up his mug, which disappeared in his big hands.

His guest wandered away from the window after a moment and took the chair he'd been offered. He watched Rourke stare down into his coffee before he took a tentative sip, as if he had a lot on his mind. Frank suspected he did. Local law enforcement often got a little nervous when the feds showed up unannounced. Rourke Kincaid being in Beartooth gave him cause for concern.

Good to his word, though, he hadn't checked with the U.S. Marshals' office. He mentioned this now and waited to hear the younger man's story, hoping it would be somewhere near the truth.

"I'm not officially with the U.S. Marshals' office right now," Rourke said. "I have a couple of weeks off."

Frank nodded. "But you aren't here on vacation."

Rourke smiled. "No. I'll be honest with you, Frank. I'm looking for someone but on my own time. Because of that, though, I'd just as soon no one around here knows my connection to the U.S. Marshals' office."

Or the U.S. Marshals' office know what he was up to. "Maybe if you told me who you're looking for…"

Rourke took another sip of the coffee and put the mug down on the small table between them. He glanced toward the front window and the crows all still on the line, before he turned back to him.

"I'm investigating a cold case in which one individual's name came up several times."

Frank wondered why he was pussyfooting around telling him, but kept quiet.

"I believe I'm looking for someone close to her."

"Her?" Frank said, lifting a brow.

"Caligrace Westfield."

"Callie? The waitress at the Branding Iron. I'm familiar with her." He didn't mention that last spring his fiancé, Nettie Benton, had told him there might be more to Callie than anyone knew. Now he realized he was not as familiar with Callie Westfield as he should have been if a U.S. marshal was interested in her. He could feel Rourke's gaze on him.

"Is there something I should know about her?"

Frank cleared his throat. Rourke was certainly not being forthcoming about what had brought him to Beartooth. He hadn't even said what kind of crime was involved.

"Let me ask you this," Frank finally said. "What are we talking here?"

"Murder. She is a lead in three separate cases at least."

That got his attention. "Where were the crimes committed?"

"Seattle area. If you know something about Cali-grace Westfield…"

Frank sighed. "I don't know *anything* actually. How-ever, last spring a friend of mine hired a private investi-gator to run a check on Callie." He saw he'd piqued the marshal's interest. "My friend was just curious." That hadn't been quite the case, but it was close enough. "My friend hadn't expected anything to come up on the girl."

"But something did."

Frank nodded. "The problem is my friend never found out what. The private investigator was killed before he could give his report." He shook his head when he saw Rourke's surprise. "The investigator was killed in a completely separate matter. But he told my friend that he found something that would surprise her." And Nettie Benton, formerly the worst gossip in the county, wasn't easily surprised.

Rourke seemed to take that information in for a moment. "How long has Callie worked at the café in Beartooth?"

Frank rubbed his jaw as he thought. "About a year or so. As I understand it, she just showed up one day, saw the sign in the window at the café, asked for the job and got it. You know she lives upstairs in the apart-ment over the place?"

Rourke nodded. "Was there a man with her? A boy-friend? Husband?"

He shook his head. "Not that I know of. Kate La-Fond…sorry, Kate French owns the café. She might be able to tell you. But I've never seen Callie with anyone."

"So she doesn't date at all?"

"Not that I know of." He frowned as he remembered overhearing a discussion at the café one morning.

"Did someone come to mind?" Rourke asked.

Frank hesitated before he said, "Carson Grant has apparently asked her out on more than one occasion. He works as a wrangler on his sister and brother-in-law's ranch. He's been back a couple of years now. Probably not the man you're looking for, though."

THE LONGHORN CAFÉ was just as small-town local as Edwin had suspected it would be. The narrow building opened into a room with three tables and six stools at a counter. The place smelled of floor cleaner and old grease. The decor consisted of a few photos of cows, and the floor was noticeably out of level.

Edwin felt his stomach turn as he stepped in. Given that it was the middle of the afternoon, the café was nearly empty, but then again, so was the town. He wondered how the café could stay in business—it and that old motel he spotted at the far end of town. But he was reminded of all the cultivated fields he'd seen flying in. Must be ranches around the area for miles. Not to mention, the town was on what Pete had called the Hi-Line—the most northern two-lane highway across the top of the state.

An elderly man sat at one end of the counter, Pete at the other. The older man was slumped over a cup of coffee, head down. Edwin headed for the pilot. Pete was busy putting away a stack of pancakes and a side of bacon. Just the thought of food made Edwin sick again, but he sat down next to him and ordered a glass of milk.

"Milk?" Pete asked with a laugh. "Did you get what you needed?"

"Not really." He'd gotten more than he'd expected, and yet he still couldn't prove that Caligrace Westfield had lived in Westfield Manor.

"So who's this woman you're looking for?" the pilot asked between bites.

"Caligrace Westfield."

He frowned. "Never heard of her."

Not a surprise. Pete was in his early twenties, and while he knew the area, he was from a town farther east along the Hi-Line.

"Whadda you say?" At the other end of the counter, the elderly man had lifted his head from his coffee and was now looking in their direction.

Edwin gave the man his full attention. "Have you heard of a woman named Caligrace Westfield?"

"Caligrace," the man said and closed his eyes. "Pretty as a Montana morning."

Edwin figured the old man might be senile, but he said, "Dark hair and eyes?"

"Black as coal sometimes." Opening his own eyes, the old man said, "But her name wasn't Westfield."

Edwin got up and moved down the counter. The man could be full of bull, just wanting attention. Edwin ran into those sorts all the time during an investigation. They were the ones who wanted to contribute—even if they had nothing to offer. They were often happy to make it up.

As he neared the man, he was surprised that on closer inspection, though not shaved and gray of both hair and beard, the man wasn't as old as he'd first thought.

"Where do you know her from?" Edwin asked.

"That home outside of town."

"Westfield Manor?"

"Weren't no manor," the man said with obvious disgust.

Knowing it couldn't be possible, he still reached into his pocket and pulled out the photograph Rourke had supplied him with. "The woman I'm looking for, though, isn't very old. If the home closed twenty-five years ago, Caligrace wouldn't have been more than—" He was going to say "five."

"Sixteen," the man interrupted.

Sixteen? Edwin did the math. No way was the woman in the photo forty-one. He tried to hide his disappointment.

"That her photo?" the man asked and took the enhanced snapshot with his thick fingers.

"It's not a great photo. But you think you know the woman?" Edwin asked even though he already knew the answer. This man couldn't have known her. The dates were all off.

"That's not my Caligrace."

"No." Edwin started to take the photo back when he realized the man was crying. He glanced toward the waitress, wondering if he'd been right the first time to suspect this man was unbalanced. But the waitress was flirting with Pete and not paying any attention to this end of the counter.

"She looks just like her mama, though," the man said, wiping his eyes before he handed back the photo. "It's good to see that she made it all right."

Edwin frowned at him. "Her *mama?*"

"That's the Caligrace I knew. But she's buried out

at Pauper's Acre," he said with a nod of his head in the direction of Westfield Manor.

"You're telling me that this woman's mother was one of the girls who lived at Westfield Manor?"

"She's the spittin' image of her mother, so I'd say, yeah, I am. The home took the bad girls, but they also took unwed mothers when no one wanted them. Caligrace was pregnant. Had a baby girl."

Edwin frowned, trying to make sense of this. "So Caligrace and her mother shared the same first name, and this woman in the photo is the baby girl she had after she came to live at the home?"

The man nodded.

"How is it that you know this?" Edwin asked, still not sure he could trust this man—or his information.

The man blew his nose into his paper napkin, took a drink of his coffee, then said, "I saw her the night the bus dumped her off. She was crying. I could see that she was pregnant. She had nothing but the clothes on her back. It was winter. I gave her an old coat I had in the back of my rig. I would have given her more, but…"

"But?" Edwin prodded.

The man looked away. "I was thirty-one, married with a pregnant wife at home and two little kids of my own." He shrugged, his hand trembling as he lifted his coffee cup again. "I couldn't help her. That's just the way it was."

So the man was fifty-six. He looked a whole lot older. Chalk it up to a hard life, apparently. A married man with a pregnant wife at home and two kids when he met the pregnant sixteen-year-old Caligrace.

"How was it that you were there that night? Did you

work there?" Edwin asked hopefully as he tucked the photo back into his jacket pocket.

"I was a sheriff's deputy returning one of the runaways that night."

CHAPTER SEVEN

"WHAT ABOUT THE CHILD Caligrace gave birth to?"
Edwin asked after he and former sheriff's deputy Burt
Denton introduced themselves. "What happened to
her?"

Burt shrugged. "Never heard."

By Edwin's calculations, the Caligrace in the photo
would have been about five at the time of the raid.
So maybe her birth certificate was right and she was
thirty. Apparently, she'd been put on the state bus that
had taken the girls away. Unless someone in town had
taken her.

"Any chance some couple felt sorry for the little girl
and took her as their own?" he asked.

"I would have taken her in a minute, but like I said,
I had enough mouths at home to feed, not that my wife
would have stood for it." He shook his head. "No one
around here took her in, but someone must have somewhere else since, according to you, she's still alive."
The man's eyes narrowed. "You didn't say why you
were looking for her."

"She might be a witness in a homicide," he said
carefully.

The former deputy merely nodded as if he recognized bull when he heard it. "I hope she has a better

life than her mother did," he said, getting to his feet. He glanced at Edwin. "Is that too much to hope for?"

"No," Edwin said. "By the way, you wouldn't have any idea where in that building the two lived, do you?"

The former deputy, in a telling gesture, looked away. "Facing the building, farthest room to the right on the third floor."

"Did the woman you knew ever tell you her last name?"

Burt shook his head. "She said her family had disowned her. She had no name, and neither did her kid. It broke my heart. I guess that's why she gave her little girl her own name. It's all she had to give the kid." He looked like a broken man as he started to leave. "I really don't want to talk about this anymore. What's done is done. Some things are best left in the past."

Edwin watched the former deputy leave, then joined Pete at the other end of the counter.

"Now what?" Pete asked as Edwin took a stool next to him.

"I have one more thing I have to do," he said. "You should come along."

Pete gave him a wary look. "If it's what I think it is, not a chance in hell."

AFTER HIS TALK with Rourke, Frank Curry climbed into his pickup and headed for the state mental hospital. It had been months since he'd seen his daughter. Not that he hadn't tried to visit. He'd gone up there anyway because he hadn't known what else he could do.

Unfortunately, after Tiffany had injured a nurse and several guards during a short-lived escape, she'd been locked up in the isolation ward. At first the doctor hadn't wanted her to have any visitors—maybe especially the father she hated.

But through the use of some heavy-duty drugs, she had been downgraded as a threat and was now able to have visitors, Frank had been told. She just hadn't wanted to see him the times he'd driven to the hospital to visit.

So he'd been surprised—and with good reason, a little worried—when he'd gotten a call from the hospital saying that Tiffany had asked to see him.

He tried not to be too hopeful. Up until a year and a half ago, he hadn't known he had a daughter. Tiffany was the secret his ex-wife, Pam, had kept from him to punish him because she'd felt he hadn't loved her enough during their short marriage. She'd raised the girl to hate the father she'd never laid eyes on. Pam had poisoned Tiffany against him to the extent that when they'd finally met, Tiffany had tried to kill him.

After she'd been sent to the mental hospital for evaluation, Frank had hoped that someone there would be able to help her. Pam had washed her hands of her daughter, making it even more painful for Tiffany.

The last time Frank had seen his daughter, he'd had to tell her that her mother was dead, murdered, and that he was a suspect. Actually, the number one suspect.

But in a turn of events, his name was cleared. Unfortunately, it was too late for Tiffany, who'd compounded her problems by making her escape and almost killing several people in the process.

Now as Frank waited in the sunroom, he wasn't sure what to pray for. If Tiffany was better, she would be charged with not only her attempted murder of him, but also her attacks on the people at the hospital.

He feared she would be going to prison.

If she wasn't better…well, then she could end up in an institution for the rest of her life.

He turned at the sound of footfalls behind him. The first time he'd laid eyes on Tiffany, he'd thought she was barely a teen. She had the look of a waif, with long, fine blond hair and pale blue eyes. She'd been seventeen, just out of high school. Old enough to be tried as an adult.

The last time he'd seen his daughter, her long blond hair had been hacked off with a pair of scissors she'd somehow gotten her hands on.

Now her hair was longer. It gave her a softer, sweeter look. For a moment, he could almost tell himself that Tiffany was better.

"I wondered if you would come," she said, stopping a few yards from him. A male nurse had come with her. He stood a few feet back, there for Frank's protection. While comforting, it was also another indication that Tiffany probably wasn't as well as he might hope.

"How could you think I wouldn't come?" he demanded. "I've come every week even though they wouldn't let me see you at first, and then you refused to see me." He sighed, hating that he came off so defensive. "Tiffany, do we have to do this?" he said, sounding as tired as he felt. She wore him out, wore him down. He'd never known what to say to her that wouldn't set her off. No matter what he did, it was wrong. His ex-wife, Pam, in her bitterness, had made sure he would never have a relationship with the girl.

"They wouldn't let me out to go to my mother's funeral," she said, narrowing her eyes at him as if it had been his fault.

"I told you there wasn't going to be a funeral." No one would have come for Pam, and he couldn't bear the town attending in sympathy for him. "Was that why you tried to escape, because you wanted to say goodbye to your mother?"

"Where is she buried?"

He hadn't known what to do with Pam's remains. There had been no one but him to handle the arrangements, so he'd had her cremated, figuring her soul was already burning in hell. Her ashes he'd had put in an urn. It sat on a shelf in his barn, since he didn't want any part of the woman in his house. He'd had no idea what to do with the urn.

"I had her cremated. I thought you might want…" He tried to read his daughter's expression. She hadn't cried when he'd told her that her mother was dead. She'd seemed…relieved. He never knew how she would react. Or if her reactions were even real. If he was truthful with himself, he was afraid of her.

"You think that someday I am going to want my mother's ashes?" She seemed amused by this.

"Wouldn't you like to sit down?" Frank asked. He'd hoped that one day they could have a normal conversation.

She didn't move, so he continued to stand, as well.

"Do you need anything?" he asked.

Tiffany cocked her head. "What were you thinking of bringing me? Maybe a teddy bear? Candy?" She shook her head. She was so young. That was what always struck him. She'd turned eighteen on a mental ward. Just the thought of what Pam had done to this girl… He felt his stomach roil. He wondered what he would have done if he'd found his ex-wife before her

killer had. He'd often dreamed of wrapping his hands
around her throat and choking the life out of her, even
though it went against everything he believed in as a
lawman.

"Why did you want to see me?" he asked impatiently.
He was sick of her games and had begun to question
why he still came up here. While the state had run paternity tests and sent him the results, he'd never opened
them. Tiffany believed she was his daughter. Did it matter if that was true or not? He felt responsible for the
way her life had turned out.

"Didn't my doctor tell you the news?" she asked.
"I'm well enough to stand trial. I've hired myself a
lawyer. No matter what you think of my mother, she
came through at the end. She left me all of her money,
money we can only guess at how she came by. But that
aside, apparently I am a very rich young woman." Her
eyes narrowed. "I would have been richer, but you
had some of the money returned to the woman in Big
Timber. Don't you get tired of always doing what you
think is right?"

"Your mother swindled the woman out of her fortune," Frank said. "I merely made sure the woman
got it back."

Tiffany shrugged. "It doesn't matter. I have plenty
of money."

"I'm happy for you," Frank said, seeing that the
idea of being rich appealed to Tiffany. He'd seen that
same glow of greed in her mother's eyes. He figured
Tiffany would use the money to get what she wanted,
which apparently was out of here. "So, you're going
to make an effort to get better? I'm glad to hear that."

"I'm making an amazing recovery," Tiffany said,

smiling. "My doctor said so. He said that my realizing the terrible things I've done and feeling remorse is a huge step in my being released. My lawyer thinks that if I throw myself on the mercy of the court…" She smiled, looking sweet and young and so vulnerable—just what a judge and jury would see. She just might walk.

He looked into her pale blue eyes and shuddered inside. He wondered how he played into her future plans. He would have to start locking his doors and sleep again with a gun beside his bed as he had when her mother was alive.

Frank hated to even think what Tiffany would do to the crows he considered part of his family. She'd killed one out of spite, and they hadn't come back for over a year.

"There is one more thing," Tiffany said and lowered both her head and her voice as she stepped closer. The male nurse went on alert.

"Mother has been coming to visit me," Tiffany said, raising her head just enough to meet his gaze. She kept her voice low so the male nurse couldn't hear her.

Only moments ago, he was thinking that Tiffany might have been faking crazy all these months and that inheriting her mother's money had made her decide it was time to stop. Now, his blood running ice cold, he saw the psychotic young woman who hadn't even blinked when she'd pulled the trigger and tried to kill him.

"She sent you a message," Tiffany said. "'Tell your father that if he marries Nettie Benton, I will come to your room one night and kill you.'"

Frank took a step back from his daughter and that

wild frightening look in her eyes. "Have you talked to your doctor about these visits from your mother?"

Tiffany let out a brittle laugh that quickly died on her lips. Her pale blue eyes darkened. "She will kill me if you marry that woman. You want my death on your conscience, Daddy?"

With that, she turned and left, the male nurse hurrying after her down the hall.

Frank stood watching her go, his heart pounding. What he'd seen in his daughter's eyes was pure evil. God protect them all if she ever got out of this place.

"I'M GOING TO look around Westfield Manor, and then I'll be ready to fly out," Edwin told the pilot. The last thing he wanted to do was go into that old building, but he needed to verify the deputy's story if at all possible.

"I'd watch out for rattlesnakes if I were you," the pilot told him. "Not to mention falling through the rotten flooring or having a beam drop on you. I guess I'm going to have to go with you." At the detective's surprised look, he added, "You haven't paid me yet."

The afternoon sun fell at a slant across the empty streets as they left the town and walked the quarter mile toward the hulking skeleton of the girls' home. The land had fallen to weeds; now dried and knee-high, they brushed loudly against their pant legs as they walked. A chill had fallen over the autumn afternoon and seemed to settle in the growing shadows.

Edwin was glad to have the pilot's company the nearer they got. No sunlight shone behind any of the broken or missing windows. The front door stood open, cold darkness beyond.

"You sure you have to go in there?" the pilot said, stopping some yards away.

Burt Denton had told him that Caligrace's room was farthest to the right on the third floor. "If you're too scared…"

"So I'll wait out here for you." The young pilot smiled. "My daddy didn't raise no fool."

The light was fading fast as Edwin stepped through the doorway. He was instantly struck by the cold and several unpleasant smells as he cautiously moved toward the stairway. He could see where the back of the building had burned. The structure smelled of smoke even after twenty-five years, but only because teenagers had been using the lower floor to party. There were beer cans and bottles strewn around a fire ring in one corner of the room and a stack of old mattresses against another. The blaze had scorched the plastered wall and burned a hole in the floor, but hadn't spread, as if nothing could destroy this place—just as the convenience-store woman had said.

The stairs felt secure enough. He took them two at a time, anxious to get this over with. The second floor wasn't quite as littered, but varmints had made nests in the corners. The remains of abandoned metal bed frames and old soiled mattresses with their guts spilled across the floor littered the common area as he took the steps up to the third floor and tried to get his bearings.

The afternoon light had dimmed this far north. Edwin wished he had borrowed a flashlight at the café. In the dusky light, he moved along the scarred wood floor down a long hallway until he found a room that faced town at the corner of the building.

Like the other rooms he'd glimpsed, this one was

bare except for the mice nest, part of a bed frame and what was left of several thin soiled mattresses pushed to one corner. He stared at the stark room and wondered why he had bothered. What had he hoped to find here?

"Are you all right?" the pilot called up from the ground below.

He gingerly stepped to the window. "I'll be right down," he called back, his voice echoing eerily. As he started to turn away, he brushed the windowsill with his fingers and felt something.

As badly as he wanted to get out of the building as quickly as possible, he turned back to the windowsill. Crudely carved into the weathered wood was one word. CALIGRACE.

"CAN WE GET out of here now?" Pete asked as the P.I. came out of the old abandoned building. He sounded anxious and a little creeped out.

Edwin felt the same way as he stopped out front to look up at the gaping dark square of glassless window on the third floor. He took a photo with his cell phone for his client, just as he had of the name carved into the wood.

"There is one more place I have to go first."

"If it's back inside that building—"

"It isn't," he said. "I need to check the cemetery." They had to move fast. They were losing their light, and Edwin was already dreading the flight. "Are you coming with me?"

Pete glanced around as if trying to decide what would be worse—staying here by himself or going along to the nearby cemetery. "Can you at least tell me what we're looking for?"

"A grave," Edwin said as he started toward the small hill. The deceased residents of Westfield Manor had been buried in a small cemetery away from the residents of the town. Old wooden markers leaned into the wind behind the barbed-wire fence. A makeshift gate lay on the ground. Edwin stepped over it and entered. Again Pete hung back, crossing his arms and looking around as if he felt a presence that had him on edge.

Some of the wooden markers had once held names, but the wind and weather had worn them away. He was wasting his time, he thought as he moved through the small cemetery, trying to read even a few letters on the markers. Most of the wood lay rotting on the ground where it had fallen years before.

He almost missed the stone marker because one of the wooden ones had fallen over it. This gravestone was only a slab of concrete, rudimentary in its construction. He figured it was the deputy's doing. The words on it looked as if they had been drawn into the wet cement with a stick: *Finally at peace poor Caligrace. God forgive.*

Edwin bent down next to it, ran his fingers over the words, then rose and took a photo with his cell phone. The wind at his back, he looked out across the empty prairie. A few dozen yards away, he saw a small weathered stone angel, the kind often seen on graves. It sat in the middle of the field among the dried weeds.

He shuddered, knowing he would never forget the loneliness and despair he felt at that moment here with these lost souls.

On the walk to the plane, neither man spoke. It

wasn't until they were in the small aircraft ready to take off that Pete said, "The waitress I was talking to? She says her mother knew some woman who knew some woman who took in a few of the girls after the home closed." He shrugged. "She might be of help." He handed Edwin a telephone number. "I had the waitress call her mother, who called the woman… You get the idea."

Edwin had been feeling morose, but now perked up a little.

"The woman lives in Billings. I could fly us there before it gets any darker. We'd have to spend the night. It's going to cost extra."

"Not a problem." Edwin checked his seat belt. "What's the woman's name?"

"Leta Arthur."

He thought about calling Rourke and telling him what he'd found out so far. As Pete taxied the plane down the bumpy wheat field, Edwin decided he'd call after he talked to Leta Arthur. He closed his eyes, held on and prayed as the plane engine revved. He prayed for the girls of Westfield Manor and for the feel of solid ground again as the plane lifted off and turned southeast.

CHAPTER EIGHT

"LAURA?" ROURKE DIDN'T look all that happy to see her as he opened the door of the cabin and found her on his doorstep. Behind him, Laura could see a bag of groceries on the counter inside and his suitcase open on the bed in the small bedroom.

"Nice to see you, too, Rourke," she said as she pushed past him, angry with herself for coming here. Why hadn't she just dropped the photos and the preliminary profile in the mail?

"Sorry, it's just that you were the last person I expected to see at my door," he said as he shut the door and followed her into the three-room cabin. "How did you find me?"

Laura rolled her eyes and said, "Seriously? I was shot in the leg, not in the head." She glanced around the cabin at the rustic Western furnishings. They looked authentic. "Interesting digs. It must take you back to growing up in Wyoming. You look as if you never left," she said, motioning to the stubble at his jaw and the way he was dressed.

He glanced around, before returning his gaze to her. "The cabin suits me since I'm not going to be here long. Laura…"

She could tell that showing up like this had him off balance. It surprised her. In all the time she'd known

Rourke, he never seemed to get flustered. It made her all the more tense and anxious about coming here.

"I'd offer you a drink," he said, "but I just picked up bare necessities so far. I haven't even unpacked," he said, motioning to his open suitcase in the bedroom.

"But you've met *her*." Laura swore he almost blushed. She bit back a curse. "So, what's she like?" she asked, hating how deep her jealousy cut.

"Not what I expected," he said, moving to the wood-stove.

Laura watched him throw more wood on the fire, his back to her. The Montana night was colder than she'd expected. Seattle weather had spoiled her.

She stared at Rourke's broad back, despising the rush of emotions that had her annoyed with him. She'd known why he'd come here. To get close to the woman and catch a serial killer. So why was she acting like the jealous girlfriend?

Reaching into her large shoulder bag, she pulled out the manila envelope she'd brought. "You *like* her." She shouldn't have been surprised. Look how far and how much he was risking coming here.

"I find her *interesting*," he said, turning to face her. "Just as I do most possible serial killers." His gaze went to the envelope in her hand. "You did a profile?"

She shook her head. "It's just preliminary." Now that she was here, she didn't want to share the photos. She hated to admit that she'd withheld them from the file. Rourke would be angry. She wished now that she'd called him, that she hadn't surprised him. That she hadn't come in with a chip on her shoulder. But it was too late to change any of that.

All she could hope for were a few stolen minutes

with him and that neither of them was angry. "I'm not keeping you from anything, am I?"

For a moment, she thought he might say she was. He seemed uncomfortable with her here. He'd been so anxious to talk about the case in Seattle—until her breakdown. She regretted it since there seemed to be a wall between them now. He was treating her as if he had to walk on eggshells around her. She wanted to scream. Or cry. Neither would accomplish what she'd come here for, though.

"I'm not going to blow your cover, if that's what you're worried about." She moved to the table set against one wall. Dropping the manila envelope on it, she removed her coat, hung it over the back of the chair and sat down.

"So, have you found her co-killer?" she asked. Might as well talk about Caligrace Westfield, since she was already in the room and clearly on Rourke's mind.

"I just got here," he said.

"You don't think she's guilty, do you?" she said, remembering his expression earlier.

"I didn't say that."

"You didn't have to. I'm afraid you're making a lot of assumptions about this woman that are false based on…" She met his gaze. "Based on what?"

"I haven't made up my mind about anything," he denied. "That's why I'm anxious to see the profile you come up with for both her and her copartner."

She pulled out her preliminary findings. "Not that much is known about female psychopathy. But there are more female serial killers than most people think. They all have something in common. They're more efficient than their male counterparts."

"Laura, you know as well as I do that, first off, women serial killers are rare. Secondly, even rarer are women who use a knife. Poison, yes. Drowning, smothering, all have been used by women serial killers against even their own children. Some have used a gun. Not a knife."

"That's why she's been able to get away with it."

He shook his head. "Aren't half of all murders by female serial killers poisonings?"

"Yes, but that's what I'm saying. Rourke, I have a feeling about this woman. She's the exception. I just read about a female serial killer who fantasized about cutting and stabbing her victims." When he joined her at the table, she continued. "I just want you to keep an open mind."

He raised a brow. "Like you are?"

She ignored the dig and looked down at what she'd come up with so far. "Your average female serial killer is thirty-two years old and white. How old is Callie?"

"Thirty."

She nodded "FSKs are intelligent. They plan their murders. It might surprise you that they're found in middle- to upper-class society and have been known to have a variety of careers, including waitressing."

Rourke crossed his arms and seemed to wait patiently for her to finish.

"Women serial killers are quiet killers, often going undetected because men—who make up most homicide departments—don't suspect them. A misconception is that women are the weaker sex, the sweet, nurturing, motherly types. But what we've found is that these women grew up in a similar childhood environment as their male serial-killer counterparts and are just as deadly," she said in conclusion.

"Isn't it true that most of the women serial killers in history acted in tandem with a male?" he asked.

"Yes," she admitted. "But—"

"*He's* who I'm looking for."

"WELL?" NETTIE BENTON asked when Frank came home. She'd moved into his house on the ranch, but spent a lot of her time at the Branding Iron Café in Beartooth, watching the work on the store. Her home, the one she'd shared with her ex-husband, Bob, had sold along with the store property. Unfortunately, she'd been happy to sell everything lock, stock and barrel and hadn't asked more questions about who exactly was buying it.

The sheriff smiled at her, and she felt her heart beat a little faster as he joined her on the couch. He was the love of her life, had been for years, even though they'd spent many years apart.

"Whoever is rebuilding Beartooth wants to remain anonymous," Frank said, as if he knew she would pester him until he told her what he'd found out. Or in this case, *hadn't* found out, she thought, judging by his expression.

"The foundation is owned by a corporation. The corporation is owned by another corporation." He shook his head. "A lot of it is offshore, so I hit a dead end. What does it matter?"

It mattered to her and he had to know that. "Why hide behind all these corporations if all of this is above-board?"

He sighed. "Maybe it really is just a benefactor who wants to do something nice for Beartooth and doesn't need or want credit for it. Could be someone who used to live here and has fond memories and a whole lot of money."

Nettie frowned. "Who do we know that would do something like that?"

"No one comes to mind, but that doesn't mean—"

"And if you were this person, wouldn't you want to be here and watch how the work is progressing? I would."

He laughed. "*You* would. But not everyone is like you, Lynette." He'd always called her by her given name. The way he said it made her blood heat beneath her skin. "Some people aren't so bossy."

She swatted playfully at him. "The store is coming along pretty quickly. I would at least want a photo of the progress, especially if I was spending this kind of money for restoration. Do you know that they're planning to make the hotel look like it did in the eighteen hundreds? That costs money."

He took her hand. "A variety of people have owned the old buildings and land in town over the years. I did some tracking."

"Let me guess. The same corporation now owns it. But wouldn't they be required to get building permits?"

He nodded. "The corporation's attorney is handling it. I'm sure when the benefactor is ready, he will reveal himself. Until then…how about we concentrate on the wedding. Have you changed your mind about eloping to Vegas?"

Had she? She met his blue-eyed gaze and felt her heart float up like a helium balloon. "I want to become your wife."

"Then let's make plans." Just then he got a call,

checked his phone and said with obvious regret that he had to go. Standing, he picked up his Stetson and leaned down to give her a kiss. "You sure you want to marry a sheriff? This is going to happen a lot until I retire."

She smiled up at him. "Positive."

"I mean it, Lynette. Pick a date. Soon."

"I'M WORRIED ABOUT YOU," Laura said, not for the first time since she'd shown up at his rented cabin unexpectedly.

"I'm not going into this blind," Rourke tried to assure her, but he could tell by her expression that she didn't believe him.

"You seem…obsessed with this woman."

He laughed that off, not about to tell her how many nights he'd dreamed about Caligrace Westfield. That made him even more aware that she might be the serial killer. Maybe his subconscious was trying to warn him—just as his former partner was.

"Let's remember, Laura, that this whole trip is probably a wild-goose chase. You said yourself that Caligrace Westfield could be a crime junkie. I'm not even convinced that she's a suspect."

Laura shook her head and then gave him one of her long, cold stares. "Don't try to bullshit me, Rourke. Remember? I know you. You wouldn't be here unless your gut told you that she's somehow involved."

He didn't bother to argue.

"I'll work you up a profile of a possible male co-killer, but my money is on the woman. She's in the perfect profession to meet a lot of men, especially in a town like Beartooth, where there seems to be more men than women."

"The women here all stay home and cook, clean and sew as women were meant to do," he joked.

Clearly Laura didn't appreciate the joke. "Tell me about the crimes," she said, getting the conversation back on track. "And the victims."

Rourke had sent her copies of what he had, but they'd learned when they'd worked together that when they talked it out, they discovered small things they hadn't noticed otherwise.

He went into the bedroom and came back with the files. "I'm glad you're helping me." *But you can't stay,* he wanted to add. Beartooth was too small, and Laura had cop written all over her—even if she wasn't still one. He thought about Caligrace Westfield's reaction to him. His cover might already be blown. Add Laura to the mix, and he feared that Callie would run.

As if reading his mind, Laura said, "Don't worry. I'm not staying."

Rourke couldn't have been more surprised when he'd opened the door and found her standing there. He'd felt uneasy around her that day since their dinner, when he'd realized how much she'd changed.

Now, though, this felt more like the old Laura, the one he'd trusted with his life on more than one occasion. Grateful for her help, he sat down across from her and opened the file. She'd taken a notebook out of her purse along with a pen.

"Three murders. The first, four years ago. The second, three years ago. The third, two years ago. None last year," he said, frowning.

"Each was a year apart?" she asked, looking up from her writing.

He glanced at his notes. He'd noticed that originally but hadn't thought too much about it. Now he checked the dates. "They were all in the fall. October third, eleventh and twenty-first."

"Maybe your killer doesn't like October."

"Or maybe that's when he has more time on his hands, for some reason."

"If there is anything to the yearly killings and that three at least took place in October…then your killer should have struck again last October. I take it you didn't find another homicide that meets the profile?"

He shook his head. "Maybe he couldn't for some reason last year."

"Caligrace had just relocated," she said as she jotted something down in her notebook. "Maybe she hadn't found her mark yet. Now that it's almost October…"

He said nothing as he thought about that.

"What do the three victims have in common?" Laura asked.

"Other than they were all murdered with a knife? On the surface, nothing. One was a bus driver. One was a chef in an upscale restaurant. One sold insurance. So each came from three different economic and social groups. All three victims were found naked, bound and gagged, with multiple stab wounds. All three were drugged."

Laura looked up from her notes and frowned. "That would definitely make them easier to manage if the killer was a woman."

"With each murder, the killer got more creative with

the knife," he continued, aware of the point she'd made about the drug.

"Did the killer bring his own knife and binding materials?"

When he didn't answer right away, she looked up. "This is why your boss doesn't think you're looking at a serial killer for all three crimes, huh. The killer used what he or she could find at the scene. Unusual for a serial killer."

"And another reason I don't believe Callie does the killing," Rourke said. "As you noted, women plan. They don't leave things to chance."

"But then again, everyone has a knife or something you can tie a person up with in their home. She would have known that if she'd been to their homes beforehand. Perhaps on a date?"

He looked at his own notes. "The killer used duct tape and a kitchen towel at the first murder, nylon stockings belonging to an ex-wife at the second and the third…handcuffs, a ball gag and blindfold in the drawer, that apparently the victim had purchased with his credit card only days before."

She raised a brow at that. "So, there is a good chance that your killer had been to each of their residences sometime before the murder."

"Premeditated?" Rourke said.

Laura nodded. "A woman would have a better chance of knowing about what was in a bedside drawer of a man's bedroom than a male killer."

"Unless the victim was gay. Or the male killer broke into the house and searched it. He could also have been in a business where he was allowed access, say a cable-TV man or someone with a utility company."

She smiled, giving him that. "What else do you have to support your serial-killer theory?"

"The knife wounds on the third victim. The killer is getting more creative. He'll kill again, if he hasn't already. I'd stake my life on it."

"That's exactly what you're doing," Laura said and pushed the manila envelope across the table to him. "Take a look at the photos I found of your serial killer."

LAURA SAW ROURKE'S gaze go to the manila folder, but he didn't touch it for a moment. "You're the only one who knows this, but I made copies of all my cases—and some that merely interested me," she said. "Don't give me that look. As if you've never broken any rules."

"Sorry, I was just surprised."

"I found the case that got you started on this…quest you're on. You were right. I did take the photos of the people behind the crime-scene tape that day."

"So you have copies of the photos I have?" he asked.

She shook her head. "These are four you haven't seen."

Rourke looked at her in surprise, then opened the envelope and removed the photos. "You kept them out of the file?" He frowned. "I don't understand. Are they of *her?*"

Laura felt the way he said "of *her?*" like a weight on her chest.

He looked at all four quickly, then more slowly. She saw the way his eye was drawn to the woman, Caligrace Westfield.

"She's looking right at the camera in these," he said after a moment.

Laura waited, watching him.

When he looked up, she saw that he'd seen the same thing she had. "She sees something…someone who frightens her."

Laura shook her head. "She saw me in my uniform and realized she was being photographed at the murder scene. Look at the shot after that one. She realizes she was probably photographed at the *other* murders. That's when she gets really scared and takes off."

He stared at the last photo for a long time before he looked up at her and frowned. "That could be one explanation."

"It's *the* explanation." She could tell that he was angry that she had kept back the four photographs. "I don't have anything else on the case that you haven't already seen," she said, knowing him so well.

Rourke nodded, still pissed.

"Why are you being so obstinate about this?" she demanded, losing her temper. "*She's* your serial killer. There is no boyfriend, no brother, no psychopathic uncle or cousin. She did them."

He shook his head as he looked down at photographs he'd spread out in order on the table. "I don't see a woman coming back to the scene of the crime. Women can and do kill—I'll give you that. But if you look at the famous women serial killers of our time, they didn't do it for sport. They were more goal oriented."

"Who says your chick here isn't goal oriented? Just because you don't know why she killed those men yet…" Anger made her stomach roil. "You've been taken in by that face of hers." She couldn't believe this. "This woman got to you even before you met her."

"I think you're reading a lot into these photos."

Laura laughed as she pushed to her feet. "*I'm* reading a lot into them? You're here because of something you saw in that woman's face. Well, keep looking at her, Rourke, because you're looking at a killer." She reached for her coat and purse. "I have to go."

He stood, his anger at her quickly turning to concern. "It's late. The deer on the highway can be bad after dark. Stay and leave in the morning. You can have my bed. I'll take the couch."

The concern in his voice plucked at her heartstrings. As if she could get any sleep knowing he was just in another room. "I have to go see my mother. That's why I'm here."

He blinked. "Where is your mother? I thought you said she was—"

"She lives in Harlowton. An hour north of here."

Rourke looked even more surprised to hear that not only wasn't she dead, but that she also lived near here.

"I didn't realize you were from Montana," he said. She could see that he was wondering why she hadn't mentioned this when he'd told her he was coming here.

"She moved to Harlowton a few years ago." He reached to help her with her coat, but she stepped back, upset with him. The damned fool was too emotionally involved in this case, in this woman. He was going to get himself killed.

"Still," he said. "It's so late. I wish you would wait and go in the morning."

"My mother's…dying." It surprised her, the amount of angst in her voice and how little it had to do with her mother. "She's sent word that it's urgent that she sees me."

His look said, "Then what the hell are you doing here?" but when he spoke, he said, "Then you should get to her as soon as possible."

CHAPTER NINE

THERE WAS NO traffic on the two-lane north of Big Timber at this time of the night. Laura wasn't that worried about deer on the highway either. There was an almost full moon that turned the landscape silver. After driving in Seattle for so many years with traffic at all hours, day or night, this was a treat.

She hadn't been back to Montana since her mother had awakened her in the middle of the night and rushed her downstairs to an old pickup waiting just outside. She'd never seen the man behind the wheel before or since. She just remembered her mother paying him when they reached the bus station in some distant town. Most of her life she hadn't known even the name of the town where they'd moved to before her mother lost her job and they had to move again.

That time, when she'd awakened, they were in Michigan. When she asked what was going on, her mother told her they were making a new start and she was never to mention the past again.

Tonight Rourke had been surprised to hear not only that her mother was alive, but also living nearby in a small Montana town. She shouldn't be angry with him for knowing so little about her. When he'd first asked about her family, she'd let him think her mother was dead. She'd made the mistake of mentioning her sister, Catherine, only once, but Rourke hadn't forgotten. He'd asked if she was coming for a visit.

What he didn't know was that she hated her sister's visits. They were only once a year, fortunately. She couldn't keep Catherine away longer.

She never talked about her family. Nor did she tell anyone else. She'd put that life behind her years ago. But she especially didn't want Rourke knowing. The last thing she wanted was his pity.

Given that she knew everything about him, it did seem unfair that he knew nothing about her. He'd been raised on a ranch in Wyoming. When his parents had retired, they'd sold the ranch and left him enough money that he never had to work. When his parents were killed in a small-plane crash, he'd already graduated from college, been working in law enforcement and had finally crossed her path at the Seattle P.D.

If she was honest with herself, she'd always believed that fate had thrown the two of them together. Seeing him again had made her realize that she'd always thought that someday they would be a couple. She knew it was crazy and certainly the feeling was all on her side. Rourke had never had an interest in her other than as a cop. Why she'd thought that would change, she had no idea.

It didn't keep it from hurting, though. Her psychiatrist insisted that if she told Rourke how she felt, she would finally be able to move past it.

Well, the best she could do now was to try to keep him alive, she thought as she came over a hill and saw the rotating white blades of the Judith Gap wind farm in the distance.

Closer, she could see the lights of Harlowton, Mon-

tana, ahead. All her misgivings about coming here hit
her in a rush. For all she knew, her mother was already
dead, taking her secrets with her.

Laura's foot came up off the accelerator. It wasn't
too late to turn around. Or she could get a motel in
town and get out of here tomorrow.

She felt that old tightening in her stomach at even
the thought of seeing her mother. She didn't want to
be here. What was the point in digging up all those
bad memories?

Ahead, she saw the highway sign. Turn around or
drive into the heart of the small Montana town to her
mother's house, where she couldn't even conceive what
might be waiting for her?

ROURKE HADN'T BEEN able to sleep after Laura left. He'd
traveled light to Montana, so it hadn't taken long to get
settled into the cabin. The fall night was still warm,
although there was talk of an early winter storm coming in later in the week.

Restless, he stepped out on the cabin porch into the
moonlit night. Laura's visit had left him shaken. So
much of what she'd said made sense. So why did all
his instincts tell him she was wrong?

Knowing he wasn't going to get any sleep, he decided to go for a walk. As he headed down the mountain
into town, he looked at the small western community.
The old buildings shone in the moonlight. The café was
closed, had been for hours. Nor were there any lights in
the apartment over it. Callie would be asleep like the
other few residents who actually lived in and around
Beartooth. Even the Range Rider bar was closed, although several pickups were still parked out front.

Some of the cowboys must have hitched a ride home rather than drive.

As he was headed back up the main drag, he heard an engine start up. A moment later, the glow of head-lights poured out onto the two-lane highway that was Beartooth's main street.

Without thinking, he stepped back into the shadows as the old pickup turned in his direction. He stayed pressed against one of the old building's stone walls as the driver passed.

Callie. He recognized her in the glow of her dash lights. Her hair was down, skimming her shoulders, her face pale in the dim light.

Rourke cursed himself for being without his own vehicle as he checked the time on his cell phone. Where was the woman going at a quarter after three in the morning?

Stepping out of his hiding place, he watched her taillights grow dimmer and thought about Laura's con-viction that Callie was the killer he'd come looking for.

She touched her brakes at the end of town near the old gas station and garage. Turning, she headed back toward the Crazy Mountains.

Where did that road go? He didn't know, but he planned to find out. Just as he would find out who she was going to meet in the wee hours of the morning up the mountain road.

He ran back to the cabin, jumped into his rented SUV and took off down the road in the direction Callie had gone. He kept thinking about the first time he'd seen her. His reaction still surprised him. Was Laura right? Was he obsessed with this woman and had been since he'd seen her face in a crime-scene photo?

If he was being honest, he'd had a theory since the first time he'd seen her image and realized she'd been at three crime scenes. He'd never thought she was a co-killer. But she was connected to the murders because she knew who the killer was. Why she hadn't come forward…well, he didn't know. Like he said, it was just a theory.

He couldn't explain it, even to himself. Just this gut feeling… He hadn't shared his theory with Laura for obvious reasons. She had made it clear how she felt. Both of their reasonings seemed clouded by their own personal feelings. Laura really believed he was falling for this woman.

He shook his head at the thought as he drove. He'd always trusted his instincts. But at the back of his mind was an inkling of worry that he was wrong. Dead wrong.

Rourke reminded himself of what was at stake as he turned and headed back into the Crazies, as the locals called the mountains that shadowed the town of Beartooth. The gravel road narrowed quickly, turning to dirt. He had to slow down. When he came to a fork in the road, he stopped, unsure which route she would have taken since he didn't know the area.

He tried the road to the right since it appeared to go deeper into the thickest wooded side of the mountains, but a few miles up the 4x4 trail, he finally had to turn around. The area was a honeycomb of old logging roads. She could have taken any one of them.

As he drove back to his cabin, he realized he wasn't so sure about his theory anymore. Laura could be right. That sweet-faced woman who haunted his dreams could very well be a serial killer who, since it was almost October, was now looking for her next victim.

Or she could be somewhere in those mountains with the man who did her killing for her. In that case, who had she already chosen for her next victim?

The house was small and old. Only a single light glowed inside. Was her mother alone? Or was her neighbor Ruthie in there with her?

Laura looked at the clock on the dash. 3:11 a.m. She knew she was stalling. How would she feel if she arrived too late? She would never know what it was her mother had to tell her. That, she realized, could be a blessing.

She sat for a few minutes longer, fighting angry tears.

"You really are quite ugly when you cry," her mother used to tell her. Laura had made it a point of not crying, especially in front of people. She didn't understand why she was crying now, but the last person she would let see her like this was her mother. Hastily wiping away the tears, she pushed open her door and stepped out in the cold fall air.

Fallen, dried leaves crunched under her heels as she walked along the broken strip of concrete walled in by weeds to her mother's door.

Whatever it is she wants to tell me, I won't let it hurt me. She can't hurt me anymore.

The screen door opened with a groan. Laura tapped at the weathered door beyond it and waited. She could hear the wind in the pines next to the house. One of the branches scraped the eave. She felt the noise getting on her nerves as she turned to look around the small neighborhood. Her mother's house sat back from the street, away from the rest of the houses. She wondered which house Ruthie lived in, since none were close by.

Moonlight cast an eerie pall over the town at this hour of the morning. She thought of her mother living here all alone. What in God's name had brought her mother here?

Turning back to the door, she started to knock again, but instead tried the knob. It turned in her hand, the door creaking open as the smell of death rushed out.

A voice from the darkness, grating as coarse sandpaper, rasped, "Is that you, Laura?"

CHAPTER TEN

IN THE SMALL apartment over the Branding Iron Café, Caligrace Westfield woke with The Headache. She closed her eyes and lay perfectly still, willing it away. For almost two years, she'd held her affliction at bay, so long that she'd thought she'd somehow escaped by coming to Beartooth.

A sob of a laugh escaped her lips. What she had wasn't a disease that could be cured. Not by any scientific means on this earth. Or a spiritual one. Still, being here in Beartooth, Montana, she'd felt freer of the curse that had forced her to become a nomad.

"You have what my grandmother did. Cherish this gift that has been given to you," her mother had told her the day she died. "Cultivate it, control it."

But that was the problem. She couldn't control it, no matter how hard she tried.

Caligrace opened her eyes and tried to focus on the clock. The Headache was blinding in intensity, making her feel sick to her stomach. Since coming to Beartooth, she hadn't missed a day of work. She wasn't going to today either.

She swung her legs over the side of the bed. The room swam, and for a moment, she thought she might retch. With cast-iron will, she rose and dressed for work. Fortunately, she wasn't required to wear a uni-

form. She pulled on a long skirt and top, then drew her
wild mane of dark hair back from her face, fighting it
into a bun of sorts at the nape of her neck.

Call Kate and tell her you can't work.

She could already smell the bacon frying in the café
below the apartment. It turned her stomach. Did she
really think she could waitress today?

The alternative was staying in this apartment with
The Headache and her growing apprehension. The air
around her seemed to crackle as she moved. She held
her breath as it sparked and buzzed. She could feel her
heart pounding so hard it made her chest ache.

Callie tried to still the thrumming in her veins. Nothing was wrong, she tried to tell herself. Nothing was any
different than it had been since the day over a year ago
when she'd arrived in Beartooth and seen the waitress-
wanted sign. She hadn't been that surprised when she'd
gotten the job. Instead, she'd had an odd sense that she'd
somehow come home.

Now she moved to the window and her view of the
mountains. It was one of those robin-egg-blue sky days.
The recent snow in the high country had capped the
high peaks. With her window open a crack for fresh
air, she caught a whiff of the cold that rushed down
out of the rugged, breathtaking mountains now afire
with the sun's morning rays.

Callie stood, a little chilled in front of the window,
as she tried to make sense of The Headache she'd
awakened with. She knew the signs. Maybe she'd been
here too long. It was the longest she'd stayed in one
place in years. The thought of leaving, though, made
her want to cry.

And yet something was on the wind. Maybe nothing more than a storm, she tried to convince herself. She often felt odd when the barometer dropped. She'd never seen anything like the storms that ravaged this small town, often snowing her in until the plows could get through and clear the roads.

For all her efforts otherwise, she couldn't ignore The Headache, though. Or what it foretold. No wonder she felt sick to her stomach. It was happening again, and there was nothing she could do about it.

Each time, though, she prayed that this time would be different. Even now, she told herself it would be. Quickly turning from the window, she opened the closet, knelt down and pried up several of the floorboards she'd loosened when she'd first moved in. The box had belonged to her grandmother. Carefully she lifted it out and, rising, took it over to the table. Lifting the lid, she caught the sweet scent of the candles that had been stored inside for years, along with the deck of worn tarot cards.

Her sweet, tiny grandmother on her father's side had been a fortune-teller, her mother had secretly informed her. Unfortunately, she'd never gotten to meet her. She'd never known any of her family other than her mother. Her mother refused to talk about her side of the family, not even by name.

Callie could hear the cook downstairs preparing for the opening of the café soon. Without much time, she hurriedly removed the cloth-wrapped bundle from the box, loosened the ribbon holding it and carefully lifted out the gun. It felt cold to the touch. Callie closed her eyes for a moment, then hurriedly dropped the small loaded handgun into her bag and put the box and its contents back in its hiding place.

NETTIE BENTON TURNED her engagement ring distract-
edly as she stared out the café window at the construction crew across the road. The men had quickly cleaned
up the mess from the fire and were already laying the
stone walls. Apparently, they weren't going to have
to replace the old foundation that had been there for
more than a century.

"I heard they're rebuilding the store exactly as it
was," she said as Kate refilled her coffee cup and took
a seat across from her. The morning rush was over, so
the café was nearly empty. Callie could handle what
few remained. Like most mornings since the store had
burned, Nettie sat and visited with Kate.

"That's what one of the men they brought in told
me, as well," Kate said. She put down a plate with a
large cinnamon roll, two forks and some butter, knowing how Nettie liked them.

At this age, Nettie was seldom surprised by human
nature. But her friendship with Kate—a woman she
had suspected of unthinkable things—had come as a
complete surprise. When Kate had suddenly shown up
in town, Nettie was sure she was hiding from something. Of course, she was, and Nettie had finally gotten
to the bottom of it. It was a source of pride for Nettie
that she often got to the bottom of things.

"Did the man you talked to mention who is behind
rebuilding the store?" Nettie asked.

"You should know," Kate said with a laugh. "You
sold it to them."

"I dealt with some *lawyer*." People in these parts
had about as much faith in lawyers as they did poli-
ticians. "At the time, I didn't care who bought it or

why. I never dreamed someone would want to rebuild the store."

"It is curious."

"Can't help but wonder why all the secrecy," Nettie said as she helped herself to a piece of the cinnamon roll, slathering it with the fresh creamery butter before taking a bite.

Kate grinned at her across the table. "Come on, I know you're dying to find out. So, what's stopping you?"

Nettie finished her bite before breaking into a smile. She'd been known as the worst gossip in the county, probably more than one county, for years. But certain events had made her realize how dangerous gossiping could be. She'd sworn off it, promising herself and her fiancé, Sheriff Frank Curry, that she was finished.

"It isn't really gossip," Kate said, as if reading her mind. "It's more like investigative work, and we all know how good you are at that."

Nettie laughed. She'd spent hours trying to uncover Kate's secrets. But her more recent foray into snooping had almost cost her her life—and had gotten her store burned down.

Looking into the benefactor who was rebuilding her store and half the town... Well, that at least shouldn't be dangerous, right? And like Kate said, it wasn't gossip. It was simple curiosity. Then again, curiosity killed the cat.

THE COWBOY TOOK the same table he had yesterday. Callie had sensed him when he'd come in. Not that she was picking up any psychic pulses from him. She'd been expecting him, so she wasn't surprised when her headache worsened.

He was somehow a part of whatever was going to happen, she realized as she grabbed a menu, a pot of coffee and a glass of ice water before heading to his table.

It was only on those days when she woke with a killer headache that she knew something bad was going to happen. Who the bad thing would happen to, she didn't know yet. But in the next few days, her headache would become blinding, and then she would have a vision of a scene that no one should ever have to witness.

She had tried everything to lessen not only the pain but also block out whatever vision was coming. Nothing had worked—certainly not drugs or alcohol or trying to distract herself.

Now as she approached the man, she told herself to just ride it out. Whatever was coming…well, she had no control over it. That was the most maddening and frightening part. Why was she the one who got these…premonitions? What was she supposed to do about them? They never let her change the outcome, so what was the point?

She'd actually gone to the police station and tried to tell someone once. The officer had been kind to her, but had made it clear he thought she was nuts. Or worse, putting him on.

Later, she'd heard he'd come looking for her, thinking she was somehow involved. She'd learned her lesson after that. She kept it to herself, dreading autumn and what was coming.

Callie felt sick at heart that it was happening again. She'd gone for almost two years without one of these major incidents. She'd actually thought they had stopped. Then this cowboy had shown up and set her nerves on edge, and now her head was splitting.

"Mornin'." She put a glass of water on his table along with a menu. As she began to fill his empty mug with coffee, he turned his gaze on her.

"Good morning."

She felt the low rumble of his voice at chest level again. "I forgot if you wanted cream with your coffee," she lied. He threw her off balance—just as he'd done the day before when she'd spilled his coffee.

When he didn't answer, she finally looked at him. His dark-eyed look said he didn't buy that she'd forgotten for a minute.

"Just black, thanks."

"I'll give you a minute to look at your menu," she said and started to turn away.

"I'll have what I had yesterday," he said. As she turned back, he reached for his menu to hand it to her. "Oh, that's right. You weren't the one who waited on me." His grin was good-natured, but there was a challenge in his voice.

It felt strange that she picked up no flashes of information from him. *Nothing*. It was as if he was protected by a wall that she couldn't penetrate. Why was that? Who was this man? Looking into those dark eyes, she was assaulted by a mix of emotions, but none she could trust or make sense of other than fear.

"Ham, eggs over easy, hash browns and whole-wheat toast." She could have told him that he also dug through the jellies until he found blackberry, which he spread thickly on his toast. That he ate only one piece of his toast and that he liked to mix his eggs with his hash browns and douse them with hot sauce and ketchup. But that was all she knew about him.

"I believe I heard Kate put your order up," she said.

He smiled and held out his hand. "Since I'm going to be staying for a while, I thought I should introduce myself. Rourke Montgomery."

She had no choice but to take his hand. "Callie Westfield." But she suspected he already knew who she was, that he'd come here looking for her. His hand was big and warm, her hand disappearing into it. "Nice to meet you, Mr. Montgomery."

The flash was small and weak. Under normal circumstances, she would probably have missed it.

The cowboy had just lied to her. But then, she'd just lied to him, as well.

ROURKE SAW THE sudden change in her. She withdrew her hand and took a step back from him. Her reactions to him kept throwing him. What had he done now?

"I'll get your order right up." She turned and was gone before "It was nice to meet you, too, Callie" was out of his mouth.

He'd had a rough night, sleeping little after he'd returned from his trip into the mountains looking for her. The coffee helped a little. He thought about calling Laura to see if she'd made it to her mother's all right, but hesitated since it was still early. Laura wouldn't have gotten to Harlowton until the wee hours of the morning and with her mother sick…dying…

When his cell phone vibrated in his jacket pocket, it startled him. He instantly expected bad news. Laura? He pulled out the phone. Edwin Sharp. Finally the call he'd been waiting for.

Glancing around the café, he saw that it was almost empty. Kate was sitting at a booth with an elderly red-headed woman some distance away. Two noisy cowboys had just come in, but they were at the counter talking loudly.

Anxious to speak with Edwin, he picked up. "I can't really talk. I'm in a café, but I can listen," he said without preamble.

"Then I'll make this quick," the P.I. said.

Rourke listened, holding any questions he had for later when he could talk freely. He couldn't believe what Edwin was telling him.

"I'm on my way now to talk to a woman who reportedly took in some of the girls from that home after it closed," the P.I. said. "I'll call you later with what I find out. But a woman named Caligrace definitely lived in that place—and died there—and she had a daughter who apparently shared her first name. No last name, though."

Rourke disconnected and looked in Callie Westfield's direction. She was filling the coffee cups of the two noisy cowboys. They were flirting with her, teasing her, and one of them was clearly trying to get her to go out with him.

One was blond, the other dark-haired, both handsome and apparently locals. Had one of them brought her here?

He watched Callie. She was putting up with them but not encouraging them. As she moved away from their table, the blond man said something about her behind.

If Callie heard, she didn't show it. But Kate heard it. She rose from the booth where she'd been visiting with the redhead and went over to the cowboys. He heard her tell them to be respectful to her waitress or they would have to leave.

They finished their coffee and got up to go. As the blond cowboy paid their bill, the dark-haired one apologized to Kate, then hung back to talk to Callie.

Rourke couldn't hear what was being said, but he could read the dark-haired cowboy's body language. He was pushing hard for her to go out with him, and apparently this wasn't the first time he'd tried to persuade her.

Callie was shaking her head. Rourke could tell she was turning him down politely, but it wasn't deterring the cowboy.

Rourke got up with his half-empty cup and walked toward the two, pretending he just wanted a warm-up on his coffee.

"I appreciate that, Carson, but the answer is still no, thank you. I need to get back to work." Callie started to move away from the man, but the cowhand caught her wrist.

Rourke moved on past to the counter where Kate had just made more coffee. As she refilled his cup, she, too, was watching Callie and the man Callie had called Carson. He guessed this would be the Carson Grant the sheriff had told him about.

"Just give me a chance," Carson said as Callie pulled free of his grip and shot him a warning look that seemed to encourage the two men to leave. Carson tossed a few bills on the counter and moved toward the door where his friend was waiting for him.

Callie glanced away from Carson to meet Rourke's gaze. She looked as angry with him as she was the cowhand as she took the coffeepot from Kate and headed for the redhead in the booth.

"Who were those cowboys bothering your waitress?" he asked Kate as the rowdy cowhands left.

"Carson Grant and Johnny Franks. They're harmless."

Rourke wondered about that. "Locals?"

"Carson just returned a couple years ago. Johnny's new to the area. They both work at the Grant-West Ranch." She looked at him as if realizing he was awfully nosy.

"I just didn't like them giving her a hard time."

Kate laughed. "Callie can take care of herself."

He nodded, remembering the look in her eye when Carson Grant had grabbed her arm. "That's good."

CARSON GRANT LET out a curse as he and Johnny Franks headed for the Grant-West Ranch pickup parked in front of the café. As Carson climbed in, he slammed the heel of his palm into the steering wheel.

"Hey," Johnny said. "What's this about?"

"That woman."

"Callie? Are you serious?"

"What's her problem? I offer her dinner at a nice place, a movie… Hell, she should be glad I want to take her out."

Johnny looked over at him in surprise. "I thought you were just joking around with her."

Carson chewed at the inside of his cheek, so angry he wanted to break something. "I'm sick of not getting what I want."

"Hey, Callie doesn't date *anyone*. She's probably

one of those women who hates men. You're better off without her."

Carson shook his head as he started the truck and backed up, making the tires squeal. "For once, I'd just like to get something I want."

Johnny made a disgusted face.

"What?" he demanded, seeing Johnny's reaction.

"It's just that I would think you'd want to set your sights higher. Hell, go after one of the Hamilton girls. At least they come with land."

Carson shook his head. One of the Hamilton girls would require too much effort. "My whole life I didn't get what I deserved," he complained. "It just gets old."

"You're preaching to the choir. My old man died without a cent. He sure as hell didn't leave me anything."

Carson let out a bitter laugh. "Mine didn't leave me anything either."

"Yeah, but your sister, Destry, at least gave you some land and a place to live."

"A few acres and a *cabin.*"

"More than I've got," Johnny pointed out.

But Carson was thinking about the monstrosity that his father had built that overlooked the ranch. "You've seen the house my father built. It's a mansion. He had the whole county talking about that place. It's even got a swimming pool. An outdoor swimming pool in this part of Montana." Carson shook his head. "W. T. Grant didn't care that he couldn't use it more than a few months of the year. He got what he wanted. People despised him for it. Me? I work for my sister on the ranch that should have been mine."

"You might want to slow down," Johnny said, hanging on as Carson took a bend in the gravel road too fast. "Killing both of us isn't going to make you feel any better about your life."

Carson swore as he let up on the gas. The truck fishtailed in the loose gravel, but he got it back under control. "You're right. Callie Westfield is nobody. If I'm going to get all worked up, it should be over one of the Hamilton girls." He let out a laugh. He knew old man Hamilton wouldn't let him within fifty yards of one of his daughters. Not that those headstrong women were his type anyway.

"I hate to see you worked up like this," Johnny said.

"It's okay. I've got a couple of meetings tonight," he said, trying to still the rage inside him. "I always get worked up before them. I know I should be glad my sister didn't cut me off completely. I'm just having a bad day."

"Count your blessings, right? Your sister is easy to work for and she pays well. Some poor suckers don't even have jobs."

Between his meetings for his alcohol and gambling issues, Carson was sick to death of counting his blessings, living one day at a time and telling himself that he didn't want a drink or to ante up at one of the local card games.

His life was a lie, he thought, as he drove toward his sister's ranch, a ranch that should have been his. He thought of his father. W.T. had been a low-down SOB; no one in the county would argue that. Better that than to be what he knew the county thought of *him*.

CHAPTER ELEVEN

"LAURA?"

She cringed at the sound of her mother's voice. She'd felt sick the moment she'd opened her eyes. She'd had the nightmare last night. It had felt so real that she'd awakened expecting to be covered in blood.

Swinging her legs over the side of the bed, she sat up. Dizziness hit her along with the nausea. She put her head down, took deep breaths and tried to still her roiling stomach.

The creak of her mother's wheelchair made her look up. She tried to focus, but her head swam. Her mother stopped in the doorway just feet away and watched her.

As Laura lifted her head and met her mother's gaze, realization hit her. "You *drugged me?*"

Laura knew she shouldn't have been shocked. Her mother had given her and her sister "just a little something to keep them quiet" when they were children. Had she really thought her mother had changed?

"Don't be ridiculous," her mother snapped. "I just gave you a little something in your warm milk to help you sleep."

Laura looked past her mother, her head still fuzzy. She felt like a child again, waking in a strange place and knowing she wasn't safe. "Is Catherine here?"

Her mother made a pained sound. "Laura—"

"She's your favorite. She's the one you want here."

Eyes welling with tears, her mother said with obvious exasperation, "Are you just trying to hurt me?"

"Fine, we won't talk about Catherine."

"Maybe we should."

"Is that why you got me home? You want to talk about my sister?"

"Oh, Laura, there is nothing I can say that you don't take the wrong way. I want to help you."

"Help me? Isn't it a little late for that, Mother?"

"I hope not." With that, the woman wheeled slowly into the other room.

Laura watched her go, wondering why she thought she could believe anything her mother told her. The woman was definitely not on her deathbed.

"CALIGRACE?" THE STOUT elderly woman asked as she leaned against the door frame and glanced at the photo Edwin had handed her. "I haven't taken in foster kids for years. I really doubt… Nope, don't remember a Caligrace." Leta Arthur began to shake her head and close the door.

"She might have gone by Callie. Dark hair and eyes, about five years old, probably small for her age—"

"Callie," Leta said, both her eyes and her door opening wider. "A quiet little thing. Had just lost her mother. I do remember *her.* What's this about? She in trouble? That's where they were all headed, you know. Wasn't any way I could prevent that. I could see it even back then. It was in the eyes." She looked down at the grainy photo of Caligrace Westfield. "But this one," she said, tapping the photo with her finger. "Cute and

quiet, but she gave me the spooks, you know what I mean?"

He thought he might. "Would you mind if I came in and asked you a few questions?" He flashed his credentials. "I've been engaged to find her."

"A private eye, eh?" She shrugged and stepped back out of the doorway.

Edwin had said goodbye to Pete once they got to Billings and rented a car, glad to have his feet on the ground.

"Not moving real fast this morning," Leta said as she led the way into the house. "Haven't even made coffee yet." It was almost ten, but she was still in her robe and slippers. She shuffled across the carpet, waving him in as her slippers made tiny static electrical sparks in her wake. She took the worn recliner. He sat on the plastic-covered couch a few yards away.

The house smelled of cats. He thought he saw one streak by out of the corner of his eye, but suspected there were many more. "What about Callie gave you the spooks?"

She thought on that for a moment. "It wasn't anything you could put your finger on. She just acted… strange. Sometimes the way she looked at me…" She shuddered.

He tried to imagine how a five-year-old could act strange enough to scare this woman. "How long did you have her?"

"Not long. My husband died and I couldn't handle so many kids, so the state took her back. Not sure where she went after that. I heard she ran away a lot. I suppose she's come to some sort of bad end, or you wouldn't be here." The woman leaned toward him. "What has she done?"

Edwin looked around the house at the many knick-knacks on the shelves, the plastic on all the chairs and couch except for the chair Leta was in. There was something petty and mean about the woman. It annoyed him that Leta was practically rubbing her hands together, she was so determined that Callie had turned out as she had predicted twenty-five years before.

Feeling equally uncharitable, he decided to ruin her day. He leaned toward her as she had done, as if to confide in her. "A very wealthy relative has left her money. I'm just trying to find her so she can collect."

"*Money?* How is that possible? The child was orphaned and in foster care."

"Callie's mother came from money. When she got pregnant, the family tried to get her to give up the baby for adoption. She ran away.... The family didn't know what happened to her. Now they've hired me to see that she gets the bulk of the family estate."

It was a conceivable enough story, actually. Leta Arthur definitely bought it. He hoped there might be some truth in it. Did Callie know anything about her family?

"So the girl is *wealthy?*"

"Too bad we didn't know about it when she was under your care. I'm sure the family would have been very grateful that you took her in."

Her eyes glittered at the thought. If only she could turn back the clock and be kind and gentle to Callie, instead of getting rid of her at the first opportunity, he thought as he got to his feet.

The woman struggled to rise from her chair. "If there is anything I can do to help you or her family—"

"Perhaps you can think of someone who worked with the girls before Caligrace came to stay with you," he suggested.

She licked her lips, frowning thoughtfully. "Gladys." He watched her search her memory for the last name. "Gladys McCormick. Yes, that's it. She ran the place right before it closed down. I heard several of the older girls mention her name. I got the impression they were frightened of her. I do hope this information is helpful."

"I'm sure it will be," he said. "Do you know how I can find Gladys?"

"No, but Marjorie might. Marjorie Cline. She's how I heard about these girls needing foster homes. The state was desperate to get them off their hands…." She seemed to catch herself. "Marjorie was a case worker. She met Gladys McCormick once." Leta made a face. "Said the woman was pure evil."

The P.I. wrote down Marjorie's address, even though he had his doubts that any of the background material could save the little girl who had come to live in this house. He feared it was too late for Caligrace, given that he'd been hired by a U.S. marshal. Even a U.S. marshal who made it clear he was "off duty."

Caligrace Westfield was in serious trouble or a man like Rourke Kincaid wouldn't be on her trail.

CALLIE RUBBED HER TEMPLES, The Headache worsening. This was as bad as it had ever been. That fact alone scared her.

"Are you all right?" Kate asked, frowning as she studied Callie's face.

She knew she must be pale. She felt faint. "Headache."

Her boss glanced at the dining room. "It's slow this morning. Take the rest of the day off. I can manage. Go on. Get out of here. But if you need anything—"

"I'll holler," Callie promised as she looked at her boss with so much gratitude that she thought she might cry. She'd spent a lifetime not letting anyone get too close. She knew too much about the people she met, and they knew nothing about her. Which, under the circumstances, she felt better keeping to herself. The flashes tired her out quickly, especially on those days when they were loud—like today.

But the headaches? They were hard enough to take physically. What they portended... That was another story.

"Thank you," she said to her boss. She liked Kate. Under other circumstances, they could have been close friends.

"Just take care of yourself. You're my best waitress."

"I'm your *only* waitress." It was an old joke, but one neither of them tired of, apparently. She reached for Kate's hand impulsively and squeezed it. For a moment, Callie almost told her. But sharing even good news, she'd learned the hard way, caused her problems. It was better that no one knew about her special...gift. Or curse, as it was.

Too bad, because she really would have loved to tell Kate not to worry any longer. After several miscarriages, Kate was pregnant with a little girl, and everything was going to be fine.

"I *will* take the rest of the day, if you don't mind."

Kate smiled. "I can handle it. I was born to wait tables."

Callie laughed. She'd heard that Kate had had a rough time of it before she'd come to Beartooth. But she'd fallen in love with Jack French and everyone said they'd never seen Kate happier.

There had been only that one dark spot—her attempts to have a child. Until now. Callie couldn't wait until her boss got the news. Kate was going to be a great mother.

LAURA WAS SITTING on the edge of the bed trying to clear her head. She was still dressed as she had been last night when she'd arrived. Apparently, she'd passed out still dressed. Had her mother put her to bed?

"Would you like something for breakfast?"

Her stomach roiled at the idea, yet she found herself padding into the kitchen. Her mother had the refrigerator open and was reaching for something at the back. "Would you like some yogurt, Catherine?"

Laura grabbed the arm of her mother's wheelchair, spinning her around to face her. "It's Laura. I'm *Laura*. Not Catherine, Mother."

"It was just a slip of the tongue. Don't you think I know you're Laura?" her mother snapped, sounding close to tears. "Catherine never spoke to me the way—"

"Stop. I can't do this." Laura hated that her voice broke with emotion. "You wish she was here now instead of me. You always chose her over me."

"That's not true. Laura, I love you both. If Catherine got more of my attention, it was because she was always acting up."

"Oh, was that it? Like I said, I don't want to talk about this."

"But we have to. I don't have much time left. I think

we should make a clean breast of what happened between the two of you."

Laura started to turn away, but her mother grabbed her arm. "I'm doing this for you. When I meet my Maker, I have to have tried to—"

"To what, Mother? Clear your conscience? Is that what this is about? Making sure I don't blame you for anything that happened?"

"You're wrong, Laura. I blame myself for all of it. If I hadn't taken the two of you there—"

"You took us to all kinds of horrible places. They all blur together. All of it does."

"You have chosen not to remember, but unless you face—"

"I remember enough, believe me."

Her mother gave her a pitying look. "If only that were true. Are you still seeing that psychiatrist the police department made you see?"

"They only did that to help me get through the trauma of being shot and almost dying, Mother."

"I saw your limp. Will you ever—"

"No, I'll always limp. Can you think of anything else horribly depressing you'd like to discuss with me?"

"I'm sorry. I wish there was something I could do to make your life better."

"My life is fine."

Her mother studied her for a long moment but was wise enough not to argue the point.

ROURKE COULDN'T SHAKE the bad feeling he'd had since last night. The last person he wanted to be fretting about right now was Laura. He needed to find a way to get closer to Caligrace Westfield—not be worrying about his former partner. Unfortunately, he couldn't get Laura out of his mind.

She'd always been so logical, never letting emotion cloud her judgment, but when he thought of some of the things she'd said last night...

He realized she was taking this case personally, and for the life of him, he couldn't understand why. It was almost as if she was...jealous. The thought made him laugh. He'd never thought of Laura that way, and he was sure the feeling was mutual. Either that or she'd kept her feelings hidden well in all the time they'd worked together.

It was this case, he told himself. He realized it didn't help that she'd worked on one of the murders. Did she feel protective of it? Or was she seriously convinced, without any real evidence, that Caligrace Westfield was the killer?

Rourke tried Laura's cell again. He hadn't wanted her to leave last night. She'd been upset about her mother, no matter what she'd said. Maybe that was all it was.

The call went straight to voice mail again. He left another message. "Just wanted to make sure you made it all right. Hope your mom is better. Call me."

Disconnecting, he frowned as he thought of their conversation before she drove away last night.

"We'll keep in touch," he'd said.

She'd looked at him, her voice breaking as she'd said, "Take care of yourself. I couldn't bear it if anything happened to you."

Rourke had heard the fear in her voice. He'd pretended not to. "You know me," he'd said and smiled.

"Yes, I do."

Laura wouldn't be the first cop to lose her nerve

after being shot, he told himself now. He just hadn't expected it of her and blamed himself.

He had been her *partner*. He should have stopped her from going down that alley. After she'd been shot, she'd thought she was going to die. She might have, if he hadn't shot the perp and called for an ambulance as quickly as he had.

As it was, he hadn't known how badly she'd been wounded. She'd had blood all over her and she'd been hallucinating.

He felt a shudder now at the memory. She'd been saying stuff that didn't make any sense as he'd held her hand and waited beside her for the ambulance.

"Is she dead?"

He'd stared at Laura, confused. "It was a man who shot you. He's dead. I shot him."

"You're sure she's dead?" Laura had tried to get up, and he'd had to hold her down. "Sometimes she just looks dead. Put your hand over her mouth and nose. Don't let her get up. If she does, she'll tell…." Laura had begun to shake then, terror in her expression.

He'd been scared that when she'd fallen she had hit her head and was now hallucinating. "Laura, the man who shot you is dead. You don't have anything to fear from him."

Her eyes, bright and brittle as granite, had locked with his. "What if she isn't dead?"

He'd stared at her, trying to make sense of her words and at the same time telling himself that she wasn't in her right mind either from the fall or loss of blood.

"If Mother finds out…"

That was when he'd known that she didn't know

what she was saying. Because her mother had been dead for years.

But her mother hadn't been dead, he reminded himself now. Her mother was alive and only now dying—just miles from here.

CHAPTER TWELVE

LAURA HAD TO lean against the wall for a moment to get her balance. Whatever her mother had put into her milk last night still had her head spinning.

Last night, after not laying eyes on her mother for years, Laura had expected her to look old, small and, since she was reportedly dying, frail and teetering on death's door.

Instead, it was remarkable how little she'd changed. She was still a big woman with a commanding presence even from a wheelchair.

Seeing her mother again had rattled her more than Laura had wanted to admit. How else had she been stupid enough to accept a glass of milk from the woman, knowing what she was capable of?

"What did you drug me with?" she demanded as she tried to get control of herself. The kitchen smelled of burned toast and maybe burned coffee, as well. There was another underlying odor that she'd taken for death when she'd opened the door last night.

Her mother had moved to the table, her back to her, her head bent as if she was crying. Laura knew that wasn't likely. Not unless it was some kind of ploy for sympathy.

"I just gave you a little something to help you sleep," her mother said, her back still to her. She wasn't cry-

ing. Nor was her head bent in any kind of remorse for
what she had done.

Laura saw that the moment she stepped over to the
table. Her mother was bent over the file on the first
murder. One of the photographs of Caligrace Westfield was in her hand.

"What are you doing going through my things?"
Laura demanded, snatching the file away. In her anger,
the contents scattered across the floor.

Laura hurriedly bent to retrieve the papers. She had
to grab the table leg for a moment as the nausea and
dizziness hit her again.

"What is all this?" her mother demanded.

"None of your business."

"I thought you weren't a cop anymore."

"I thought you were dying." Laura swallowed back
the bile that rose in her throat and fought to keep the
contents of her stomach down. "I'm a profiler now."

"A what?"

"I study criminal behavior. It lets me develop a psy-
chological profile of an offender based on a specific
crime or crime scene." She rose slowly because of the
nausea, the papers in her hands. "Give me those."

Her mother handed over everything but one of the
enlarged photos of Caligrace Westfield.

When Laura reached for it, her mother's gaze locked
with hers. "Why are you investigating Westfield?"

At first she misunderstood, thinking her mother
must have read the last name on the file, including
the preliminary profile she'd done of the suspect: C.
Westfield. "She's a suspect." She stuffed everything
back in the folder before returning it to her overnight

bag, which her mother had also gone through, apparently. "Like I said, it's none of your—"

"Why would you be interested in that place?" her mother demanded in that hoarse rasp of a voice.

Laura felt her skin crawl. "What *place?*"

The older woman's eyes widened in alarm. "Westfield *Manor.* Or are you going to keep telling me you don't remember? Just like you don't remember this woman in this photograph," she cried, waving Caligrace's photo in front of Laura's face.

Suddenly Laura felt too weak to stand and barely got a chair pulled out before dropping into it. Caligrace Westfield's photo *had* looked familiar the first time she'd seen it, but there wasn't any way she could know the woman.

Leaning over, she cradled her head in her hands, afraid she was going to be sick. "You're confused. Westfield is only the woman's last name. It has nothing to do with…"

"That place you say you don't remember?" her mother crowed, triumph in her voice. "So you do remember. Then you must also remember what happened to your sister there."

"My *sister?* What about what happened to *me,* Mother?" Laura shot to her feet and, stumbling over her mother's wheelchair, rushed into the bathroom to throw up.

MARJORIE CLINE LIVED at the local nursing home in Lewistown, Montana. She was a tiny, frail woman with a head of stark white fuzzy hair like a halo. The moment she saw Edwin, she burst into a big smile, her blue eyes sparkling.

"Well, look who's here!" she cried excitedly.

At his confused expression, a nearby nurse came over. "Are you here to see Marjorie?"

"Yes, but—"

The nurse nodded and smiled sympathetically. "She thought you were her son. It's all right. She has Alzheimer's."

"Oh, I'm sorry to hear that." The nurse couldn't imagine how sorry. "I had hoped to talk to her about—"

"Let me guess. Westfield."

Edwin blinked in surprise.

"I'm surprised that it took this long for someone to finally be interested in what apparently went on up there. It was all Marjorie talked about when she first came here."

"Maybe you could help me, then." He showed her his credentials and asked if she could spare a minute to talk.

"I was just getting ready to go on break. I can tell you what Marjorie used to go on about. I'm not sure how much I remember."

As it turned out, she remembered a lot. Edwin listened to horror stories about the filth, the lack of food, the corruption.

"They should have strung up that woman who ran the place," the nurse said.

"Did Marjorie mention the woman's name?"

"Gladys McCormick. I heard after the state closed down the place that they tried to find the woman, but apparently, she had skipped the state, disappeared." The nurse shook her head. "Marjorie said there is a graveyard behind the place. That's where they put those poor girls since no one wanted to pay to have them buried properly, let alone in the city's cemetery."

He thought of the one crude gravestone and the angel out in the field, away from the others.

"Before Marjorie got as bad as she is now, that's been a couple of years ago, she went on a trip to Yellowstone with her son. On the way, she swore she saw Gladys McCormick. She made her son stop so she could confront the woman, who said she was mistaken. I think it was very upsetting for her son. He didn't take his mother anywhere after that, doesn't come to visit at all anymore."

Edwin couldn't bear to look at the sweet, little old woman anxiously watching the main door. "Where was this that she thought she saw Gladys McCormick?"

"Oh, Marjorie *swore* it was her and that the woman lied through her teeth. It was in Harlowton."

"If the woman wasn't Gladys McCormick, did she tell them the name she was going by?"

The nurse shook her head. "I don't think Marjorie thought to ask, and of course her son didn't. Marjorie even called the local police and wanted them to go arrest the woman for the murders."

"Murders? There was more than one?"

"Oh, I know the grizzly one made the news, but Marjorie swore there was another one. Of course, no one had ever heard of that one." The nurse looked away for a moment and sighed. "That was another reason no one believed her. Marjorie swore Gladys covered up the second one. She said it was one of the girls."

Edwin thought of Caligrace's mother. Was it possible Gladys had found out that she was the one who had contacted the deputy the first time blood was shed inside that place and made sure Caligrace didn't talk again?

"Did you tell the police this?"

"I called them and told them the story Marjorie had told me. They came here and spoke to Marjorie, but they caught her on one of her bad days. She wasn't making a lot of sense. Then they talked to her son. He swore that he didn't know what his mother was talking about. That they didn't even see anyone in Harlowton, let alone accost some poor woman." The nurse made a face. "As far as I know, the police never tried to find the woman Marjorie swore she'd seen."

ROURKE FINALLY REACHED Laura late in the afternoon. She sounded as if he'd woken her up, and he mentally kicked himself. She must be exhausted from the late-night drive, not to mention the stress of her mother's condition. No wonder she hadn't been answering his calls.

"I just wanted to make sure that you made it to your mother's all right," he said.

"You really don't need to worry about me."

Rourke feared that he did. "Look, you have enough on your plate right now. I don't want you to worry about—"

"Don't. I need something to keep my mind occupied, especially right now. Have you discovered a possible male co-killer?"

He hesitated. "There are two cowboys."

"Give me their names and I'll see if I can find a connection between them and Callie."

"I'd appreciate that, if you're sure—"

"I'm sure."

"Carson Grant and Johnny Franks. Carson is apparently from the area. Johnny hasn't been here long."

"I'll see what I can find out about them for you. Also, I'm working on the profiles." He heard a door slam, then the rev of a motor as she apparently went outside.

She sounded more like the woman who'd been his partner for those years on the Seattle P.D. Maybe there wasn't any reason for concern. "That's great. Thank you. How is your mother?"

"Dying. How is Callie?"

Callie. "I'm making some progress. She's…complicated."

Laura made a disparaging sound. "Don't lose sight that she could be the person who cut up those other men."

"I haven't forgotten. I should mention, Carson Grant has been hitting on Callie. She keeps turning him down, but—"

"But you think there could be something there."

He hated to admit it. "Thanks for your help, but do me a favor. Keep in touch. I don't like to have to worry about you."

"Then don't," she said, but he could hear it in her voice. She was touched. He realized he should have been making these calls a lot more over the past year.

"I'm really sorry about your mom. I'll come up for the funeral—"

"There isn't going to be one, but thanks. I need to go." And just like that, she was gone.

Rourke tried to put his worries about Laura out of his mind as he went over the murder files. He kept thinking he was missing something. Either that or he was on a wild-goose chase.

It was late when he finally wandered outside to the cabin porch for some fresh air. Through the pines, he could see the café. The night was cold and clear, the sky alight with stars. The moon was just coming up, a golden orb peeking over the tops of the trees.

At the sound of a vehicle, he glanced toward the café in time to see Callie driving away in her pickup. Where was she heading for the second night in a row?

This time, he was going to find out.

CALLIE HAD GONE upstairs to her apartment and tried to sleep, praying it would lessen the headache. Or at least keep her from thinking about Rourke Montgomery. If that was even his name. He'd lied about something when they'd met, which was no more shocking than the fact that she'd gotten the small, dim flash.

Why would a complete stranger feel the need to lie to her? That was the question that nagged at her and kept her from sleep. That and the headache.

When she finally couldn't stand the confines of her apartment over the café any longer, she'd gotten up. It was after midnight. The town outside her apartment was dead quiet. But she couldn't stand being hemmed in by the four walls any longer. Her head was still throbbing. If she was right and the stranger in town was the cause of her headache, then putting distance between herself and the town could help.

She'd changed into jeans, boots, a flannel shirt and coat and headed for her pickup. The moon had come up and now glazed the Crazies in an icy cold silver. It cast the quiet Beartooth in an eerie pale light. Callie loved this time of night. She'd always been a night owl, requiring little sleep.

As she pulled out to the main drag, she debated where to go. Left would take her to Big Timber on the paved highway. The last thing she needed, though, was another town with people. She turned right and drove along the main street, passing the remains of what had once been a thriving mining town. Stone buildings still stood, though most had been empty for years and were in need of repair. But she could see that work had begun on the old hotel. Another reminder of the change that had blown into her life.

At the edge of town, the pavement ended, and she turned toward the Crazy Mountains, her headlights cutting through the tall pines. The dirt road wound back through dense pines broken only by groves of aspens. Some still had an array of gold, red and orange leaves that glowed in her headlights. The farther she went, the more narrow and twisted the road became until it topped out, then dropped in switchbacks to the blue-green lake below.

This was one of her favorite spots. She'd found the lake by accident and now came here many nights. Soon winter snows would drift in the road, closing it until late spring. That made her sad because she feared she would be gone by spring.

She pulled to the edge of the lake, parked and got out. Few people came here even during normal daylight hours. This time of night, she always had the place to herself. The high mountain lake was surrounded by towering green pines. Moonlight played off the crystal clear icy cold water as the large boulders left from the glacier age formed pockets of shadows along the edge.

Tonight the lake glistened in the warmth of the moon, the sky around her so filled with stars that it almost felt like daylight. The fresh cold fall air filled her lungs. As she released it, she realized she felt better. She'd been right to escape town, which told her she was just as right about Rourke.

So who was he and what was he doing in Beartooth? She feared she would know soon enough.

At the sound of a vehicle approaching, she turned. Headlights bobbed on the road. She couldn't see the cowboy behind the wheel as the vehicle grew closer, but she sensed him.

Her head began to pound. If she'd had any doubt, she didn't anymore. *He* was the source of her headache. He'd followed her, and now here she was, in the middle of the night at an isolated lake in the mountains, alone with him.

ROURKE WAS SURPRISED as he came over a rise and spotted the blue pickup—and the lake at the end of the road.

He'd stayed back, keeping his distance as he'd followed her out of town. This time he'd seen which road she'd taken back into the mountains. Now, though, he was caught. She'd seen his lights as he came down the road. He decided he would have to talk his way out of this. Or at least try.

Driving on down to where she was parked, he pulled in, cut his lights and climbed out. Callie was leaning against the side of her truck as if waiting for him as he approached. If she'd come here to meet someone, the person hadn't arrived yet.

"Hey," he said, closing the distance between them.

"Hey." There was a distinct edge to her voice.

"I'm sorry. You probably wanted to be alone."

"But you followed me anyway. Why is that?" she asked as she reached inside the open window of the pickup and came out with a handgun.

He raised his hands as she pointed it at his chest. "Are you going to shoot me?"

"Am I going to have to?"

"Not if I can help it," he said, trying to decide if she would actually pull the trigger. She seemed comfortable with the gun, holding it as if she was no stranger to the weapon. He thought again of Laura's argument that some female serial killers used weapons like guns and knives.

"Again, why did you follow me?"

"I was worried about you. I was afraid you were walking in your sleep."

"I wasn't *walking*," she pointed out.

"Actually, there have been cases of sleepwalkers driving some distances then returning home with no memory of it." He glanced back at the road cut into the rock cliffs they'd driven down. "Dangerous place to be sleepwalking—or sleep-driving."

"Could be just as dangerous to follow someone here."

He shook his head. "Not on a beautiful moonlit night. That is why you came here, isn't it? For the view? Or maybe you're like me and you just couldn't sleep?"

She didn't answer.

He looked out at the water. "I had no idea this lake was here. It's so peaceful."

"It's usually peaceful here this time of the night because there is no one around," she said, still sounding upset with him.

"I could leave."

She sighed. Even holding a gun on him, she didn't look dangerous. Thinking that, of course, could be his last mistake, though. The moonlight played on her face. She looked…beautiful. He was more aware of her soft rounded curves, more aware of her as a woman, and he quickly warned himself to be careful. He'd seen her effect on Carson Grant. Callie had the poor cowboy eating out of her hand.

Callie leveled the gun at his heart. "Tell me the real reason you followed me."

He smiled. "It's really no mystery. I couldn't sleep. I saw you leave." He shrugged. "I've been getting up the nerve to ask you out. I didn't want to ask you at the café…."

She scoffed at that. "You are not the kind of man who has to get up his nerve."

"You're wrong about that. I'm actually pretty shy. But following you was a dumb idea."

She seemed to relax a little.

"Could I put my hands down now?"

"First, tell me what you're doing in Beartooth."

"I'm looking for a small ranch to invest in."

She considered that for a moment. "You know anything about ranching?"

"I should," he said with a laugh as he looked past her toward the lake. It really was beautiful, but nothing compared to her in the moonlight. "I grew up on one in Wyoming."

"That what you were talking to the sheriff about yesterday?" she asked. So, she'd seen them, had she?

He nodded. "I was asking about the area. Usually, the sheriff is a good person to ask. Sounds like there isn't much crime here."

"You might be surprised," she said, but lowered the gun. "I guess no one has told you what happened at the general store the night it burned down."

"I heard." He was more interested in the woman standing in front of him. "What lake is this?" he asked, staying where he was so as not to spook her. She wasn't going to shoot him, but she didn't trust him either.

"Saddlestring." She was still watching him, still wary of him, the gun dangling from her fingertips at her side.

"It looks cold and deep."

"Were you thinking of going for a swim?"

"I would if you went in first."

She chuckled. "Have you had any luck with this approach with women?"

"Not much."

"That should tell you something."

"But if I had asked you out yesterday morning at breakfast like I wanted to, what would you have said?"

"Thanks, but no, thanks."

"See?"

She shifted on her feet, the gun at her side.

"I should go and let you enjoy the peace and quiet."

Callie didn't say anything as he tipped his Stetson, turned and walked toward his SUV. Laura would have given him hell for turning his back on a woman with a gun. Especially a possible serial killer.

"If you do this again another night, at least bring a couple of bottles of cold beer," she called after him.

He smiled to himself but didn't turn. "I will."

CHAPTER THIRTEEN

CALLIE HAD EXPECTED to see Rourke at breakfast. When he hadn't come in by lunchtime, she found herself watching for him.

"Anything wrong?" Kate asked, sounding amused.

"Nope."

"No headache today?"

"Nope." That wasn't quite true. It was still there, a dull ache at the back of her skull. Whatever was coming was still on its way. She just never knew when the trouble would hit—just that it would.

"I haven't seen your cowboy yet today," Kate said.

"He probably left town," Callie said as she began to clear dishes from one of the lunch-crowd tables.

Kate chuckled. "That's probably it. Or maybe you scared him off."

Callie smiled to herself. Not even holding a gun on Rourke Montgomery had scared him off. No, he was still in town. She could…sense him even though she wasn't getting any flashes of information about him.

"Too bad you can't scare off Carson Grant as easily," Kate said. "You know, if he gets to be too much, I could talk to the sheriff—"

"I can handle Carson," Callie said as she started past her with her arms full of dishes.

Her boss smiled. "Still, if you ever need my help…"

"Thanks. I appreciate it, but I'm fine." Also not exactly true. Carson had been a real pain earlier. He just wasn't taking no for an answer.

She'd known what he wanted from the first day she'd started work and he'd flirted with her. For months now he'd been teasing her, trying to get her to go out with him. Unfortunately, she could read him loud and clear—even if she hadn't been psychic. There was a jittery nervousness to him, so from the start she'd known he was a man with demons other than his addictions, both gambling and alcohol.

If anyone had asked her, she could have told them that Carson Grant was just hanging on by the skin of his teeth. She suspected he would be falling off the wagon any day now.

The bell over the café door tinkled. Callie didn't have to turn and look. She kept on heading for the dish room in the kitchen as Rourke came through the door. He brought the fall scents with him on the cold mountain air. She breathed it in and smiled, then quickly chastised herself as she felt the dull ache at the back of her head.

Rourke was somehow connected to the trouble. The thought made her heart ache, as well. This was why she tried not to get involved with the people around her, so she didn't hurt so much when the bad things happened.

But as she dropped off the dishes, washed her hands and headed back into the café, she prayed that nothing would happen to Rourke. Not that she could stop it, though.

ROURKE HAD SPENT the morning with a real-estate agent, looking at small ranches. He'd made some headway last night with Callie, but she was smart. Also, this was a small town. Word traveled fast. If he wasn't really looking for a ranch, Callie would hear about it.

Now, as he came in after the lunch rush and took his usual seat, he saw that she was busy clearing off a table. Nearby, he spotted Carson Grant and his friend Johnny Franks. They were also watching Callie.

She looked tired, as if she hadn't gotten much sleep. Welcome to the club, he thought. He'd spent a restless night—what was left of it after he'd returned to his cabin. All morning, as he'd gone from one beautiful ranch to another, he hadn't been able to keep the woman off his mind.

"Are you all right?" Rourke asked when she came over to his table.

"Fine," she said as she filled up a cup with coffee and handed him a menu.

But she wasn't fine. He felt as if she was on edge and worried that he was making her that way.

"I'm sorry about last night," he said.

"What part of it?" She met his gaze with a challenging one.

"The part where you pulled a gun on me."

She smiled, and he felt a wave of relief. Whatever was bothering her, he didn't think he was completely responsible for it.

Carson called to her. "I could use some of that coffee."

"I'll be back to take your order," she said to Rourke.

He realized Carson could be part of the problem as he watched her return to the cowboy's table. He could see the way she moved through the café that she wasn't quite as efficient as she usually was. Kate had noticed it, too, apparently, because she was watching Callie, a frown on her face.

Rourke thought about his talk with Laura early this morning when she'd called. She'd said she'd been working on the profiles for him, and the more she did, the more she feared she was right about Caligrace.

"It's been over a year since there was a murder that we know about," she'd said. He'd heard street noises. He'd just assumed she was calling from outside again because she didn't want to disturb her mother. "So, why hasn't your killer struck again?"

"Maybe he has," he'd insisted.

"Maybe *she* has. But I don't think so. She left the Seattle area. Maybe to make a new start. But now you show up. Unless your instincts are completely wrong…"

She'd hit on the core of the matter. Could he trust his instincts? They'd let him down before. What if he was making the same mistake now?

"Rourke, I think you are closer to the killer than you know. The killings that we know about were all in October. You do know what today is, don't you? October 1. So if it's Callie and I'm right about her, then she's going to get more agitated until she snaps. She's going to kill again and soon."

It's not her, he'd wanted to argue. But as he watched Callie now, he couldn't help but worry. She wasn't herself; anyone could see that.

"Rourke, you have to believe me. Caligrace Westfield is your killer," Laura had said. "There is no boyfriend, no brother or lover who is doing this. No co-killer. She is going to be feeling more stress. Don't tell me you haven't seen it."

He'd seen it. The woman carried a gun in her purse,

for crying out loud. She was scared. Something was bothering her or scaring her. The question was: What? A murderous past? Or was there more to it?

"Rourke, this woman has put some kind of spell on you," Laura had said, even more adamant. "You have to be careful. You're applying pressure, something that maybe she hasn't had for this past year. If I'm right, she's going to start unraveling, and when she does…"

The sound of breaking dishes yanked him out of his thoughts. Callie stood over the broken plates full of food she'd just dropped on her way to one of the tables. She looked like a woman unraveling.

Kate hurried to her as Callie knelt down to pick up the shards. "Let me do this. You'll cut yourself."

"I don't know what happened." Callie looked close to tears. "I've never done that before."

"It's all right," Kate assured her. "Get me the broom and dustpan. We'll get this cleaned up. It's no big deal. Just make sure the cook starts the meals over." She closed a hand over Callie's arm and gave her a shake. "Did you hear me? Go get—"

Callie finally moved. "I'll get it." She rose to her feet, clearly rattled. Her gaze shot to him. Something in her eyes—

Before he could put a name to it, she turned and disappeared into the back of the café. It was like everything that Laura had been saying. So why was he refusing to believe it? Because he didn't want to.

Rourke heard the cowboy with Carson Grant say, "You're right. You're definitely getting to her." The two men laughed. "You got her falling at your feet."

Clearly shaken, Callie let Kate lead her back to the

empty counter. Rourke could see Kate trying to find out what was bothering the young woman.

He hated to think that Laura was right, that he'd let this woman get to him, that he was this close to a serial killer and refused to believe it. He picked up his menu, even though he'd lost his appetite.

Out of the corner of his eye, he saw a man approaching the café. The man wore a large coat that appeared threadbare even from a distance. He had a backpack thrown over one shoulder, and he was limping as if his worn boots hurt his feet.

A moment later, the bell over the café door tinkled, and a gust of fall air rushed in along with the man.

Rourke heard a sound like a gasp and turned to see Callie's eyes widened in alarm.

From behind the counter, Kate was also looking in the direction of the man who'd entered the café. She said, "Everyone just stay calm, and let me handle this."

Turning toward the vagrant-looking man, Rourke saw he had pulled a gun and was pointing it at Kate. "Give me the money in the cash register now!"

She moved cautiously to the register and opened it.

Rourke swore under his breath. The man's hand was shaking. With nerves? Or a need for drugs? Either way, he looked desperate, a man with nothing to lose—the most dangerous kind.

Kate handed over the cash.

"This is all you've got?" the man demanded.

Rourke could see this situation going south at any moment. To make matters worse, Callie was edging toward the man. What did she plan to do, try to take the gun away from him?

"I know you have more money," the man said. "You must have a safe or a box you keep it in."

Cursing under his breath, Rourke pulled out his wallet and got to his feet. "I have money."

The man spun toward him, swinging the barrel of the gun so it was now pointed at Rourke's heart as he approached. From his surprised expression, he hadn't seen Rourke until that moment.

He held out the wallet. "No one wants any trouble. Here, take this. It's got a couple hundred in it."

"Stop right there!" The man looked even more jumpy. Not good. "Drop the wallet. You," the man said, motioning to Callie. "You bring it to me."

"It's no problem," Rourke said, ignoring the man's order and putting himself between the gun and Callie. He was almost to the man. He could see the man's finger twitching on the trigger. Rourke knew he'd be damned lucky not to get shot before this was over.

Just another step or two…

"I said to drop the wallet." The man tried to steady the gun as he readied himself to fire.

Rourke moved with the speed of his training. He pretended to drop the wallet, to bend down, but when he came up, he launched himself at the man, shoving the gun to the side as he spun into the fellow with an elbow and wrenched the weapon away.

As the man doubled over from the first strike, Rourke spun back, catching him in the side of the head with the gun. The man dropped like a bushel bag of potatoes.

"Call the sheriff," Rourke said to Kate, who stood openmouthed behind the counter.

She blinked, then grabbed her cell phone and hit 911.

"Nice moves," Callie said, her dark eyes studying him with new intensity. "You're quite the hero."

He scoffed at that. "It was stupid. If I had been thinking clearly…"

She shook her head, not buying it. "Next you're going to tell me that you picked up those moves watching late-night TV."

"You guessed it. Speaking of moves, you were certainly cool as a cucumber." She still was. Kate was shaking and clearly upset. But not Callie.

"I knew he wasn't going to shoot anyone."

"Oh, you did, huh?"

She looked uncomfortable. "I didn't think the gun was loaded. I could have been wrong." She shrugged.

But she hadn't been wrong. When he'd taken the gun away from the man, he'd seen that the clip was empty. Rourke realized as he felt Callie's gaze on him that he'd possibly just blown his cover for nothing.

CHAPTER FOURTEEN

LAURA WAS RELIEVED when her mother had taken to her bed. It had allowed her to work on Rourke's case and to keep her from thinking about the crazy things her mother had said. The woman was certifiable. Why hadn't Laura seen that before and had her mother put someplace where she couldn't hurt anyone?

When her cell phone rang, she was glad to see it was Rourke. She'd been afraid she wouldn't hear from him after their discussion earlier this morning.

"How are you and your mother doing?" he asked.

"As well as can be expected," she said, just glad to hear his voice. It always made her heart beat a little faster, she thought as she took the phone outside so her mother couldn't hear. "What have you heard from your P.I.?"

Rourke seemed just as glad for the change of topic. "He's been up north in Flat Rock, tracked Callie to a girls' home up there. They called the place Westfield Manor—which he thinks is how Callie came up with her last name. He talked to the woman who took her into foster care for a while and now he has a lead on the woman who ran the place. Maybe you or your mother might have heard of her since two years ago she was living in Harlowton? The woman's name is Gladys

McCormick. Maybe your mother hasn't been living there that long, though."

"No, she hasn't," Laura said, feeling as if the ground under her feet had turned into quicksand. "I'm sorry. I need to go. My mother... Thanks for calling."

As she looked toward the house, she saw a face at the window, but it quickly disappeared. "Catherine?" Her blood turned to ice. Just her imagination playing tricks on her?

Laura shuddered, hugging herself as she was drawn toward the house the same way she'd been drawn into that alley a year ago, even though she'd known something dark and horrible was waiting for her.

She pushed open the back door and stepped in, stopping to listen. The refrigerator in the kitchen hummed noisily, the smell of burned toast and coffee still strong.

Somewhere deeper in the house, a floorboard groaned. She listened for the creak of her mother's wheelchair and heard nothing. In the living room, she caught a whiff of something nauseatingly sweet.

Her sister's perfume?

Sometimes she would catch a hint of it in her apartment in Seattle and be forced to spend the next hour searching every inch of the place. Catherine had always been good at hiding when they were children. Laura would finally find her curled into a ball in some dark hole, her blue eyes wide with some terrible secret.

As she started down the hall, she saw that the only closed door was to her mother's room. Her pulse jumped, her footsteps quickening. If Catherine was in there with her... *"Mother?"*

Laura shoved open the door. It hit the wall with a bang, the sound echoing through the room. The first thing she saw was her mother's wheelchair lying on its side. Already moving, she lurched into the room and stopped dead next to the bed. A chill washed over her, dimpling her skin with goose bumps.

Her mother lay on the bed on her back, her arms folded over her chest.

"Mother?"

Laura started to lean down closer, her heart in her throat. Her mother didn't appear to be breathing. She—

The old woman opened her eyes.

Laura couldn't hold back the scream as she stumbled back.

ON HIS WAY to Harlowton to try to track down the elusive Gladys McCormick, Edwin's cell phone rang. He figured it would be Rourke, but to his surprise, the name that came up was Leta Arthur.

"Mrs. Arthur?" he said into the phone.

"Did my friend help you?" she asked without preamble.

"Unfortunately, Marjorie was having one of her bad days." He didn't tell her what the nurse had relayed to him about Gladys McCormick. He didn't feel like being that nice to Leta. Also, he thought looking for the elusive Gladys McCormick would turn out to be a wild-goose chase anyway.

"Well, maybe this will help. I have another name for you. I've been making some calls to help the family with this," Leta said. It always amazed him what greed could do to help the cause.

"This woman worked there only a short time, but she might know something more that the family will appreciate," she was saying. "The woman's name is

Harper, Lisa Harper. She lives in Judith Gap, which is south of Lewistown. She actually worked at the girls' home for a while."

Judith Gap. He'd seen it on the map he'd picked up. It was just up the road from where he was driving. The rental car had a navigation system, but he was old school. He liked a real map.

"I've already called her and told her you were coming by. Just mention my name." Leta rattled off the address. "You can't miss it. The house is right by the school."

"You've been most helpful," he said.

"It's the least I can do."

The house was small and sat on a hill. The wind howled around it, kicking up dust and sending anything not nailed down flying. On the way into town, he'd seen the wind farm. The massive blades of dozens of huge white windmills turned hypnotically against the crystal clear blue of Montana's big sky.

He'd heard there was a snowstorm blowing in. Given the fierceness of the wind, he just hoped he didn't get caught in it. He fought his rental-car door to get out, then stood, letting the wind buffet him as he took in the view. Mountains bordered two sides of town, the tops dusted white with snow. Behind the mountains to the west, he would see a line of dark, low-hanging clouds.

He turned to the house. The curtains were drawn, the old house looking uninhabited. Slowly he climbed the rickety steps and crossed a leaf-strewn porch to reach the front door. Like the house, it was weathered.

He knocked as the wind whirled the dried leaves across the porch and waited, then knocked again. Inside the house, he heard the scrape of something being dragged across the floor and suddenly felt uncomfortable.

When he was little, his mother used to take him to the old folks' home on the edge of town to see his grandmother. Those memories were like nightmares. The smell of old age, urine and impending death. The grasping gnarled hands reaching for him from cloaked shrunken figures in wheelchairs.

He braced himself as he heard the familiar sound of an elderly person shuffling toward the door. The door opened a crack, and a weathered, scowling face peered out.

"Lisa Harper?" The too-familiar smell of decay swept out as if suddenly freed from being imprisoned in the house for months.

"What do you want? I don't have any money and I don't want anything anyway," she snapped and started to close the door.

"I want to talk to you about Westfield. Leta Arthur said she'd called you about my stopping by?"

The door stopped closing about an inch from the jamb. "I can't imagine why anyone would care about that place after all these years."

"The U.S. Marshals' office does, Mrs. Harper. Unless you want to talk to them…"

The door slowly opened. "There is no Mrs. It's just Lisa Harper. I never married."

He nodded, hearing the bitterness in her tone as he got his first real view of the woman leaning on the walker.

At one time, she'd been a large woman. Now her wide shoulders were slumped, the meat on her gone, leaving little more than her bony skeleton.

Her head, though, was still large, the face square, the scowl lines embedded into her pallid flesh. This had not been a happy woman, he suspected.

She left the door open, the only invitation he was going to get, apparently. He would have been much happier talking to her on the porch, but he doubted the woman could withstand the wind gusts, even if there had been somewhere to sit.

Wishing he was anywhere but here, he stepped into the dark gloom of the woman's living room. The decor was as old and worn as the house and the woman.

As she shuffled toward a worn quilt-covered recliner, he sought out a chair. Everything was covered with either blankets or pilled afghans.

Sitting down on the edge of the sagging couch, he pulled out his notebook and pen as the woman worked her way back into her chair. She let out a groan, as if the effort had used the last of her energy. He suspected it had.

"What can you tell me about Westfield?" he asked, just wanting to get this over with as quickly as possible. "Leta mentioned you worked there?"

"Just until I could get another job and get out of there."

"When was that?" he asked.

"Twenty-six years ago."

At least her memory seemed intact. "Do you happen to remember a young woman named Caligrace? She had a young daughter. The girl would have been about four years old, dark hair and—"

"I was the cook. I stayed in the kitchen. When I wasn't working, I locked myself in my room. That place was the scariest I've ever worked."

"Why do you say that?"

"The woman who ran the place was a bitch—excuse my language, but she was. And those girls? Thieving, lying, horrible girls that no one wanted, most of them pregnant or hauling around babies that no one wanted."

"Do you remember the name of the woman who ran the place?"

"Gladys. I'm surprised I even remember that." She shook her head. "I was there only a few months that fall. I've never been so cold. One of the girls died, and we had to keep her body in the basement because the ground was frozen and we had to wait for the state to come and bury her."

He shuddered inwardly. "It must have been horrible."

"I couldn't get out of there soon enough."

He closed his notebook and rose to his feet. "Thank you. I appreciate your—"

"Aren't you going to ask me about the murder?"

"You were at Westfield Manor then?"

She laughed hoarsely and repeated with contempt, "Westfield *Manor*."

He lowered himself gingerly back to the edge of the couch and tried to breathe through his mouth as he opened his notebook again. The chill that ran the length of his spine felt like a sharp cold blade. "What do you remember about the murder?"

"One of the male caretakers was stabbed to death in his room. The killer was never caught, but we all knew it was someone inside the home. The doors were locked at night, not that it kept some of them in or others out. But the killings were done by someone who lived there. The knife used was one stolen from my kitchen."

"Weren't you terrified?"

"Why would I be? She was only killing men."

"She?"

"Everyone knew it was one of the girls. Which one?" She shrugged. "I suspect they were all capable of it. For all I know, Gladys herself could have done it. The woman lied about everything. Like when that girl fell down the stairs. Everyone knew she was pushed."

LAURA STOOD AT the top of the basement stairs, staring down into the dark. *Don't go down there.* Her every instinct told her to let the past go. But her mother had dug it up like a grave digger determined to look death in the face no matter how gruesome. Or how painful.

A need she couldn't explain made her reach inside the doorway and feel around for the light switch. Her mother was determined that she remember every hellhole she'd lived in as a child, including Westfield Manor.

She hadn't known the name of the place. They had all run together to her.

"After your father left us, I didn't have a choice but to take any job I could," her mother had said earlier after almost frightening the life out of her.

"What do you want from me?" Laura had demanded. "Forgiveness? Fine, you're forgiven for dragging me and Catherine around the country from one horrible place to another. Now you can die in peace."

Her mother had begun to cry. "I can't bear the thought of what will happen to you once I'm gone."

"I'll be fine. It isn't like you were able to stop the bullet that took my leg or any of the other life-changing events in my life."

"No, I haven't protected you, have I?"

"You sound tired. You really should get some rest."

"I *am* tired. The doctor said I could go at any time. Remember that prayer I taught you when you were a child? 'Now I lay me down to sleep. I pray the Lord my soul to keep. If I should die before I wake...' You left out that last part."

"Probably because I expected to die in my sleep. Or worse."

Laura flipped the switch. A dim light blinked on deep in the darkness below her, revealing a set of steep narrow wooden stairs to the basement.

"This case you're working on," her mother had said. "Is it with the man you used to have as a police partner?"

"Homicide, but yes."

"Laura, there is something I have to tell you."

"I don't want to hear some horrible thing you need to get off your conscience that I will have to live with for the rest of my life."

"You have to stop investigating Westfield," her mother had said.

"This case isn't about that. I already told you that. It's about some girl who lived there."

She had started to leave her mother's bedroom, when the woman grabbed her arm, forcing Laura to turn back to her. "I know you must have recognized her the first time you saw her photo."

"Mother, I told you—"

"Caligrace. She looks just like her mother."

"I told you. I don't remember all the homes we lived in. Maybe she looked familiar. Maybe the name Westfield—"

"Your partner is investigating the murders!" her mother had cried. "Your *cop* partner. Oh, Laura, he's setting you up, don't you see that? He *knows* about us. He *knows* about…Catherine."

She had shaken loose her mother's grip and taken a step back from the bed. "It's just a coincidence that this woman was at Westfield when we were. It has nothing to do with Catherine. Or you. Or me. You have always tried to poison my mind. I'm not letting you. Just die and take your secrets with—"

"Whether you believe it or not, I love you." She'd reached into her pocket, pulled out her hand and held her closed fist out to Laura.

Laura had stared at the wrinkled hand for a moment before she'd let her mother drop a key into her palm. "What is this?"

"They say the truth will set you free. For your sake…" Her mother had closed her eyes. "It's in the basement. Your father's old trunk."

Swallowing her fear now, Laura descended the steps into the damp, earthy-smelling space. It wasn't a true basement, more like a crawl space under a house, because the floor was dirt, the ceiling so low she had to bend over to keep from bumping her head on the joists.

In the dim light, she spotted the trunk in a corner. It was an old army one with a large padlock on it, making Laura think of the day she'd asked about her father.

"He was in the army. His name was Roger."

"Roger?" Catherine had laughed and rolled her eyes as if she thought their mother was joking with them. *"Roger Dodger?"*

"You didn't know his last name?" Laura had asked innocently. She was all of eight.

"Of course I knew his last name. He lived with us for a while after you girls were born, but we never married. He was a nice man. Sweet, nice-looking," their mother had said almost a little dreamily. "But he wasn't cut out for a wife and a couple of crying kids." Even at a young age, she'd heard the bitterness.

It was too dark in the basement to unlock the padlock. Anyway, the trunk wasn't so large that she couldn't pick it up. Pocketing the key, she lifted the trunk and carried it up the stairs into the kitchen.

The funky smell of the basement followed her. Putting the trunk on the kitchen table, she went back to close the basement door. She hadn't looked in all the dark corners under the house, hadn't wanted to know what else might be down there.

Back in the kitchen as she started to unlock the trunk, she stopped to look behind her. The house suddenly felt too quiet.

Moving slowly, almost tiptoeing, she walked down the hallway toward her mother's bedroom.

The door was closed again. Laura was sure she'd left it open. Gooseflesh skittered over her skin. She stood listening before slowly opening the door.

Her mother still lay on the bed. But one arm dangled over the side, the hand splayed open. Her mother's pillow was on the floor next to the bed. Something about that made Laura step into the room. She knelt to pick up the pillow and noticed there was a spot on it that looked almost like blood.

Drawing closer to the bed, she stared down at her mother. There was blood on her lip. Her eyes were open wide, her face frozen in a grimace. Laura felt her heart lunge as she caught a whiff of her sister's perfume.

Dropping the pillow, she stepped back from the bed. A floorboard creaked somewhere in the house.

"Catherine, I know you're here." Her voice broke with the fear she felt whenever her sister showed up. Bad things happened when Catherine was around. "Oh, Catherine," she said as she stared at her mother. "What have you done?"

She thought she heard her sister's laugh on the wind that buffeted the side of the house. The laugh was mocking, just as it had been when they were children.

Laura stood in the doorway of her mother's room. Her shock had given away to a numbness. She tried to feel something other than sick with regret. Look what her mother's precious Catherine had done. Even now, her mother would still have loved Catherine more, she thought as tears filled her eyes.

Standing there, she'd never felt so alone. She thought of the trunk she'd brought up from the basement and what might be inside it.

Throw it back down the stairs. Don't let your mother win. She's gone. She can't hurt you anymore.

The doorbell rang, making her jump. She held her breath. It rang again.

Stepping out of the room, she shut the bedroom door behind her as she moved down the hallway feeling sick to her stomach.

On the front porch, a large dark figure pressed the doorbell again before moving from the small window in the door to the larger window that looked into the living room.

Laura watched the man cup his hands to his eyes as he leaned against the glass to peer inside. She moved quickly to the door and opened it.

"Hello," he said and handed her his card. She glanced at it. Edwin Sharp, P.I.

"I'm looking for Gladys McCormick. I understand she lives here."

Laura leaned against the doorjamb. "She did. I'm sorry, but she passed away earlier today. I'm her neighbor. I was just closing up the house for her."

CHAPTER FIFTEEN

No matter what Frank said, Nettie was convinced her theory would net her the name of the Beartooth Benefactor.

She spent her mornings in the café, watching her former general store being rebuilt. No expense was being spared to return it to its former glory.

That made her both sad that it wasn't hers anymore and proud of whoever was restoring it. And grateful, too. She couldn't have afforded to rebuild the store as it had been.

But it wasn't the workers that she spent most of her time watching. She took in the cars that drove by, especially those that went by slow. She watched for anyone taking photos or just hanging out on the street.

With all the activity, her quest kept her busy.

"Frank said he's been pushing you to set the date," Kate said as she refilled Nettie's cup with coffee. "What's going on? I thought you were anxious to marry him."

"I am," she said, still watching the street. "I just can't leave right now."

"Oh?" Kate asked and glanced toward the window. "Are you having second thoughts about selling the store?"

"I need to know who's behind this."

Kate chuckled and sat down opposite her. "I thought

you'd have the mystery solved by now." She frowned. "If this person wants to stay hidden that badly, maybe you should forget what I said about investigating. Look what happened last time."

"I doubt the Beartooth Benefactor will kill me for exposing his identity."

"Is that what we're calling him?" Kate chuckled. "I wouldn't be so sure he wouldn't kill you. Let's face it—anyone investing as much money as they are here has to be more than a little crazy. Beartooth as a destination resort?" She scoffed. "So you might want to just let your curiosity not get the best of you this time."

"Why do you think he's doing it?" Nettie asked, looking out the window again.

"Other than being crazy?"

"Frank thinks it's someone who used to live here who's, like, on his deathbed and wants to do something for the town."

"That's one theory."

"That cowboy, the dark handsome one, did he say what he is doing in town?" Nettie asked. "Didn't he arrive the same day as the crews did?"

Kate nodded. "I heard he was looking for a small ranch to invest in."

"What do we know about him?"

As the bell over the front door tinkled, Kate shrugged and pushed to her feet. "I think he's interested in my waitress, so there better not be anything underhanded about him."

Nettie blinked as Kate left to wait on whoever had come through the door. She'd forgotten all about Callie Westfield. Last year she'd hired a private investigator to find out what he could about Callie. As it turned out, he'd said he'd found something that Nettie would find interesting, but unfortunately, he hadn't lived long enough to tell her what that information had been.

Was it possible Callie Westfield was the Beartooth Benefactor? Working as a waitress was great cover, if that were the case. Callie could watch the town change, listen to what everyone thought about it, and no one would be the wiser that she was behind it.

Or maybe Callie and the cowboy were in it together.

With a sigh, Nettie realized how improbable that was. No, she thought Frank was right. It was some-one from around here. Someone with a soft spot for Beartooth.

GLADYS MCCORMICK WAS DEAD. Edwin put in a call to Rourke, knowing that the U.S. marshal was going to be as disappointed as he was.

The woman who'd answered the door said she was a neighbor and knew nothing about Gladys or where she might have worked, Edwin told him. "Apparently, Gladys stayed to herself, the neighbor said. She'd never even met her until Gladys called to say she wasn't well. The neighbor went over this morning to find Gladys dead. I guess the mortuary had just picked her up be-fore I got there."

"That's too bad." Rourke sounded distracted.

Edwin thought about that street in Harlowton in front of Gladys McCormick's house. He'd thanked the neighbor and walked back to his rental car, tired and ready for this assignment to end. But there had been something else bothering him as he'd looked back at Gladys McCormick's house. He'd felt…spooked. He'd been in some dark places in his life, none quite as dark as this case, though, he'd thought, remembering being in Westfield Manor.

"I know you must be disappointed," he told Rourke now. He hadn't expected to get much out of Gladys McCormick—especially after what he'd heard about her. But he'd wanted to meet her and see if she was as evil as everyone said.

"I could try to get into the house after the neighbor leaves…" Edwin said, even though it was the last thing he wanted to do.

"I think you might do better finding out more about the murder that was committed at the girls' home," Rourke said. "Can you talk to that deputy you met again? Get me everything you can. I'm especially interested in the date of the murder."

Edwin thought about just placing a call to Burt Denton, but the man hadn't wanted to talk about it anymore. He knew if he hoped to get any useful information, he was going to have to go back to Flat Rock. And he'd have to again see the burned-out shell of Westfield Manor and that room on the third floor. Even when he closed his eyes to sleep at night, he saw those crudely carved letters in the windowsill. Caligrace.

But this time, he was driving.

"I WAS THINKING about what you said, and I'd be bitter, too, if it was me," Johnny Frank said as he and Carson Grant pulled up in front of Grant-West Ranch's main house.

"Bitter? I thought you were the one telling me just the other day that I was lucky my sister gave me a job, a little land and a cabin to live in," Carson Grant said as he sat taking in Destry's new home. She and her husband, Rylan, had built it after their marriage. Now they had two small noisy twins, another kid on the way and what should have been Carson's inheritance.

"I was wrong," Johnny was saying now. Johnny had found out that Destry wasn't even W.T.'s blood. Carson's father had left everything to his bastard daughter. "The W Bar G should have been yours, lock, stock and barrel. You're the old man's *son.* Who leaves everything to someone else's daughter? No, that just wasn't right."

"I gave it all up in a moment of weakness, okay?" Weak—wasn't that what his father had always thought of him?

"Who gives up a fortune in a moment of weakness?"

"It's a long story and not one I want to rehash. Destry got the ranch, married Rylan West and now they own the largest ranch in this part of the state. I'm happy for her."

"Well, I'd be bitter as hell and trying to get what was rightfully mine back, if I were you."

"You're not me," Carson snapped.

"Okay, but your old man's cook lives better than you do. How in hell did she get the mansion your father built?"

"Simple. She loved him and I hated his guts." He cut off any further conversation by shoving open the pickup door and climbing out. He didn't want to talk about it, not today. He had other things on his mind. Number one on that list was Callie Westfield down at the café. He'd been chasing her relentlessly for months.

"Give it up. She's making a fool out of you," Johnny had said after they'd left the café earlier. Carson had realized the man was right. She'd been tempting him since day one. He'd gone too long not getting anything he wanted. He wanted Callie, and tonight he was going to have her.

"Wait here. I need to talk to my sister for a moment," he told Johnny.

"Is everything all right?" Destry asked him when he came into the ranch kitchen. He could hear the kids making a racket down the hall. Destry, determined to be involved in the running of the ranches, had hired a nanny to take care of the little rug rats a few days a week. He could hear the elderly nanny trying to rein in the brats.

"Things are great. Well, not great yet." He flashed her a big smile as he helped himself to a cup of coffee. "But they will be."

She instantly looked worried. "Carson, I haven't seen you like this since…"

"Since I was drinking and gambling?" He shook his head. "It's nothing like that. I've met this woman, and no, she's nothing like the last one I brought home." Cherry had been a Vegas showgirl with dollar signs in her eyes. "I just wanted to let you know that I might be a little late in the morning."

Destry smiled. "You have a date?"

He nodded, even though it wasn't quite true, since Callie didn't know about it yet. It was going to be a surprise.

OUTSIDE IN THE early-fall darkness, Rourke stood breathing in the cold night air after his talk with the P.I. A chilly wind rustled the dried leaves on a nearby aspen and sighed through the boughs of the dark pines. The snowcapped peaks behind Beartooth seemed to glow icy white in the dark stillness.

Rourke felt antsy, uncertain, and told himself it was the snowstorm that he'd heard would be hitting in the next twenty-four hours. What was he doing here? He thought of his boss. Brent Ryan was certain he was wrong. Laura thought he was sacrificing everything that made sense in his life. He knew she was scared for him. Scared that he was going to get himself killed. After Edwin's call, he thought she might be right.

Mentally, he ticked off what he now knew at least with some certainty about Callie.

An unmarried, pregnant woman named Caligrace had given birth to a daughter in a girls' home jokingly called Westfield Manor on the edge of the town of Flat Rock, Montana, approximately thirty years ago.

When the home closed, the daughter, also apparently named Caligrace, was about five. She had gone into the foster-care system. But because of the lack of records at Westfield, there was little way to track her.

When she turned seventeen, she got herself a fake birth certificate and called herself Caligrace Westfield. Before that, she'd apparently been bounced around from one foster home after another.

She had attended five universities, mostly on loans using fake credentials. She'd majored in psychology, gotten exceptional grades, but hadn't graduated during those five years. She'd had numerous jobs for the past thirteen years, some of them in the Seattle area, most of them waitressing.

While living at the Westfield girls' home, there had been a murder, killer still at large.

Rourke knew that couldn't be a coincidence, but the Caligrace Westfield he knew would have been too young to have committed the murder. However, she still could have known about it—especially if her mother was involved.

He didn't need the profile Laura was working up to know that Caligrace had the kind of past that bred serial killers.

She had a textbook serial-killer background—if she was male. Women serial killers were rarer. Their reasons for killing were often more mercenary.

He glanced toward the café. It had been closed now for hours. A single light burned in the apartment over it. Rourke glanced at his watch. It was late. Callie should be asleep. Or maybe she was like him and was having trouble sleeping again tonight.

Suddenly the light in the apartment blinked out. Apparently, she was going to have better luck than him. He started to turn toward the door to the cabin, when he noticed a pickup parked down the street from the café.

In the glow of a cigarette, he saw Carson Grant waiting in the truck. A few minutes later, Callie came driving out.

UNABLE TO SLEEP, Callie headed to the lake. She told herself she needed the peace and quiet, but a part of her wondered if the cowboy would show. If he did, then that meant he was watching her apartment—watching *her*.

Tonight would tell the tale.

The lake was beautiful in the moonlight. She parked and got out, hugging herself against the cold night air. When she heard the sound of the vehicle engine, she tensed and reached inside the pickup for her gun. As the vehicle grew closer, she realized it wasn't Rourke's SUV engine she was hearing.

As the truck pulled up next to the moonlit lake, she

saw the driver and swore under her breath. Carson
Grant. He cut his lights and engine and got out. She
eased the gun into the waistband of her jeans, covering it with her jacket.

She didn't want trouble, and if she played this right,
there wouldn't be any. At least she was hoping that
was the case. Any fool knew that Carson had followed
her here. She didn't even have to guess what he had
in mind.

Staying next to her pickup, she said, "I hope you
have a good reason for being here."

He grinned. "I got an invitation."

"That right? Wasn't from me."

"Ah, come on, Callie. A woman doesn't drive to
such a remote spot in the middle of the night unless
she wants company."

"This woman does," she said, her hands on her hips,
just inches from the gun. She got a strong flash that
filled her with dread. She knew exactly what Carson
was doing here. Worse, he was making her head throb.
"You just need to turn around and—"

"I heard you come down here," he said, looking
around before settling his gaze on her again. "I figured
you were meeting someone, but don't see anyone." He
took a step toward her.

ROURKE HAD WATCHED Callie turn at the edge of town
where the pavement ended, and he'd known she was
headed for the lake again. Only this time, Carson Grant
was following her.

He'd hurried back inside for his gun, two beers and
two glasses, then climbed into the SUV and followed.
The moonlit night allowed him to drive without his

lights on once he'd turned onto the dirt road that led back into the pines.

He told himself that the two could be meeting at the lake, something they'd set up earlier, but all his instincts said just the opposite.

As he came over a rise, he caught a glimpse of taillights before they disappeared around a curve as the road switchbacked down to the lake.

He shifted down and followed, stopping a quarter mile from the lake. The night air was cold as he cut the engine, got out and started down the road, moonlight playing through the pine boughs to splash silver across his path.

Moments later, he heard the raised voices. By the time he reached the pines at the edge of the lake, Carson and Callie were standing a few yards apart. They'd lowered their voices, but he could tell by Callie's stance that she hadn't invited Carson here.

Neither of them saw him as he approached from the trees next to them.

"I told you I wasn't interested," Callie said and reached under her jacket.

Rourke knew she was going for her gun, but Carson must have known it, as well. He lunged at her and grabbed her arm, making Callie cry out as he took the gun away from her and pointed it at her chest.

"Were you planning to *shoot* me?" Carson demanded. "What kind of crazy-ass woman are you, pulling a gun on me? I've been *nice.* I asked you out to dinner. I wanted to do this your way." He thrust the weapon at her. "But, sweetheart, you just changed the rules." He grabbed Callie's arm with his free hand.

Rourke quickly stepped up behind him. "Put down

the gun," he ordered, pressing the barrel of his own weapon into the side of Carson's neck. *"Now!"*

Carson turned, swinging around, leading with the gun.

Rourke had anticipated the move and quickly disarmed the cowboy, throwing him to the ground.

He handed Callie back her gun. "You might want to put that away."

Turning to Carson, who was still sprawled in the dirt, he said, "The lady asked you to leave her alone. I suggest you take her at her word and do so from now on."

"Lady?" Carson mocked as he got to his feet and dusted off his jeans. "What business is it of yours anyway?"

"I'm tired of watching you harass her. She said no. Let's leave it at that."

"We aren't finished," he yelled at Callie as he picked up his hat from the dirt and stuffed it down on his head.

"We are," she said.

Carson didn't seem to hear her as he turned on Rourke. "You're going to regret getting into my business. Remember the name Carson Grant. You'll be seeing me again."

With that, he stormed over to his pickup and left, the tires of his rig throwing off dirt and gravel.

Rourke listened to the roar of the engine until it died away, then turned to Callie. "Are you all right?"

"That depends. Did you bring something to drink?"

"Beer," he said and grinned. "I'll be right back."

SHE HEARD THE CLINK of glass. A moment later, as Rourke approached, she saw that he had his fingers looped around the necks of two beer bottles and two glasses. "You didn't have to get fancy," she said, motioning to the glasses. "I've been known to drink out of a bottle."

"Not for our first moonlit drink together," he said as he opened a beer and expertly poured part of it into the glass. He handed it to her along with the bottle, then motioned to a log next to the water.

As she sat down, he joined her.

"You just happened along again?" she asked after taking a drink.

"Nope. I knew there would be a full moon tonight. I was counting on you not being able to sleep." He opened his beer, poured and took a long drink. "Beer by moonlight. But I only brought two, so Carson had to go."

She took a sip of her beer. "Your timing is impeccable."

"The truth is, I couldn't sleep either. I happened to see Carson Grant sitting in his truck outside your apartment. When he followed you down here, I had a feeling you hadn't invited him. I knew I could be wrong—"

She smiled over at him. "Thank you."

He gave her a nod. "Glad I could be of assistance."

"Kind of like at the café earlier with the robber," she said. "Watching late-night TV has taught you all kinds of moves."

Rourke grinned at her. "You have no idea."

She chuckled, wishing she didn't like him so much. The cowboy thought he knew her. That was his first mistake. All her instincts warned her not to trust him. He'd lied about needing to get up his nerve to ask her out. She feared what else he was lying about. "Why Beartooth?"

He shrugged. "I like the area, thought I might raise me some cattle and alfalfa."

She studied her beer in the moonlight. He was no rancher. The way he'd unarmed the robber at the café and now Carson...

"I can't see you as a rancher." She turned just enough that she could see his profile and waited.

"I don't know why not. I told you I grew up ropin' and ridin' in Wyoming on a ranch. Maybe I miss it more than I thought I would." His look dared her to challenge him.

"You didn't like Wyoming enough to buy there?"

"Have you seen Wyoming other than Yellowstone and the Tetons?"

She shook her head. She hadn't.

"It's inhospitable. Anyway, I like this," he said, waving his beer toward the moonlit lake. "This area is breathtaking." He glanced over at her, his look saying the lake wasn't the only thing that took his breath away. But he'd been smart enough not to say it. "So what brought *you* here?"

"A job."

He laughed softly. "Sorry, didn't mean to pry."

She thought he would ask another personal question, but to her surprise, he didn't say anything.

They sat in a companionable silence, drinking their beers as the moon made a slow, steady arc over the lake. A breeze stirred the pines behind them, whispering like lovers in their dark boughs.

Callie breathed in the night scents, the lake and pines predominantly stronger than the dried grasses at the water's edge. She felt herself relax in his presence. It wouldn't last; she knew that.

But for tonight, it felt good not to be on guard. Even as relaxing as it was, she couldn't help but be aware that she still hadn't picked up any flashes from him. At least the headache wasn't as bad as it had been earlier with Carson. Still…she could read Carson. She couldn't read Rourke, and that made her uneasy.

She told herself she didn't need to know any more about him. But she feared she did. Who was this man? Why was he different? And maybe more to the point, what was his real interest in her?

CARSON HAD NEVER been so angry. He could spit nails. As the lights of Beartooth appeared ahead, he saw his life through clearer eyes than he had in a long time. Johnny was right. He'd never gotten what he wanted because someone was always taking it away from him. First his father, then his sister and now some cowboy passing through town.

As he reached the edge of town, he knew he couldn't go back to the tiny cabin he'd been living in. Not sober, anyway. He should have been living in his father's mansion instead of W.T.'s former cook living there.

Swinging into the parking lot of the Range Rider bar, he wondered if the whole damned town had been laughing at him behind his back all this time. He was pretty sure they had been.

What made him even more angry, he thought as he got out of his pickup and headed inside, was that he'd tried so damned hard to be the son his father had wanted. Then he'd tried to be the brother Destry demanded he be. He'd given up everything, gambling and drinking and his rightful inheritance.

He pushed into the dim darkness of the bar, the air ripe with the smell of beer. What he wouldn't do for a drink right now. Fortunately, there wasn't but a couple of cowboys at the other end of the bar. He didn't want company.

"Carson," the owner said, sounding surprised to see him. The few times he'd been in here since his father had died, he'd had a cola. Not tonight.

"I'll take a shot of tequila with a beer chaser."

Clete lifted a brow. "Seriously?"

"Did I stutter?" Carson snapped. "You're running a bar, aren't you?"

Clete held up both hands. "Just asking."

"Well, don't," he said, slapping some money on the bar. "And keep 'em coming."

After the first couple of drinks, Carson pulled out his cell phone and dialed a number he used to have on speed dial. "Anything happening tonight? I'm looking for a game."

"Carson Grant?"

"I'm back." He was practically salivating at the thought of a poker game. It had been so long since he'd held cards in his hands. His fingers itched for the feel of them, the smell of them, the rush that came with each hand.

The man on the other end of the line laughed. "How soon can you be here?"

Carson gulped down the rest of his drink. "I'm on my way. Keep a chair warm for me."

Tonight he'd play some cards, maybe even win some money. This was all Callie's fault, his falling off the wagon, he told himself as he got a six-pack for the road. Tomorrow he would decide how to make Callie Westfield pay for making him look like a fool all these months.

CHAPTER SIXTEEN

CALLIE WATCHED ROURKE finish his beer and then, with a sigh, stand up from the log where they had been sitting beside the lake.

She swallowed the last of the beer in her glass as she got to her feet. The empty glass hung from her fingertips as she turned to look at the cowboy. He was drop-dead handsome and as sexy as any man she'd ever met, but there was a tenderness in his eyes when he looked at her, and that was her undoing.

Standing on tiptoes, she suddenly leaned toward him and gently kissed his lips. No flash. She had no idea what he was thinking. All she'd felt was a rush of desire.

He didn't move, didn't seem to breathe as his dark eyes locked with hers. "If that was a thank-you kiss—"

"No," she said and put her glass down on the log. "*This* is a thank-you kiss." Throwing caution to the wind, she circled his neck with her arms, her gaze again locking with his before shifting to his lips.

She felt as if she was playing with fire. If she wasn't careful, she would definitely get burned. As she drew him down for the kiss, he wrapped his arms around her waist. Her lips touched his, and he pulled her into him, his hard body no surprise, as he deepened the kiss.

Callie could feel his heart pounding. Or maybe it

was her own heartbeat loud in her ears. "You learned this on TV, too?" she whispered against his mouth.

He groaned in answer and grabbed the nape of her neck, burying his fingers in her hair.

Callie felt her blood run hot as her bare skin rippled with goose bumps. But it was the headache—more like the lack of it—that shocked her almost as much as the passion Rourke evoked from her. In his arms, his mouth on hers, she felt nothing but desire.

LAURA HAD CALLED the mortuary to say her mother had passed in her sleep. A local doctor had come, checked the woman's vitals and pronounced her dead.

When asked who she was, Laura had said her name was Catherine McCormick. She'd even shed a few tears, explaining that she'd heard her mother was dying, but hadn't arrived in time.

Then she'd taken the trunk and the few belongings she'd brought and left her mother's house. She hadn't known where she was going. She'd driven south toward Big Timber—and ultimately Beartooth and Rourke.

But at Big Timber, she'd looked over at the still-locked trunk on the passenger-side floorboard and decided to get a motel. She wasn't up to seeing Rourke. Not yet.

Once in the motel, she worked on the profiles. But the trunk with its stupid padlock kept pulling at her. She told herself that she needed to keep her mind on Rourke's murder cases and the mysterious woman he had become consumed with. Rourke didn't need to know about her past. No one did. It was too painful. Too humiliating.

Finally, she'd shoved the trunk under the bed, wish-

ing that she'd left it in her mother's basement. She
wouldn't open it. As she'd driven in, she'd seen a burn
barrel behind the motel. It wouldn't take much of a
flame to ignite the old paper she suspected would be inside the trunk. There would probably be records of the
awful places she'd lived, including Westfield Manor.
Whatever horrors her mother had left for her would be
best destroyed. She liked the idea of them going up in
smoke as if none of it had ever happened.

Taking out her laptop, she went to work on finding
out everything she could about the two names Rourke
had given her: Carson Grant and Johnny Franks.

Rourke had told her that Carson Grant had been hitting on Callie. A local boy from a well-known family. She'd known the type her whole life and wasn't
surprised that he'd gotten into all kinds of trouble,
including being a suspect in a murder case. Gambler,
drinker, rowdy cowboy.

He currently lived in a cabin in a remote corner of
his sister's ranch. He'd been clean and sober for a while.
Laura figured that couldn't last too much longer. He
was too young, no real responsibilities, no roots. It was
only a matter of time before he went off the wagon.

She stared at his photo, wondering how long it would
be before Callie decided to kill him.

ROURKE BREATHED IN the sweet, mysterious scent of
Callie Westfield as his mouth took possession of hers
again.

She moaned, sending his already pounding heart
drumming harder. He wanted this woman, wanted to
get under her skin, wanted to know her intimately.
He knew how dangerous it was. He didn't care. She'd

been a mystery to him for too long. Now she was in his arms, her mouth opening invitingly to his, her breath mingling with his, her tongue—

Callie suddenly pulled back, her gaze locking with his again. He was breathing hard. He didn't want to let go of her.

She took a breath, her cheeks flushed. Her arms moved from around his neck. She pressed her palms against the front of his shirt—but she didn't push him away, and he didn't loosen his hold on her, afraid if he did she would slip away.

He watched her catch her breath, her dark eyes searching his face before her gaze locked again with his.

"Tell me I'm not wrong about you," she whispered.

"Tell me I'm wrong about you," he wanted to plead, but instead he said, "I guess that depends on what you're thinking about me right now."

Her smile was slow, her eyes bright with moonlight and desire. "That you're going to break my heart."

"I hope not. I sure don't want to."

She cocked her head, studying him. "You don't know how much I wish I could read *your* thoughts right now."

"You would be disappointed. I don't think much with you in my arms, and when you're kissing me, my only thought is your mouth." The truth of that made him smile. He certainly wasn't thinking like a U.S. marshal. He could hear Laura's warning. *Don't get too close.* He realized he could have just kissed his first serial killer.

"Have you had your heart broken before?" he asked, curious as both a man and a marshal.

Callie pushed back gently, still studying him. He loosened his hold, and she slipped from his arms, turning her back to him. He took a deep breath, mentally kicking himself for spoiling the moment. He let the breath out slowly as she picked up her empty beer bottle and glass.

"That was probably a mistake," she said, her back to him.

"If you're talking about that kiss, nope, that was definitely not a mistake."

She turned to look at him, eyes narrowing. "And if I was talking about something else?"

He wanted to say that only time would tell. Instead, he joked, "The mistake was *stopping* kissing. But then, maybe it wasn't."

She smiled. "I'll bite. Why not?"

"Because if we hadn't stopped, you would have wanted to make love in the moonlight by the lake."

Callie laughed. "Is that right?"

"I'm certain of it."

"What about you?" she asked, cocking her head to the side.

"Oh, I think you could have persuaded me, but I prefer to wait until the third date—not the first."

She chuckled. "You're considering this a first date?"

He grinned and rubbed his thumb slowly along his lower lip. "First kiss. First date, don't you think?"

Shaking her head, she smiled at him. She had a great smile. Sometimes it even reached her eyes.

"Think you can sleep now?" he asked.

She nodded slowly. Was that disappointment or relief he saw in her eyes?

"Good, then you don't mind if I follow you as far as town," he said, taking her glass and bottle from her and picking up his own. "I would hate to see you run into Carson Grant again tonight."

LAURA COULDN'T SLEEP. Like a scene out of a Poe tale, she could hear the trunk under her bed calling to her. Giving up fighting it any longer, she climbed out of bed and dragged out the trunk.

She realized she had no choice but to open it. She had to see what was inside. Her fingers trembled as she pulled out the key to the padlock, and then in a fit of terror, she shot to her feet to pace back and forth. Her mind listed all the reasons she should have destroyed the contents.

Reaching for her phone, she started to call her psychiatrist, but stopped herself. She knew what he'd say. The same thing he had been saying all along. She had to face her past, shine light on those dark holes of blank memory from her childhood and face her fears.

She stopped pacing to stare at the trunk. Why hadn't she burned everything like she'd planned? Because she had to know all of it. Her mother had saved it for *her*. Saved it for this moment when she came face-to-face with her past.

Wasn't it possible there would be something in the trunk that would prove Callie was the killer?

If she had any hope of saving Rourke...

But she feared it was too late. "No, it won't be too late until he finds himself tied to a bed and a knife to his throat," she said to the empty room.

Her mother had hidden this trunk in the basement. Locked it so no one else could see what was inside. Maybe especially her sister, Catherine?

That thought made her head hurt. She saw the clock

by the bed. She didn't have any more time. If there was something in that trunk…

Moving to it, she fished the key to the padlock back out of her pocket and bent down to insert it into the lock. It snapped open, feeling icy cold beneath her fingers. Removing the lock, she told herself it wasn't too late. She could still burn the contents.

She thought of Rourke and felt a weight on her chest that made it hard to breathe.

With a curse, she reached down and grabbed the edge of the trunk lid and lifted it. The old metal creaked, reminding her of her mother's wheelchair. For just a moment, she saw the pillow in her hand, the spot of blood on it, the blood on her mother's lip.…

Laura threw off the disturbing image as she looked down into the trunk at the jumble of papers. Off to one side of the loose papers, she spotted what at first looked like a book.

With trembling fingers, she picked it up. A diary. Her mother had kept a diary? She opened it to the first page, her fingers trembling.

In her mother's handwriting was *Westfield 1987–88*.

WHEN ROURKE REACHED town after following Callie back, he parked on the main drag in front of the café. Originally he'd planned to just make sure she got inside her apartment without any trouble.

But after parking, he decided to walk the perimeter to be certain Carson wasn't hiding in the dark like he had been earlier lying in wait for her.

As Rourke made his loop around the café, he was surprised to find that Callie had gone up to her apartment, turned on the lights and then come back down.

She was waiting for him at the bottom of her outside stairs.

Moonlight played on her face, making her dark eyes bright. Her hair, which she'd had pulled back earlier, now framed her face, the raven locks against her pale skin. She couldn't have looked more beautiful. Or more desirable. He felt a tremor inside him like nothing he'd ever felt before. Red flag warnings were going off like fireworks in his head.

She smiled, and the moment he stepped to her, all he could think about was kissing her again. His mouth took hers hungrily, the kiss all passion and need as he pulled her into his arms. Lifting her off her feet, he pressed her against the side of the building. He could feel the soft curves of her body, the heat she radiated warming the October night.

Neither of them must have heard the vehicle approaching. Before they knew it, they were caught in blinding-bright headlights. Ducking back into the shadow of the building, they burst into nervous laughter, desire sparking like fireflies between them.

"Third date, huh?" Callie said, sounding as breathless as he felt.

The light glowing in her apartment just yards away drew him like a moth to a flame. He knew how dangerous this could be, and yet…

"I suppose we could consider this our second date," he said, his voice husky with desire. "Maybe if I left and came back…"

She laughed and gave him a playful push. "Don't get ahead of yourself, cowboy."

"Go out with me tomorrow night. Dinner in Big Timber. Say yes."

Callie took only a moment to consider. "Yes," she said, then raced up the stairs, stopping at the top to look back at him before disappearing inside.

He watched her go, asking himself if he hadn't just made a date with a serial killer.

LAURA'S PSYCHIATRIST SOUNDED half-asleep when he came to the phone.

"You say it's an emergency? What's happened?"

How could she explain it? She couldn't. "I feel as if I'm going to fly to pieces, just explode, and at the same time, I'm terrified. I can't sleep. I can't eat. Something terrible is going to happen."

"What caused this setback?" Her psychiatrist was an older man with white hair and bushy eyebrows over pale blue eyes. She often thought of him as the grandfather she'd never had.

She swallowed and tried to find the words. "I've told you about my former partner."

"The one you're in love with. Did you finally tell him how you feel?"

"No." The mere thought made her shudder. "I saw him tonight with a suspect. I saw them together. Kissing."

"How did you feel?"

"How do you think I felt?" she cried, then dropped her voice. She knew she shouldn't have gone to Rourke's cabin looking for him. When she'd found his SUV gone at such a late hour, she'd driven down by the café. That was when she'd seen them.

"I was heartbroken, but also furious with him. This woman could be a serial killer. I'm afraid...I'm afraid he's falling for her, falling into a trap."

"You want to save him from himself?"

She wanted to kill him. "I don't want to see anything happen to him."

"We've discussed this before. The best way to overcome a fear is to face it. Tell this man how you feel about him."

Laura shook her head but said nothing.

"You've held on to this for far too long. Trapped emotions fester. Worse, they tend to overpower, become much larger and more overwhelming than they actually are."

"I think he's falling for this woman. I think he fell for her the moment he saw her photo." She knew how crazy that sounded.

"Maybe he is just doing his job. Didn't you tell me the last time we talked that hc went to Montana to get close to this woman so he could find the true killer?"

"You don't understand. This woman—"

"It isn't about another woman, Laura. You said he has no idea how you feel. You *have* to tell him. No matter what happens, it will be out. You won't be holding it inside you and letting it eat away at you."

"She's going to kill him," she said in a whisper as she fought back tears.

"This secret is setting back your recovery, Laura. You are strong. No matter what happens when you tell him, you will get past it. Have you had any more panic attacks?"

Other than the one she'd had when she'd seen Rourke kissing Caligrace Westfield by the café? "No."

"Why are you so afraid of this man?"

"I'm not afraid of Rourke." That was definitely not

her fear. "I'm afraid what I'll... I don't know what I'm afraid of."

"This is your first real contact with him since your accident." He referred to her being shot in the alley as if it was an accident, like wrecking her car or falling off a ladder.

She wanted to correct him, a part of her aware that being shot was no accident. In her heart, she knew that she had been heading for that dark alley her whole life, destined to almost die in it. Wasn't that why she'd become a cop?

"You have always had a death wish," her mother had said when she'd foolishly called to tell her she'd been shot. "When you became a policewoman, I thought, 'Now she has found a way to fulfill that wish.'"

"I feel like I'm the only one who can save Rourke," Laura said now to her psychiatrist. "I'm just afraid it might be too late."

"Why this feeling of urgency?"

"I know that sounds crazy, but I've been plagued with this premonition of doom from as far back as I can remember. Since Rourke brought me this case, I feel as if it's a time bomb. I can hear it ticking." Her voice broke. "I'm so scared." How could she tell him that Caligrace Westfield was at the heart of her secret fear?

"I don't believe the problem is the case, Laura," he said, not unkindly. "Or this other woman. Tell Rourke how you feel. This isn't your case. You can't save him."

"What if this woman kills him?"

"Kills him? Or steals him from you?"

"Either way I will lose him. I can't live with that."

CHAPTER SEVENTEEN

THE FORMER DEPUTY didn't seem all that surprised to find P.I. Edwin Sharp standing on his doorstep in Flat Rock, Montana.

"I thought you might be back." Burt Denton sighed. "My wife is away," he said as he stepped aside to let Edwin in.

As Edwin entered the house, he heard the drone of the television. A weatherman was forecasting the upcoming winter storm he'd been hearing about on the way up. He hoped to be someplace warm and dry before it hit.

Burt Denton's home was a two-story farmhouse, the walls filled with pictures of Burt's children, the furniture worn and old. Edwin looked around and got the feeling that the "wife" had been gone for some time.

"Might as well come in the kitchen," Burt said.

"I hope you don't mind talking about the girls' home and the people who lived there," Edwin said after declining coffee. His stomach had been upset now for several days. He told himself it was the flying, but he suspected it was the case.

When he'd driven into town, he couldn't miss the hulking structure of the girls' home. A cold wind had blown a tumbleweed down the main street ahead of his car. The whole town had an end-of-the-world feeling as he'd parked in front of Burt Denton's house.

Now he took a seat at the Formica-topped table in the large kitchen. He could see where there had been knickknacks on the shelves along one wall, but all that was left was a faded outline of them.

Burt looked resigned to talking about Westfield and ultimately Caligrace as he took a seat. "What do you want to know?"

"You knew the woman who ran the place, Gladys McCormick?"

His face registered dislike. "A horrible woman."

"I noticed that the place burned at some point."

"That was her doing. She burned all the paperwork, no doubt covering her own behind. When they needed clothing or more food or even the bare necessities like a little more heat, she told them there just wasn't money for it and that they'd gotten themselves into this mess, so they could only blame themselves if they went hungry or didn't have a warm coat come winter."

Edwin didn't have to ask where Burt had gotten this information. "You helped Caligrace and her daughter with what you could." It wasn't a question. Nor was Edwin surprised when Burt gave a slight nod.

"It cost me my marriage eventually." The admission came hard, Edwin could see. That he'd been in love with the woman was obvious. "I wish I could have done more. I wrote to the state, I threatened to put Gladys in jail, but my hands were tied, and the state didn't do anything until after the murder. I tried to rally the community to help, but people here had their own problems. They would point out that Gladys didn't treat her own kids much better, and maybe a little hardship might turn all those girls around."

Edwin felt a start. *"Gladys had children of her own?"*

"Two daughters," Burt said. "Twins—two identical dark-haired girls with blue eyes."

"How old were they?"

"They must have been about twelve, thirteen." He saw Edwin writing this down and added, "One of them, I could never tell them apart, acted much older than her age. Every time I had to go out there, she'd flirt with me when her mother wasn't looking. Wild as a Montana blizzard, that one."

"Do you remember the girls' names?"

He frowned, started to shake his head, then stopped himself. "Wait, the wild one. I heard her called Kathy, I think. She called her sister Lee, I think. I wouldn't swear to it. I tried to steer clear of them."

The P.I. looked at his notes, then said, "So, tell me about the murder."

"The male was killed after I got word about the rape."

"Who was raped?"

"That's just it—I never knew for certain. Once I got to the home after I got word—"

"Who sent word?" he asked and realized he already knew before the words were out of his mouth. "Caligrace." Edwin made a notation. "And you say that Caligrace told you that one of the girls had been raped."

Burt nodded. "But when I got there, even she wouldn't talk. Gladys had put the fear of God in all of them. Not that I can blame them for being afraid of her." He shook his head. "You want to know what the worst part was? The girl who got raped? The rumor was that it was one of Gladys's own daughters. I never knew which one, but can you imagine a mother like that?"

"I can't imagine why the mother wouldn't want the man arrested."

Burt shrugged. "If it was the wild girl that got raped, maybe the mother thought she'd asked for it. It wouldn't be the first time I've run across a mother like that," he said with disgust. "Or maybe the man was too valuable as an employee. I know it must have been hard for Gladys to get anyone to work in that hellhole. The man who got killed was a punk twenty-two-year-old who'd been in trouble before. He probably liked working in a place with that many wild young girls."

"You wouldn't know where I might find Gladys McCormick's daughters, would you?"

Burt shook his head. "Right after that is when I called the state and they finally came for the girls. But it was too late for Caligrace. She'd fallen ill." He looked close to tears, just as he'd been at the café the first time Edwin had met him.

"What killed her?"

Burt shrugged. "The doctor said it was pneumonia, but I think it was heartbreak." He swallowed and met Edwin's gaze. "Her little girl?"

"Callie," Edwin offered.

"They found her in the room when they found the murdered man. Apparently, she'd witnessed all of it."

"She saw the killing?"

"And probably the killer."

"Who did she say it was?"

Burt shook his head. "She didn't seem able to speak after that. Walked around in a daze. Caligrace was terrified that her daughter would never come out of it. Then when she fell ill…"

Edwin could see the man's anguish. Burt would have gotten them both out of there if it wasn't for the family he already had, a family he'd apparently lost over the whole mess.

"So she didn't live long enough to see her daughter recover?"

"Not that I know." Burt shook his head. He looked even older than he had that day in the café. "It only got worse after that. Before the state showed up, Caligrace got word to me that there'd been an accident."

Edwin looked up from his notes.

"One of Gladys's daughters had fallen down the stairs and had broken her neck. Word was that the girl had been *pushed* down the stairs."

"You don't mean it killed her?" Edwin asked in surprise.

"Well, that's where it gets crazy. When I got to Westfield, Gladys said the girl was fine, that both her daughters were just fine. I asked to see them. She told me that they were sleeping but that she would get them if I would wait."

"Did Gladys know how you'd heard?"

He nodded. "By then Caligrace was real sick, but I didn't know how sick until it was too late. A few minutes later, the wild one, Kathy, came out, denied she'd been pushed down the stairs, said something rude and went back to bed. Then the other one came out half-asleep, said she didn't know what I was talking about. They both seemed fine, so I left."

"This was the day after the murder?"

Again he nodded. "I didn't get word until the next

morning that Caligrace had died." He shook his head. "She was buried the morning before the state came and took the girls. I tried to put it behind me."

"So, what you're saying is that someone else told you one of the girls pushed one of the twins down the stairs and killed her?"

"One of the girls from the home told me that she'd been sent by Caligrace, who *thought* one of the twins was dead, but apparently she survived the fall, if it had happened at all. By then Caligrace could have been hallucinating. I heard how sick she'd been from one of the girls before the state took them away."

"Did the girl say who she thought had pushed Gladys's daughter down the stairs?" he asked.

"Her twin sister."

THROUGH THE BRANDING IRON CAFÉ window, Nettie watched Frank drive up. Another car pulled in next to his as he climbed out. It took Nettie a moment to place the older woman he spoke to. She hadn't seen Charlotte since last year, when she'd visited the recluse.

Charlotte had left Montana to become a movie maven back in the early 1960s. Her brother, Bull, had gone after her four years later. The woman he'd brought home was still beautiful, but broken.

The story was that she'd married some rich older man, Archibald Abrahams, who'd gotten her a few parts in some small movies before he'd died. There'd been some question about the husband's death, the word *poisoned* floating around and rumors of a torrid love affair with a young movie director.

True or not, Charlotte had never married again after her return. Like a character in a film, she'd spent her life pining away for a career that had never happened and a man who'd gotten away.

Frank stopped to say a few words to Charlotte and then came into the café, joining her at the table.

"Was that Charlotte Westfall?" she asked as she saw the woman drive away.

"She's going by her married name, Charlotte Abrahams, now. She'd heard the rumors about Beartooth's reconstruction and had to come out to see for herself, she said. Lynette." He reached across the table and took her hand. "Let's get married."

She was busy watching Charlotte drive away. "What happened to her money?"

"I beg your pardon?"

"The fortune Charlotte's rich old husband left her?" Last year it came out that Frank's ex-wife, Pam, had stolen all of Charlotte's fortune. "Did the money ever turn up?"

He nodded solemnly. "It was found in Pam's bank account after her death. Pam left everything to our daughter, Tiffany, but I made sure Charlotte got every penny back."

Nettie looked into his handsome face. He'd aged well, but when she looked at him, she saw the young man he'd been when the two of them had first fallen madly in love as teens.

"Does Tiffany know what you did?" She saw the answer in the lines around his eyes. "She must be furious with you."

He chuckled at that. "What's one more thing to hold against me."

Nettie realized he hadn't mentioned his latest visit

to the mental hospital, and she hadn't asked. "You told her when you went to see her?"

"She'd already heard." He seemed to hesitate. His gaze lifted to hers. She saw the worry as well as the love. "Tiffany also heard about our plans to get married."

Nettie suppressed a shudder. "She threatened us if we got married."

He shook his head. "She threatened to kill herself."

Nettie gasped, her hand going to her mouth. Her eyes filled with tears. "Oh, Frank."

"We're getting married, Lynette. I won't let Tiffany and her mother rule my life any longer with their threats."

"What if she does it?"

He looked away. "God help me, but sometimes I think it might be the only way that girl can find any peace." He shifted his gaze back to her. "Lynette, I had hoped that Tiffany might get better, but I don't think she can. She has money, and she's hired a lawyer. She thinks she is going to be set free."

Nettie felt her heart lurch at the thought. "What do you think?"

"That if I have to, I won't let that happen. Tiffany is dangerous. I'm afraid she is going to spend the rest of her life either in a mental hospital or a prison cell." He shook his head. "Pam did such a number on that child, filling her so full of hate…. It isn't just that Tiffany tried to kill me. She hurt others when she escaped from the hospital. Who knows how many more people she will hurt if she gets the chance?"

Nettie reached across the table and took his hand. "Are you even sure this girl is your flesh and blood?"

"I feel responsible either way because I didn't realize just how sick my ex was."

Nettie scoffed at that. "It would be just like Pam to try to pass this girl off as yours to hurt you."

"She can't hurt me anymore. Pam's dead and Tiffany...well, hopefully, will be in a place where she can't hurt anyone else either. Neither of them is going to keep me from marrying you. We're setting a date right now. I don't want to live another day without you as my wife. So, what's it going to be?"

"Frank—"

"If you force my hand, I swear, Lynette, I will pick you up right now, toss you over my shoulder and carry you to the nearest justice of the peace."

"For better or worse?" she whispered.

"In sickness and in health."

She nodded. "The justice of the peace it is."

He squeezed her hand. "That's what I was hoping you'd say. Judge Andrews is waiting for us at the courthouse."

ROURKE COULDN'T HIDE his disappointment when he reached the café to find that Caligrace wasn't working and her pickup was gone. He wanted to see her, especially after last night. The kiss had been unexpected, he thought now, smiling in spite of himself. He was looking forward to their date tonight and hoped she hadn't changed her mind.

The U.S. marshal in him felt as if he was making progress. It hadn't skipped his attention that the woman was leery of him—and possibly other men, as well. Maybe she had been hurt in the past. Laura would say it gave Callie motive to murder men.

Nor had he lost sight of his original goal. He'd come here to find a killer. That hadn't changed. But the more time he spent around Callie, the less he believed her to be involved. He hoped that on their date tonight, he could get closer to her. He had to gain her trust. He had to find out why she'd shown up at those three murder scenes.

Rourke had to put his mind at rest about the woman. He *was* getting closer. The fact that he liked her, was attracted to her, wouldn't matter if he found out she was involved in the murders. He was the law. Catching bad guys was what he did. He'd worked his way up to where he was today. He wasn't about to give up everything, not for a case, certainly not for a woman.

But even as he thought it, he felt a strange ache. Not desire, although he'd certainly felt it last night. No, this was something deeper, something more primal. He felt something he hadn't felt with any other woman. He couldn't even put it into words. He'd felt… drawn to her in a way that was alien to him. In a way that made him think about settling down.

He shook off the thought. It was only a case. If anything, he was probably afraid for Callie. Afraid, too, that he might be wrong about her.

Laura was right about one thing. He was obsessed with the woman. He wanted to get into her head— under her skin. The cop in him wanted to know why. What made a killer? Was there a tipping point where one person raised exactly like another became a killer and the other became a schoolteacher, a preacher or even a cop?

Callie felt like the key to a mystery he'd spent his career trying to solve. What was it about this woman that made him believe if he could just get close enough, he would find his killer?

"Coffee?"

The sound of Kate's voice jerked him out of his thoughts.

He cleared his throat and said, "Please. You handling things today by yourself?" he asked, hoping maybe Callie was coming in late.

"Just me. And I'll warn you right now, I'm not as patient or competent as Callie, but I'm meaner, so don't give me any trouble," she joked as she poured him a cup.

"I'll keep that in mind. It's nice that you give her a day off once in a while."

Kate merely smiled and then took off to refill coffee cups at the large front table where the local ranchers hung out.

Rourke had taken the same table he always did since the place was half-empty. He didn't need to bother with the menu. It was as basic as any menu could be. When Kate swung by, order pad ready, he said, "Ham, eggs over easy, whole-wheat toast and hash browns."

She scribbled down his order, slopped more coffee into his cup and was gone.

He stared out the window at the construction workers moving like ants around the general-store site. They were making good progress. For a moment, he wondered who in their right mind would try to rebuild Beartooth. He kind of liked it the way it was. He had a feeling Callie did, too.

When his order arrived, he ate, feeling time slipping away as he reminded himself that he was no closer to finding the killer. What would he do when his two weeks were up, if he hadn't solved this?

The thought of leaving Beartooth before he'd finished seemed inconceivable.... Or was it leaving Callie? He had to clear her. He couldn't leave this until he could prove she had nothing to do with the murders. Or that she had.

So unless he was on a wild-goose chase—which he often feared was the case—then there had to be someone close to her who was committing the murders. But who? So far he hadn't seen Callie with anyone—except himself and Carson, he thought, recalling last night at the lake.

Unless there was more to her relationship with Carson Grant than he knew.

When his cell phone vibrated, he saw it was Edwin and took the call outside. He had to walk around to the side of the building because of the noisy construction across the street.

"What did you find out?" he asked without preamble and listened as the P.I. filled him in. The more he heard about Callie, the more his heart ached for her.

"She *saw* the murder?" he asked in shock.

"And the *murderer,* apparently. I don't know how long she went without speaking. Apparently, she was better by the time she was taken to a foster home after Westfield closed down."

Rourke could well imagine Laura's take on this. He didn't need her to tell him what that kind of trauma at that age could have done to her. It could have made her into a killer.

He had a sudden thought. "What was the date of the murder?" He heard Edwin shuffling through his notes.

"October five."

"October five," he repeated and let out a curse. There was definitely a pattern, and he had a pretty good idea that it had begun that night in Westfield.

"You think your killer is mimicking the first murder?"

"It would appear that way," he said, feeling sick.

"There's more. Gladys McCormick had two daughters of her own. According to the deputy, one of them was raped preceding the murder. Gladys denied it. But the deputy said he got called up there again about another murder. Your girl's mother had heard that one of Gladys's daughters was pushed down the stairs and that she thought the girl had either died or was badly hurt. Again Gladys denied it. He saw both girls later and they seemed to be fine. But the rumor was that one of the twins pushed the other down the stairs."

Rourke let out a low whistle. "What do we know about these twin girls?"

"Very little. He wasn't even sure of their names."

"Find them."

Lost in thought after breakfast, Rourke walked back to his cabin. Callie had seen the man murdered—and apparently seen the murderer. He couldn't wait to find Gladys McCormick's daughters. If it was true and one of them was raped prior to the murder…and then one of them pushed the other down a flight of stairs… there had to be a connection to the killing and therefore to Callie.

"Rourke?"

He spun in the direction of the voice, shocked to find Laura in the shadowed corner of his porch. As she stood from where she'd been sitting on an old chair, he realized he hadn't seen her car. Had she planned it that way?

"Laura?"

Her face seemed to crumple as she stepped to him, and suddenly she was in his arms, sobbing her heart out.

"Your mother?" he asked.

She nodded against his shoulder.

"It's all right. It's all right," he said, patting her back, but he had a feeling it was far from it.

CHAPTER EIGHTEEN

As ROURKE LED her into the cabin, Laura let him believe she was upset over her mother's death. She was embarrassed enough for breaking down the way she had. She wasn't about to tell him that she'd come looking for him last night and that she'd seen him with Callie Westfield. Nor that witnessing the kiss had broken her heart as well as terrified her at how foolish he was being.

But breaking down like that? It was so unlike her. Why wouldn't she be upset, though, after seeing the man she loved kissing another woman? The thought made her laugh inwardly. Not just kissing another woman. Kissing a woman who was in all probability a killer.

"I'm so sorry about your mom."

"I really don't want to talk about it."

He nodded as if he understood. Not likely. "Can I buy you breakfast? We could go down to the café—"

She shook her head. "I don't want to see Caligrace Westfield."

"She isn't working today."

"Really?" Laura wondered where she was, then. She could have just gone into Big Timber or Bozeman shopping. Or maybe she was meeting her co-killer. Rourke didn't seem to know any more than she did. "Also, I don't want anyone overhearing what I have to tell you."

"Laura, I appreciate your help, but you don't need to be doing this now with everything..."

"All the arrangements for my mother have been taken care of. Can we please talk about something else?"

"How about some coffee?" He set about making a pot, allowing Laura time, she knew, to pull herself together. She looked around the cabin, too anxious to sit until he insisted.

"I know you haven't had time to do the profiles—"

"I did," she said. "If these murders are being committed by a male associated with the woman, then the two of them could be luring these men in. She seduces them. He kills them."

"I suspect he is more like a protective male in her life who thinks he is saving her," Rourke said. "Maybe he is. Maybe these men did something to her that makes him feel they need to be punished."

"Or it could be a case of sexual dominance by one or both of them." Laura took a folder from her purse. "We have a lot of information on male serial killers. These are things that they often share in common." She ticked them off on her fingers, seeing that he already knew them.

"Multiple problems at home, instability in the family unit, the father often gone or a disruptive influence because of alcohol, drugs or sexual abuse. Most moved a lot, had no attachment to people or the community where they lived for a short time."

"Thus reducing the child's chances for finding opportunities to develop positive relationships," he said, nodding.

"Most offenders didn't have a satisfactory relationship with their fathers. Either the father was gone entirely or on drugs or alcohol, so not there as a parent. Often their mothers were unavailable emotionally. A lack of justice was another factor, feeling like they got a raw deal. Many complained that their parents were preoccupied with their own problems, leading to the offender coming up with a fantasy life to escape. Often that fantasy life involved violence and began to dominate their thoughts."

"Dominance through aggression," Rourke said with a nod. "Murder gives them a feeling of being in control."

"This is Caligrace Westfield's background, from what you've told me. What does it tell you?"

"That not every child who grows up under these types of conditions turns into a serial killer."

ROURKE COULD SEE that Laura was upset with him. "I know what you're saying," he agreed, getting up from the table to refill their coffee cups. "My gut tells me that Callie is somehow connected to these murders. But that she isn't the killer."

"Then who is?"

"That's what I hope to find out tonight."

Laura lifted a brow.

"I'm taking her out to dinner." He saw her expression as he poured her more coffee. "Don't worry. I'll be careful. I have to take it slow. She's jumpy."

"That should tell you something. You still think there is someone in the shadows doing the killing."

He nodded.

"She knows he's there?"

Rourke frowned. "That part is what bothers me. She's aware of the murders on some level…."

Laura sighed. "Do I need to remind you that some women are capable of killing their own children?"

He had a sudden image of a woman filling a bathtub, smiling to her children, just before she held each struggling child under.

"I'm not one of her children," he said, hating that he sounded defensive.

"No, but if she's a black widow, you're already caught in her web."

He returned the coffeepot to the stove. "If I didn't know better, I'd say you were jealous."

She laughed. "Just trying to keep you alive."

When he turned, he caught a glimpse of her pain. "I'm so sorry about your mother."

"I told you. We weren't close."

"Still—"

"You can't possibly understand. You had a…*family.*"

"And you didn't? You've never talked about them. I thought you said once that you had a sister—"

"Catherine. She shows up when she feels like it."

"That would explain why I've never met her."

"Catherine makes an appearance every year or so just to remind me that I can't get her out of my life no matter how hard I try."

She could feel Rourke studying her in shocked surprise. "I'm sorry you're not close."

"We're too close for comfort," she said with a laugh. "Sometimes I'm too much like her. She is a lot meaner than I am."

Rourke laughed. "So you're the *good* sister?"

She met his gaze and nodded solemnly. The cabin suddenly felt too small. "Stop trying to change the subject. It's October. Your killer is going to strike again—and soon, according to her pattern."

He didn't tell her that he'd seen a change in Callie.

Laura sighed as if she could see she wasn't getting anywhere with him. "Here are the profiles," she said, sliding them across the table to him. "I also did some research on Carson Grant and Johnny Franks. Carson Grant was a suspect in the death of a local girl, Jenny West."

"West?" Rourke said. "Carson's sister, Destry, is married to a West. Rylan West, I believe."

Laura nodded. "Jenny was his sister. Carson took off right after the murder and didn't come back for years. When he did, he was deep in debt, gambling debts following him. He's been clean now for almost two years. He works for his sister after his father cut him out of the will."

"That explains a lot," Rourke said, nodding. "The cowboy has a chip on his shoulder."

"Johnny Franks is a drifter. He hooked up with Carson about the time Callie came to town. He has a rap sheet for assault."

"Any tie between him and Callie?"

"Not that I could find. Any more from your P.I.?" Laura took a sip of her coffee, cupping the mug in her hands as she looked over the rising steam.

Rourke knew what he had to tell her would only make Callie look more guilty. "The murder at Westfield was committed on October five."

She put down her mug. "So there *is* a connection."

"There's more," he admitted. "According to the deputy up there, Callie witnessed the murder at Westfield. She was *five,* so there is no way she was involved. But apparently, she was found in the room. The girl suffered at least temporary trauma from the ordeal."

Laura stared at him. "So she not only saw what happened..."

"There is a good chance she also saw the killer."

LAURA GOT UP and moved around the small cabin. "Well, if Callie saw the killer, then why hasn't she come forward with a name?" she demanded, feeling a little lightheaded.

"I don't know. Maybe because of the trauma, she doesn't remember."

"Or that killer doesn't play into these murders. Maybe it was a onetime thing and not relevant to these cases." She turned to look at him. "Surely you've considered that Callie is acting out what she saw that night at such a young age."

"Of course I have," he said. "But I'm not convinced the original murder is relevant to these cases. What if this is a case of co-killers, just as I originally thought, but both of them are women?"

Laura raised a brow in surprise. "You have someone in mind?"

"At first I thought it might be Gladys McCormick. If it's true and one of her daughters was raped by the man, she would be the most obvious person to exact justice."

"And *now?*"

"I think it might have been one of the girls."

"How about Callie's own mother?" Laura said.

"Wouldn't that account for Callie not telling who committed the murder?"

"Yes, but her mother is dead. I think it stands to reason that the man was killed by someone in that house."

"You're back to one of the girls who lived there?" She continued to move around the cabin, too nervous to sit.

"I'm thinking it could have been one of Gladys McCormick's daughters."

"Vengeance against the man who raped her sister?"

"Maybe. Or the sister who was allegedly raped could have done it. That would explain why Callie didn't tell. She would have been fearful of Gladys McCormick, because I would imagine her mother was. That fear would probably also encompass the woman's daughters."

"How old were these daughters?"

"Twelve or thirteen," he said, nodding at her point. "I know they were young."

"If Callie really was in the room and saw the murder…a child put in that kind of horrendous circumstance…" Her voice broke. "I can't imagine what that kind of trauma could have done to her."

"It would have been even worse for the girl who was raped," Rourke pointed out. "Then if she killed the man…"

"I would imagine your killer sees men as a threat. Not all men, maybe only men who get too close or men who hurt her in some way." She met his gaze. "I don't think you realize how dangerous this woman is." She could see that he still wanted to believe his precious Callie was innocent. "So these co-killers…if one of them is Callie… You're actually going on a date with her tonight? At best, she will set you up. At worst, she will cut your heart out herself."

She hadn't meant to say it with such anger.

Rourke looked at her in surprise as she picked up her purse to leave. "Laura, why are you making this so personal?"

"*I'm* making it personal?" She slung her purse strap over her shoulder. "You were half in love with Callie before you even met her. I see you getting more caught up in her web every day."

Rourke sighed. "Just because I don't think she's guilty—"

"I see you falling for her, and it breaks my heart because I can't see this ending but one way."

"I *like* her. I'll admit it. But you're wrong. I haven't forgotten that she's a suspect."

"Haven't you?" She blurted it out. "I saw you with her last night, Rourke."

He had the good sense to look chagrined. "I'm trying to get close to her, remember? She's…she's hiding something."

The admission took Laura by surprise. So maybe he wasn't so sure Callie was innocent.

"And that doesn't make you nervous?" she demanded.

"It makes me nervous as hell. Laura, I know what I'm doing."

She could have argued that. "So, you think she just can't remember or doesn't want to? You know, either way there might be a way to find out. Maybe if she returned to Westfield, to the place where this all started… Never mind. It's a crazy idea."

"No, it's not," Rourke said. "If the killings are a

manifestation of that earlier trauma, then maybe she would remember the killer."

"It's a long shot." She could see that he was taken with the idea.

"Somewhere in her memory is the real killer. If she can access it—"

"Then you will have solved your case," Laura said. "That's all this is, right? Just another case? How would you get her to go with you, though?"

Rourke didn't seem to hear her. "I can't do anything until I hear from the P.I. I hired. He found out that Gladys McCormick had two daughters, identical twins. He's trying to find them. He left a message earlier that he thinks he knows where at least one of them is. He's going to call tonight."

Laura felt all the blood rush from her head as she continued to move around the room. "Why are you interested in *them?*" she asked, her back to him.

"It makes sense that one of them could have been involved in the murder at Westfield, given what Edwin learned about them. After the alleged rape and the murder, the deputy said he was told that one of the sisters pushed the other one down the stairs. Originally, it was believed that the girl had died or was badly hurt. Apparently, that wasn't true, but these girls are at the heart of what happened in that place. If anyone knows who the killer is, I'm betting one of them does."

She felt a cold chill move through her as she found herself standing by the kitchen counter and saw what Rourke had written on his notebook next to his plugged-in cell phone. *"Edwin. Billings Imperial Hotel, room 1112. Call tonight."*

"There's something I need to tell you," she said,

turning to face him. Her voice broke. She feared she
would burst into tears. After her earlier breakdown, he
would think she was losing her mind. She wasn't all
that sure she wasn't.

"What is it?" Rourke asked in concern.

"I've been meaning to tell you for some time. I
just didn't know how." She looked at him. He was the
most handsome man she'd ever known, but that wasn't
why she'd fallen in love with him. Rourke wanted justice in a world where there was too little. But he was
also kind and compassionate. He felt things deeply.
He cared.

"I'm not surprised that you don't want to believe
Caligrace is the killer," she said. "You see that innocent face of hers and you want to believe the best. I
understand that."

"Laura, what is this *really* about? Your mother?"

She wanted to scream that it *was* about her mother,
about sister Catherine, about her. Catherine was close
by; she could feel it. Her sister could be showing up
any day. Catherine couldn't stand seeing her happy.
She had a way of making her feel bad about everything, especially Rourke. Her sister knew how she felt
about the man and taunted her about it.

"You and Rourke are never going to happen. You're
only kidding yourself. You keep thinking that one day
he will just miraculously fall in love with you? Never
going to happen. Now, Rourke and me… Well, I think
I might be more his type."

"Stay away from him," Laura had pleaded with her
sister. She knew how Catherine was when she wanted
something. Her sister destroyed things. Laura had spent

years keeping the two of them apart, even though Rourke had often mentioned that he'd like to meet her sister.

Laura looked at Rourke now, wanting to warn him. Catherine could show up anytime out of the blue as she'd done for years.

"What would Mother say if she knew how you treated me?" Catherine would whine. "Didn't she tell you to be nice to me?"

Catherine had always been their mother's favorite and they both knew it. "Try being nicer to Catherine" was her mother's mantra for years.

She'd always been nice to her sister. It was Catherine who wasn't nice to *her*. It was Catherine who always got her into trouble. Catherine who, if she let her, would ruin her life.

Laura took a breath, let it out and, clasping her hands together tightly, said, "You're right. I am taking this personally because…I'm in love with you."

A heavy silence filled the cabin, colder than the approaching snowstorm outside.

Rourke cleared his voice. "Laura—"

"You don't have to say anything." Why had she blurted it out like that? Why had she listened to her psychiatrist? She didn't feel better. She felt horrible. She wanted to die. She wanted to launch herself at Rourke and beat her fists against his chest.

She turned away, unable to bear the sympathy she saw in his dark eyes. From behind her, she heard him rise and move toward her. Closing her eyes, she braced herself for his touch. If only he would take her in his arms and hold her and tell her he felt the same way.

He took her shoulders in his hands and turned her around to face him. "Laura, I had no idea."

She laughed through the sudden tears. "I know."

"How long have you—"

"Almost since I met you, but it doesn't matter. I just had to tell you."

"You know I care about you."

"I also know you've always thought of me only as your partner...."

"And a good friend," he said.

"Yes." It felt like a lie, though. If they had been good friends, he would already know what she *wasn't* telling him. "There's more."

His eyes widened a little. He glanced at his watch. He needed to get ready for his date.

She could feel her heart hammering against her ribs. She tried to swallow the lump in her throat. He was right. This wasn't the time.

"I just wanted to tell you that I have a job interview back in Seattle. I need to get going. I wanted you to know that I was leaving."

"A job interview? That's great." He looked relieved. He certainly didn't look sorry to see her go. "You'll call me, won't you? We can talk once you get back home, after the interview."

She nodded and wiped hastily at her tears.

He seemed not to know how to say goodbye to her, so he walked her to the door.

"Goodbye, Rourke," she said as they parted company. "Enjoy your date."

As she walked down the hillside to where she'd parked her car, she told herself that maybe things would have been different if he had loved her. Or if he had let her tell him about the old trunk. But she knew she was just fooling herself. Once she told him about her and sister Catherine… Well, no matter what she did now, she didn't see how there would be a way to save Rourke.

CHAPTER NINETEEN

CALLIE STOOD IN front of the mirror, hating how nervous she felt. "It's just a date." That made her laugh since she didn't *date*. She'd tried it a number of times, but knowing what your date was thinking ruined it.

With Rourke…the only time she'd felt anything was when he'd lied, and that could have been simply her instincts kicking in, since the flash she'd felt had been so weak. She pushed away the memory, not wanting to think about it.

She couldn't believe how excited she was about this date. She and Rourke had had fun at the lake. She *liked* him and was looking forward to this dinner. She was grateful she didn't know what he was thinking, what he was really doing in town or why she still had that dull headache that foretold of something bad to come.

Wasn't it all right to believe in the best for once? Wasn't it possible that he was just who he said he was and that maybe there was a chance…?

She refused to let her thoughts go any further. For tonight, she was going to enjoy herself having dinner with a handsome, charming cowboy. She'd deal with whatever was coming when it happened. Nothing was going to ruin her night, she thought as she looked out the window, hoping to see him drive up.

But at the back of her mind she was thinking, *Don't*

disappoint me, Rourke, as she spotted Carson Grant's truck parked down the street. She couldn't tell if he was in the truck, but she had a bad feeling he was and that he was watching her apartment. He was too far away for her to pick up anything from him psychically. But hadn't she known he'd meant what he'd threatened, that it wasn't over between the two of them? Carson was determined that she was going to go out with him, no matter what she or even Rourke had to say about the matter.

Just then, he pulled up in his rented SUV. She pushed Carson out of her thoughts. She would deal with him when she had to. Thinking only of her date, she found herself smiling as she watched Rourke get out of the SUV. No man looked better in a Western sports jacket, jeans and boots than he did, she thought as she watched him make his way to the stairs. She checked herself again in the mirror. Her cheeks were flushed, her eyes bright and shining. She couldn't help smiling at how giddy she felt.

It's just dinner, she told herself, then whispered, "Yes, but please let me have tonight. Just this one night."

She'd heard that a winter storm was blowing in. It was all the ranchers in the café had been talking about today. A few years ago a storm had blown in and killed thousands of head of cattle just over the border in North Dakota. It could just as easily have happened in Montana, since not even the weathermen had predicted the severity of the storm. So she could understand why the ranchers were concerned.

Her, personally? She would love it to snow and make this an even more magical evening. Callie only wished she could blame the dull throb at the base of her skull on the impending storm. But she knew that whatever was about to happen, it wasn't far off, and that it would be bad. It always was.

"You look amazing," Rourke said, his dark eyes shining as he held Callie at arm's length and took her in. She wore a blue dress that slipped like a warm breeze over her curves. Her dark mane was down, floating around her shoulders. She looked like an angel.

As he helped her on with her coat, he thought of what Edwin had told him about her childhood and felt a well of sympathy. It was amazing that she'd survived that life. He thought of the small child who'd witnessed a gruesome murder and hadn't spoken for who knew how long. It broke his heart.

But at the back of his mind, he worried. What had it done to this beautiful woman? He hated to think. Maybe he would find out the truth tonight and, hopefully, live to tell about it.

He was no fool. He was carrying tonight under his Western jacket. Nor would he have been surprised to hear that Calllie had her pistol in the large purse she'd brought along. While looking at this woman, he couldn't believe she was a killer. But he wasn't taking any chances, no matter what Laura thought.

Laura. He was still upset from her earlier visit. He'd had no idea she was in love with him. Was he that blind to everything around him? He questioned whether he had any business being in law enforcement.

"Is everything all right?" Callie asked.

"Sorry, I'm worried about a friend of mine," he said. "But this night is too special to be worrying. Let's go have some fun." He opened the apartment door, holding it for her, as they left. "I love nights like this," he said as they descended the stairs.

A cold wind blew down out of the mountains. Earlier, he'd seen cattle gathering together, a sure sign that a storm was blowing in.

At the bottom of the stairs, Callie stopped to look up at the Crazies. The mountains towered over the town, a deep purple against a sky that seemed to sparkle a midnight blue.

"It really is going to snow," she said, a smile in her voice. "I can smell it on the air."

"You like winter?" he asked, a little surprised.

She glanced over at him. "Don't you?"

"I haven't seen a real winter storm since I was a kid in Wyoming," he said, realizing that he had missed it in Seattle. "In Wyoming, the storms often came with gale winds that whipped the snow into art sculptures in the yard and made the ranch into my own private wonderland. A lot of times the bus couldn't get through the drifts, so there wouldn't be school for days until the plows could get to us. The neighbor boys would hop on a tractor and come over to play. If the drifts were high enough, we'd jump out of the barn. If not, we'd leap into the ones next to the shed."

"A few storms like that came through Beartooth last year where the snow blew in around the buildings. It was so beautiful. I don't mind the snow, especially on those nights when the huge flakes float down. It's... mesmerizing."

She was mesmerizing, he thought as he watched her turn her face up to the approaching storm.

"Don't tell anyone, but I made a snowman last winter," she said with a laugh as they walked to his SUV and he opened her door.

"Why wouldn't you want anyone to know?"

"Because I'm thirty years old, and here I am, out in the dark, pushing huge balls of snow around."

"I wish I could have seen it," he said as she slipped into the passenger seat.

As he climbed behind the wheel, she laughed and said, "I think Kate knew I was the one who made it because I borrowed a carrot from the kitchen. Someone left an old floppy hat in the café months before that, so I used it and tied on a scarf."

He saw her smile to herself at the memory. "I bet he was beautiful."

"*She* was," Callie corrected. "She was very regal. I was sad when she melted."

He saw her glance down the street to where he'd seen Carson parked earlier. The pickup was no longer there, and he sighed with relief. When he'd seen Carson's pickup, he'd hoped there wouldn't be trouble tonight.

"I hope you're hungry," he said as he drove toward Big Timber.

"I'm always hungry. You're going to be sorry you invited me to dinner. I'm not one of those women who eats like a bird."

"Good, because we aren't having birdseed. I thought we'd go to The Grand. I hear they have good food. I'm hankering for some Montana beef, rare."

"I took you for a rare-beef kind of guy."

He laughed at that. "I took you for a tofu kind of girl." He cut his gaze to her as he drove, thinking of her living those three years in Seattle. "Granola all the way."

"So you think you know me," she said and smiled as she settled back against the seat.

"Not yet."

THE LAND FELL away from the Crazies to the Yellowstone River. In the headlights she caught glimpses of the summer-dried shades of pale yellow to faded grays and soft brown.

Callie loved the way the seasons changed here. In the spring, this lush farmland would turn into bright green pasture, dark green alfalfa or waves of golden grain. Summer, the creeks and rivers would run clear, cutting through willows and chokecherry bushes heavy with fruit along their edges.

During the summer, she had soaked up the heat, trying to capture as many warm hours as possible during the fleeting days. Fall always blew in as if waiting anxiously in the wings. The aspens would suddenly burst with bright red and orange leaves that fluttered in the breeze.

Old Man Winter, though, was never far behind. Its winds stripped the leaves from the aspens, whirling them in the air so the days smelled of earth and decay. And one day she would look out, and all she would see were the bare branches, spindly and gnarled, etched against an ominous sky.

"I'll be glad when winter comes," Callie said, looking out the window. "I've never liked fall. There is something…sad and depressing about it. It always feels like an ending to me." She felt him shoot her a look. "Winter can be cold but beautiful. It's as if the snow purifies everything, you know?"

He nodded, but she didn't think he did.

"It's the in-between that I don't like."

"Well, you aren't going to have to wait long now. There's definitely a snowstorm coming in tonight."

ROURKE DROVE, THINKING about what she'd said. Worry worked at him, making him anxious. He didn't have to wonder what Laura would have made of Callie's "confession" about fall. He reminded himself that her mother had died in the fall. All the terrible things that had happened to her had happened in the fall, which only made him more anxious to know this woman. Know what she was feeling, thinking and, more important, what she was going to do next. His need to know more about the woman in the seat next to him only increased his anxiety. He fought the urge to question her on the twenty-mile drive into Big Timber, but restrained himself by turning on some music. "I hope you don't mind country."

She shook her head and began to sing along with the song on the radio, clearly no stranger to the music genre. She had a good voice, clear and sweet. He felt himself relax a little and almost regretted that he'd brought his gun. He'd foolishly also picked up his badge and stuck it in his coat pocket.

Was he worried that he might have to use it tonight? Technically, he wasn't even a U.S. marshal. But he was still the law, and that he'd even grabbed the badge showed him how much he wasn't ready to give it up.

The Grand was an old hotel and restaurant on the main drag of Big Timber. Rourke parked diagonally out front and went around to open her door. The night had gotten colder, the wind kicking up dust and debris, a prelude to the icy bite from the approaching snowstorm. He quickly hustled her inside, where it was warm and cozy.

The warmth and smells seemed to welcome them as they stopped at the door to take off their jackets before moving down the bar to one of the booths at the back. Fortunately, the place wasn't packed. There were only a few people eating, a few more at the bar. The approaching storm must have kept a lot of people away. It was also early.

"I'm curious," Callie said after they'd ordered drinks and an appetizer. "Tell me more about Rourke Montgomery."

He smiled, hating the reminder of his lie. "I'm just as curious about you. I'll tell if you will."

"YOU FIRST," CALLIE said after their drinks and appetizer were served. She leaned forward, smiling as she took a sip of her beer. "Tell me who you are, the real you."

Rourke shrugged and took his time. "I was born in Wyoming. My parents owned a ranch, like I told you. They eventually sold it."

"You didn't want it?" she asked, sounding surprised.

He seemed to think about that for a moment. "I couldn't see myself back in Wyoming. I'd moved on."

"Moved on doing what? You never said what you do for a living."

Rourke shook his head. "No, you don't. It's your turn. Give," he said. "Tell me about the real you."

"There really isn't much to tell. I grew up in Montana."

"So, you're from here. I didn't realize that. From Beartooth?"

"I lived all over the state, moved around a lot. It's such a beautiful state, I just wanted to see it all." That wasn't quite true, but she doubted Rourke was telling her everything either.

"So, you're a native Montanan. I'm jealous. I love the state—at least what I've seen of it so far."

She smiled. "Even Beartooth?"

"Especially Beartooth and Saddlestring Lake." He grinned at her, then asked, "Do you still have family here?"

"No. Your turn. So, what do you do?"

"I'm kind of in between jobs right now," he said, almost looking embarrassed, she thought. "I've done all kinds of work, from wrangling to training horses. Truth is, my parents' ranch was fairly large. I got quite a bit of money after they sold. I don't *have* to work." He cringed. "I hate to admit that."

"There is nothing wrong with being lucky," she said, even though she couldn't see him just hanging out with nothing to do. He didn't seem the type. She studied him openly for a moment, surprised that she was wishing she could read him. But so far, she believed he was telling her the truth.

She hated being such a suspicious person, but it came with the territory, didn't it?

"Your turn," Rourke said.

"I'm a waitress," she said and laughed. She was grateful when their meals arrived because she could tell that Rourke was still curious about her—just as she'd sensed he'd been the first day she'd laid eyes on him.

Too curious for a man who was probably just passing through, she thought as she watched him cut into his steak.

EDWIN FROWNED AT the knock on his hotel-room door. He glanced at his watch. Eight. He couldn't imagine who it could be. He realized that he hadn't called Rourke again since he'd only just returned to his room. Had the U.S. marshal decided to pay him a visit?

Moving to the door, he started to open it, when he got a strange feeling of dread. He laughed it off. He didn't scare easily, but this whole case had left him uneasy, even a little paranoid.

"Who is it?" he asked through the door.

"Housekeeping."

Housekeeping at this hour of the night? He unlocked the door and opened it to find a young dark-haired woman holding a stack of towels.

"Sorry to bother you so late," the woman said.

He wasn't sure what registered first, her voice or her face. He was already reaching for the towels, when he recognized her. The dark hair had thrown him since the last time he'd seen her, she'd been a blonde. There were those few seconds of confused, then alarmed recognition as she placed the towels into his hands and grabbed his wrist. He felt a shock of surprise an instant before he felt the needle.

Flinching, his gaze flew up to meet hers as the towels fell to the floor at his feet. "You're—"

"Catherine McCormick. I hear you've been looking for me."

Before he could react, she shoved him back, kick-ing the towels into the room as she entered and clos-ing and locking the door behind her.

Edwin stumbled back, tripping over the edge of the bed and almost going down. His mind spun as some powerful drug raced through his bloodstream.

His gun. He had to get his gun.

She was on him before he could take two steps, surprising him with how strong she was. He opened his mouth to speak. Or to cry for help? It didn't mat-ter. Nothing came out. Whatever she'd drugged him with had quickly rendered him mute. He could feel his body becoming numb.

As she pushed him down on the bed, she still hadn't spoken a word. He stared at her face, terrified by what he saw in her eyes. Dark evil. His cell phone rang over on the table by the window. She let it ring as she pro-ceeded to undress him, stripping him of all his clothes until he was naked.

His fear escalated into sheer terror. He knew enough about this case that the last thing he wanted was to end up naked and tied to a bed.

When she tried to pull him to his feet, he couldn't stand. She pushed him off the bed, then grabbed his arms and dragged him across the carpet and into the bathroom.

A cell phone rang as she lifted him into the cold empty tub. Her cell phone this time, he realized. She glanced at him as if seeing him for the first time and then stepped out of the room to take the call.

He lay in the tub, his head resting against the edge. His mind screamed for him to do something. But it was useless. His muscles didn't respond. He was helpless.

Worse, he had no doubt that he was about to die. His only hope was that it would be quick.

ROURKE HADN'T LEARNED anything about Callie that he didn't already know. She'd been vague at best. But could he blame her for wanting to hide her past? Her mother had been sixteen, pregnant, unmarried and living in a girls' home where horrible things happened.

How much would a five-year-old remember of that? Enough that the girl had taken the name of the place, he reminded himself with a chill. A part of her was still tied to that past. Did that include murder?

"So, how did you end up in Beartooth?" he asked after they'd taken a few bites of their food.

"I had no plans, really. I was just driving down the interstate when I saw the Crazy mountain range. It was so beautiful that I took the first road I came to that headed in that direction, and it brought me to Beartooth. Fortunately, I'd had some experience waiting tables, and Kate just happened to be looking for a waitress. I like to think it was fate. Like you, I've done a lot of odd jobs in my life."

"I did some traveling around for a while after college. I liked just seeing where the road would take me. Did you go to college?"

"Tried a few colleges, learned a lot. I never saw the need for a degree. I couldn't see myself staying in one place long enough to grow roots." She shrugged almost apologetically. "I guess I'm just a free spirit."

"Nothing wrong with that," he said, smiling over at her, hoping that was why she moved so much, but all his instincts told him she was a woman on the run. It was what she was running from that worried him.

They ate, complimenting the food and then talking about their favorite meals. He wasn't surprised to learn that she liked all different kinds of cuisine, including Thai.

"Not much of that in Montana, is there?" he asked.

"You'd be surprised. There's some around. You just need to know where to find it."

Was she flirting with him? She was. "Maybe we'll have to try it if there's one that's not too far away."

She gave him a mysterious smile in answer. Yes, he liked her, he thought as he looked across the table at her before lowering his gaze to his food. He liked her more all the time. While he'd always thought that falling for someone was scary, nothing was scarier than feeling himself drawn in even more by this woman.

Maybe a gun wasn't the only weapon she carried in her purse. Or maybe she planned to pick up a steak knife before they left the restaurant tonight.

He told himself that sounded more like Laura than the way he was feeling about Callie, when he looked up and saw Carson Grant come through the door on a gust of wind. Before the door closed, he saw that the storm had finally hit. Snow whirled out on the street in a kaleidoscope of huge flakes.

CALLIE SENSED HIM even before she turned to see Carson enter the restaurant. He'd already spotted Rourke and now sneered, giving a tip of his Stetson to them before climbing onto the closest bar stool and shaking the snow off his coat.

She looked down at her plate, her appetite gone. Fortunately, most of her meal was also gone. "If you'll excuse me," she said, putting down her napkin. "I'm going to the ladies' room, and then I thought maybe we could get dessert to go?"

Rourke smiled. "Great idea."

"We can eat it at my apartment," she said brazenly and left the booth. Once in the bathroom, she leaned against the door for a moment to steady herself. The bathroom looked as if it was from the original hotel with its black-and-white tile and older fixtures. She'd sensed Carson because of the malevolent aura around him. She'd never felt it so strongly as she did tonight. Her head throbbed, no longer a dull ache.

That terrible feeling of déjà vu washed over her. She couldn't bear the thought that it was happening again.

She stepped to the sink and pressed a cold wet paper towel to her cheeks. She tried to fight off the darkness that seemed to come over her. She wouldn't let anything spoil this evening. Nor would she let the headache.

Straightening, she looked at herself in the mirror. *You have tonight. Make the most of it.*

On her way back to Rourke, she passed a table with several small children sitting with their parents, when she got a flash. The family radiated warmth and happiness. They were all having fun, the parents interacting with their two daughters. She smiled at the little girls, wishing as she hadn't in years that she'd had a childhood that had looked like that, that had *felt* like that.

Just then, the smallest of the little girls started to reach for her glass of milk. Callie had been so intent on the little girls that she saw the whole thing happening long before it did.

She quickly stepped to the table and rescued the glass as it started to shoot off the surface. Catching it without spilling a drop, she returned it to the little girl. The parents looked at her in surprise and then thanked her.

"No problem," Callie said, but as she turned toward the booth where she and Rourke had been sitting, she saw his expression.

He looked…shocked. She realized he must have been watching her approach, so he'd witnessed the whole thing. As his gaze met hers, she saw what she'd feared in his eyes. He *knew*.

ROURKE BLINKED, DISBELIEVING. He'd never seen anyone move that fast. It was as if Callie had known beforehand that the girl was going to spill her drink. With a start, he remembered another time at the café when he'd seen her move to a table to save a plate that had gotten too close to the edge. Both times, there had been no warning, and yet…

He stared at her, his mind reeling. She'd somehow known both incidents were going to happen before they did. It was the only way she could have gotten to the table fast enough. The realization stunned him because of the ramifications.

If Callie had second sight…

His heart began to pound. Then she could *know* about the murders. No scanner by her bed. She could have *seen* them, and that was what had led her to the crime scenes. But then she would have also seen the killer at each murder—just as she had as a child.

His heart began to pound at the thought that she really might hold the answers to the crimes. She might be the one person who could tell him who the serial killer was.

Or she could be the killer.

No. He knew he was reaching, but what he had

seen could explain why his instincts told him she was the connection. If true, how strong was her gift? He remembered her reaction to him. What had she seen?

He realized with a silent curse that if she really did have some psychic ability, then she would know who he really was and what he'd come to Beartooth to do. That thought left him cold.

"Ready?" Callie asked, smiling as she saw the two containers on the table. "I hope that's dessert."

"It is. I didn't know what you liked, so I got a couple of different ones." He hadn't realized that he'd stood and was holding her coat. He nodded numbly and helped her with her jacket.

He told himself he was overreacting. He couldn't even be sure of what he'd seen, let alone what it might mean. He was jumping to crazy conclusions. Callie wouldn't have gone out to dinner with him if she knew why he'd come to Beartooth. *Or maybe she would have if she planned to kill you tonight.* Laura's voice in his head.

Maybe she wasn't psychic after all. Maybe he'd imagined what he thought he'd seen. Or maybe she just had quick reflexes. Or maybe…

As they were leaving, Carson said something. Callie hurried her step, as if wanting to get out of there without a scene. Rourke didn't want trouble. Especially tonight.

Once on the street, he took a deep breath. Snowflakes whirled around them from the dark sky overhead. The cold night air helped clear his head. Now he wasn't so sure what he'd seen earlier—if anything.

It was obsession, he thought as he looked over at Callie. He couldn't turn back. Whatever was going to happen tonight...he was ready. Each thing he learned about Callie was like a layer that he peeled away, only to find there were more and more layers. What would he discover if he peeled enough away? He shuddered to think.

Even if she wasn't the killer, she knew who the killer was. He couldn't discount that she might be the co-killer, maybe the one who reeled them in for the real killer, and maybe he'd already gotten too close.

"I hope Carson didn't spoil your night," Callie said.

"Not mine. How about yours?"

She smiled and took his arm as they walked toward the SUV through the falling snow. "I'm having a wonderful time. I can't wait to see what you have planned for dessert."

He smiled over at her, telling himself that if she did have some type of psychic ability, then she would already know.

As they reached the car, she took the two dessert containers from him.

"Don't shake those like they're Christmas presents," he warned. "I want you to be surprised."

She eyed the boxes, then him and smiled. "I'm always surprised around you."

He wondered about that as she slipped into the SUV, and he went around to climb behind the wheel. With any luck, he would find out once they reached her apartment.

CHAPTER TWENTY

CALLIE UNLOCKED HER apartment door. Behind her, Rourke stood holding the desserts. She loved that she had no idea what he'd gotten—just as she had no idea what he was thinking right now.

The falling snow made the night seem to glitter. The cold air felt good in her lungs. She couldn't remember ever feeling more alive. Even her headache was better. Her skin prickled with excitement as she pushed open the door.

At the back of her mind, the tiny voice of reason warned that she was making a mistake. She didn't know this man. Worse, all the signs indicated that whatever was coming, he was a part of it.

She stepped in, turning on a small lamp. It cast a warm glow in the corner of the room, chasing away the dark shadows. Behind her, she heard Rourke close the door and lock it.

Her heart was pounding, her blood running hot, as she slipped off her coat and stepped to him. She knew that if she had any sense at all, she'd offer him dessert and nothing more. His arrival in town and her headache couldn't be a coincidence. She knew how badly this could end, and yet no man had ever made her feel the way she did.

True, part of the attraction was that she couldn't

read him. But that was also the danger. He was a mystery to her—just as she suspected she was a mystery to him. She'd seen his interest in her from the very beginning. That alone should have made her smart enough not to take this any further.

He'd carried in the dessert boxes. She took them from him, setting them aside, and looked up into his handsome face. He was waiting for her to make the first move, but she could see the same aching need in his eyes that had her nerves strung like piano wire.

Looping her arms around his neck, she drew him down, her mouth hungry for a taste of him. Her tongue teased his, making him groan as he grabbed her around the waist and pulled her hard against him. A moan escaped her as she felt the heat of him, the need, as he buried his free hand in her hair and deepened the kiss.

He swung her around, pushing her against the wall as he pressed his hard body into hers. Shifting a little, he cupped the swell of her breast. She felt her nipple straining hard against the fabric of the silken dress. Drawing down the neck of the dress, he freed her nipple and pressed his hot, wet mouth to it. He sucked it into a hard, aching point, sending heat racing to her center.

"Rourke," she cried out as his hand slipped under the hem of her dress to the cool silken fabric of her panties. His fingers found the heat of her. Just the touch of him, and she lost it, trembling as all reason left her.

ROURKE CARRIED HER into the bedroom. Warning bells were going off in his head. He had to remind himself of who he was, why he was there and, more important, who this woman was. A suspect. A captivating and beautiful but dangerous suspect. Get too close and he could find himself tied to a bed with a knife to his throat.

He could feel her still trembling in his arms. She seemed so small, so vulnerable. Rourke gently set her down on the bed. She met his gaze and slowly drew her dress up over her head, discarding it to the floor. Her dark eyes shone as she pulled him down next to her and began to unsnap his shirt.

He closed his eyes, reveling in the touch of her warm hands against his bare skin. As she unbuttoned his jeans, he opened his eyes again to look at her. Only a little light bled into the bedroom from the adjoining room. He held her gaze as he shrugged out of his clothes.

Taking her in his arms, he slowly removed her undergarments. He laved her nipples with his tongue and kissed a path down her flat, warm stomach to the dark V at her center.

She writhed and cried out again and drew him back to her. He pressed his body to hers, soaking in the warm smoothness of her nakedness against his own as he kissed her. The kiss was gentle, loving, but quickly turned passionate as he rolled her over on top of him.

Callie straddled him, throwing back her head as she took him inside her. He gazed at her amazing face, the long curve of her neck, the rounded firm breasts and the wild dark hair that hung around her like an aura. He'd finally given in to what he was feeling. He'd fallen for this woman.

ROURKE WOKE WITH a start. For a moment, he didn't know where he was. The unfamiliar room had a chill to it, making him aware that he was naked. And alone.

He tried to sit up but found his legs were tangled in the sheets. The clock next to the bed glowed a dull green. 3:44 a.m. He kicked at the sheets, freeing himself as he rolled over, remembering his earlier lovemaking with Callie.

Only Callie wasn't in bed next to him.

The covers were thrown back on her side of the bed. He felt the sheet. It was icy cold. She'd been gone for some time.

Getting up, he pulled on his jeans and padded barefoot into the living room. The desserts were where she'd set them earlier in the evening, untouched. The apartment was small enough that he could tell right away that she wasn't there. But still, he glanced into the open door of the bathroom before looking out the window to where her pickup had been parked. The falling snow had filled in the space where the vehicle had been.

Callie was gone—and judging from the snow where her pickup had been parked, she'd been gone for a long time.

THE BOOZE HAD worn off. So had the gambling glow. Carson Grant tried to open his eyes and realized with a start that he was blindfolded and tied to a bed.

His head swam. Where was he? He couldn't remember. His last recollection was of leaving the poker game not quite broke and realizing he was starving. He'd pulled into the truck stop in Big Timber, half-sick to his stomach. As he'd climbed out of the ranch pickup, he'd complimented himself on not losing more than he had. Once he got paid this week, he would pick up another game and make up for what he'd lost and then some. So far, luck had been with him only in the fact that his sister, Destry, would never have to know.

That was what he'd been thinking when he'd pulled open the door to the truck-stop all-night diner and collided with the young woman coming out. "Callie?"

He couldn't remember much else, but he must have forgotten all about his hangover and his hunger and his bad luck at cards and brought her back to his cabin for a drink. Then what? That was where his memory ended.

As he tried to sit up, he realized that his wrists were bound to the ornate iron headboard of his bed. He heard the familiar creak of the bedsprings as he tried to pull free. He was definitely in his cabin.

A cool breeze moved across his skin, making him realize that he was naked. He smiled, hoping it really had been Callie and that now she was playing some sex game. *Bring it on,* he thought.

"Hey," he called out. "Getting a little cold here by myself." He tried to move his feet but realized that, like his wrists, they, too, were bound to the bed frame. He wasn't sure he liked this as he heard the floorboards of his old cabin creak. "Take off the blindfold at least, so I can see you." Carson didn't mind kinky *or* rough, but he liked being the initiator.

Something skittered over his bare thigh, making him start. He pulled harder on the bonds at his wrists as realization hit him. He was at the mercy of this woman, and if he was right and it *was* Callie… Or maybe she'd just said that was her name.

He tried not to panic. He would play her little sex game, and when she was through, he'd show her a thing or two. But he could feel his heart pounding too hard against his ribs. His chest rose and fell, faster and faster, as his fear rose with it.

A sound made him stop struggling. He held his breath. She was right next to the bed. He could hear her breathing. She was only trying to scare him. This was about the night at the lake. Hell, maybe this had been Callie's plan all along. Get him back to his cabin, ply him with drinks—he vaguely remembered digging a couple of cans of beer out of the fridge while the woman showed herself around the cabin. So, why couldn't he remember her face?

He frowned as he remembered seeing her standing in front of the window, the snow falling in a wall of white on the other side, her naked body silhouetted against the cold light as she turned toward him.

Another floorboard creaked. Another brush of something cold over his skin, this time along his rib cage. He jerked at his bonds, getting pissed off now. "Untie me right now, you hear me? A joke is a joke, but this is no longer funny."

A harsh whisper next to his ear silenced him. At first he thought he'd heard wrong. Then his captor repeated the same three little words.

"Beg for mercy."

ROURKE HAD TURNED from the apartment window, when he heard the sound of Callie's pickup engine. He stood for a moment watching her get out and head up the stairs. She had her head down, a weariness to her as she began to climb the stairs. A cold fear filled him as he turned back to the bedroom. He quickly shed his jeans and crawled under the covers.

She came in quietly. Laura would have said she

"sneaked" in. He lay perfectly still as he listened. His pulse raced, his heart thundering, as he debated what to do. Follow his instincts or get his gun and be waiting for her when she entered the room, possibly armed with a knife?

All the other victims had been drugged, he reminded himself. Wouldn't she offer him something to drink first? Or was she looking to end it all tonight?

He rolled over, his back to the door, and waited. He heard her step to the bedroom doorway. She was standing there looking at him. He could hear her breathing, breathing hard. He doubted it was from the climb up the stairs, considering what good shape she was in.

Rourke felt an icy finger of unease race up his spine. He tried not to shudder. He told himself that if she had wanted him dead, he would have awakened tied to her bed.

He listened as she disrobed. A few moments later, she slid into bed behind him. He couldn't pretend sleep any longer as he felt her ice-cold skin brush against his.

Turning, he looked into her face. Her eyes were red, as if she'd been crying. "You're freezing. Where have you been?"

When she spoke, her voice broke. "I went for a drive. I…I…" Tears welled in her eyes. One spilled over and coursed down her cheek. He caught it with his thumb without thinking and wiped it away.

"You can be honest with me, Callie," he said, his voice hoarse with emotion and a lingering terror of what she was hiding. "Talk to me."

She searched his face. How had he thought this woman had second sight? She didn't know what he was thinking or feeling. She couldn't have.

"I've never met anyone like you," she said in a whisper, her voice hoarse. "I don't know how to… Last night…all of it. I'm scared, Rourke. I've never cared this much, never wanted…" She threw her arms around him. He drew her close, holding her tightly as he fought his doubts about the naked woman in his arms.

He closed his eyes.

Callie was lying. Wherever she'd gone, wherever she'd been, it hadn't just been a drive. And yet, all his instincts told him she wasn't a killer. Not even a co-killer.

Laura was right. He'd gotten too close. Worse, this was where he wanted to be. He felt the passion between them spark and ignite. When she kissed him, he shoved away his misgivings, telling himself that whatever she was hiding from him, it wasn't murder.

When he woke again, the sun was out, and Callie was standing over him with something in her hand that caught the light.

CHAPTER TWENTY-ONE

SHERIFF FRANK CURRY and his new bride, Lynette John-son Benton Curry, were standing in line at the airport for an early flight, when they saw his second in command headed for them. The winter storm had blown through, leaving the sky a cold, cloudless robin-egg blue as the blinding sun made the seven inches of fresh snow glitter like diamonds.

"Don't worry. Whatever it is, it won't interfere with our honeymoon," Frank told Lynette as he watched Undersheriff Dillon Lawson approach. Even though he feared just the opposite, he said, "We're going to Hawaii to sit on the beach and sip umbrella drinks and watch the sun set over the water."

"But not today," she said. "Dillon isn't here to wish us bon voyage, Sheriff."

Frank looked into his wife's eyes and smiled. This woman knew him, loved him—was finally his. He'd wanted this for most of his life. Finally, they were one. Nothing could keep them apart. He kissed his bride and turned to face whatever had brought the law after them.

Dillon dragged off his Stetson and, apologizing to Lynette, lowered his voice and said, "I'm afraid I need a word with you, Sheriff."

Not Frank, but Sheriff. "Lynette, if you'll excuse us for just a moment." He stepped to a quiet corner with

Dillon, dread weighing down his footsteps. Like Lynette, he knew his undersheriff wouldn't be here unless it was urgent. His first thought was Tiffany.

He tried to swallow the bile that rose in his throat. Surely Tiffany couldn't have heard already. Surely she wouldn't follow through with her threat—

"I just got a call from a hysterical Destry West. When her brother, Carson, didn't show for work today..." Dillon met his gaze. "She found him at his cabin. It's bad, Frank."

He'd heard Carson had been seen drinking and was rumored to be gambling again. For years, Frank had suspected Carson would meet a bad end. "How bad?"

"Murdered." Dillon lowered his voice, even though there was no one close by. "His mutilated body was found naked, tied to his bed. There's no keeping a lid on this. We're already getting calls at the sheriff's department. The whole county is in a panic. I figured, under the circumstances..."

"You figured right," Frank said, tamping down his disappointment. By this evening, he'd so hoped to be barefoot on the beach with his new bride. "You've secured the crime scene?"

Dillon nodded. "The coroner is on his way there now."

"Don't let anyone touch the scene until I get there."

"You want me to be *honest* with *you?*" Callie demanded.

Rourke saw the object in her hand flash in the light an instant before she threw his badge at him.

"You're a U.S. marshal?"

"Not at the moment. I'm on leave." He sat up in the bed. "I told you I did a lot of things."

Her eyes narrowed. "What else did you lie about?"

"I've been as honest with you as you've been with me," he said. "Why were you going through the pockets of my coat?"

She crossed her arms over her chest and looked as if she was fighting tears. He saw that she was dressed for work already. "Because I just had this bad feeling…"

"The same kind of feeling you got last night at the restaurant before that little girl almost spilled her milk?"

She recoiled at his words. "I don't know what—"

"What I'm talking about?" he said, swinging his legs over the side of the bed. "You knew she was going to spill her milk before she reached for her glass, so don't lie. I *saw* it." He snatched up his jeans from the floor and pulled them on, then took a step toward her. "I've seen it before at the café, but it didn't really register until last night. You knew that robber wasn't going to shoot you because you knew there weren't bullets in the gun before I did."

She hugged herself, looking scared. "You don't understand."

"I think I do. There was a neighborhood woman when I was growing up. She…saw things before they happened. She knew things that she had no way of knowing other than second sight. I saw it last night at the restaurant."

CALLIE MET HIS gaze with a defiant look. "If I had this 'sight,' as you call it, then why didn't I know you were a U.S. marshal until I found your badge?"

"You apparently knew enough to look through my pockets."

"I had to know if I could trust you."

"You *can* trust me," he said quickly and stepped to her to take her shoulders in his big hands.

She winced at his touch, remembering how gentle he'd been last night during their lovemaking. She *had* trusted him, even though she'd known better, and yet her desire for him had outweighed her caution. What a fool she was.

"What are you really doing in Beartooth?"

"First, you tell me if I'm right about your…gift."

Callie studied him for a moment, realizing she didn't want to lie to him. And what would be the point anyway? He'd seen it last night at The Grand. He already knew.

"I pick up what I call flashes of information from people. Like what they're thinking. Sometimes I can see a person's future. And before you ask, I don't get anything from you. I never have." She saw his incredulity. "See why I try to keep it a secret? Now you're wondering if I'm lying and I really can read you." She shook her head. "Not that you believe me, but you're the exception. I've never been able to pick up anything from you."

"You want me to believe that I'm the only person you can't read?"

"There have been a few others, but it's rare." She met his gaze. "This is why I don't tell anyone. They never believe me, and then they start acting strange around me. They make me feel like I'm a freak."

She started to turn away, but he wouldn't release her.

"I don't think you're a freak."

"Really? Then, Marshal, why do I feel like you came to Beartooth looking for me?"

A loud knock at the door made them both jump. "Callie?" a male voice called.

She recognized the sheriff's voice and felt her heart drop. Rourke must have recognized the voice as well, because he suddenly looked worried.

"Is there something you need to tell me?" he whispered as he let her go to grab his shirt.

She almost laughed in his face as she watched him quickly dress. There was so much and yet nothing she could tell him. Stepping away from him, she closed the bedroom door behind her and, taking a deep breath, went to open the door to the sheriff.

"Good morning, Sheriff. What can I do for you?"

"I'm looking for Rourke Kincaid. I was hoping—"

Kincaid. The name she'd found on his driver's license in his wallet. So the sheriff had known the truth.

"As a matter of fact, he just stopped by," she said and stepped out of the way as Rourke, now fully dressed, joined her.

"I need to talk to you," the sheriff said to him.

"If you two will excuse me," Callie said, "I was just on my way to work." She slipped past them, down the stairs and into the back of the café.

"Are you all right?" Kate asked the moment she saw her. "You're white as a sheet. Oh, honey, I guess you heard about Carson Grant. It's so horrible what happened. It's all anyone is talking about this morning."

LAURA SAT IN the middle of the floor with the diary from the trunk and all her mother's papers scattered around her. She didn't know how long she'd been crying. In fact, it had surprised her to feel tears running down her face onto the paper in her hand.

There were stories in the sparse notes her mother had kept on each of the girls under her care. Each story broke her heart. Young girls, some of them scared and pregnant, all girls who everyone had given up on.

She felt their loneliness, their isolation, their fear. She'd been one of those girls—just as abandoned as any one of them. And her sister… Just the thought of Catherine made the tears come harder.

"So you do remember now," she heard her mother say as if in the room.

Laura picked up the diary. Yes, she remembered Westfield. She remembered the cold, the isolation, the alienation. The other girls hadn't trusted her and Catherine. Laura had tried to befriend some of them. Catherine hadn't bothered. It was as if she knew no one was ever going to like them in the places they lived because of their mother's job.

They were both Gladys's daughters. Most of the girls feared them, just as they feared Gladys. What they didn't seem to realize was that Catherine was one of them. She coped by being as mean as any one of them. She loved that they were afraid of her.

It was all in the diary from that year.

Her mother had never talked about her childhood, about her life. All Laura had known was the hard woman who'd raised two daughters alone. A bitter, resentful woman who'd forced her daughters to grow up too quickly.

Laura wiped at her tears and looked around the room as her cell phone rang. Rourke?

Her muscles were stiff. How long had she been on

this floor? She couldn't remember her last meal or when she'd last slept as she tried to get up to find the phone. She had the surreal feeling that she hadn't been out of this motel room in days. But that couldn't be true, she thought. It had been only yesterday that she'd told Rourke how she felt—and lied to him about an interview back in Seattle.

Finding her phone, she saw that it wasn't Rourke. Her heart dropped, since she'd expected him to call. But he was probably busy. *With Callie after their big date last night.*

She cleared her voice then answered, "Hello?"

"Laura?" It was her psychiatrist. "I wanted to check on you. The last time we talked… Are you all right?"

"Fine."

He made a concerned sound. "You missed your appointment."

She'd forgotten all about it. "My mother died."

"Oh, I'm sorry to hear that. Does this mean that you and your mother reconciled before her death?"

"I arrived too late. She'd already passed."

"Oh, that's too bad. You've always said that she was the only one who could provide you with the lost memories of your childhood."

"Maybe it's a blessing," she said, looking at the diary in her hand. "What if I couldn't handle what she told me?"

He was silent for a few moments. "Perhaps."

"I told him. Rourke." As she sat on the end of the motel bed, she said, "I told him how I feel." She clenched her teeth for a moment in anger. "It wasn't exactly freeing."

"I'm sure that must have been difficult for you, but

now he knows. It isn't something you have to carry around with you."

"No, I guess not," she said as she set the diary on the bed and pushed it away.

"Now you can move on."

"Yes. Move on." Her stomach growled. "Actually, I was just getting ready to go out for something to eat."

"I won't keep you, then. Shall I assume you will be available for your appointment next month?"

"Why not?"

"Laura, are you sure you're all right?"

She smiled to herself at his concern. "Do you realize you're the only one who really cares about me? That's not a bad thing, really, is it? I mean, it's nice." She thanked him and disconnected.

"WHAT IS THIS ABOUT?" Rourke demanded after Frank ushered him into his office and closed the door.

"I need to know more about the crime that brought you to Beartooth—in particular, why it led you to Callie Westfield," the sheriff said as he motioned him into a chair across from his desk. Frank had insisted he follow him to his office after talking for only a few minutes at Callie's apartment.

"That's why you came looking for me this morning?" Rourke demanded. "What's going on? You dragged me all the way down here—"

"There's been a murder."

Rourke felt as if he'd been sucker punched. "A murder?" He thought immediately of Cassie and the missing hours from last night. "Who was murdered?"

The sheriff studied him as if he thought Rourke

might have been expecting this. "Carson Grant. He was found tied to his bed and tortured with a knife."

Rourke let out a curse.

"That's what I thought. It's the same M.O. as the murders that brought you here, isn't it?"

He took off his hat and raked a hand through his hair as he tried to pull himself together. "When did this happen?"

"According to the coroner, probably some time between midnight and four this morning. I didn't press you for information when you arrived here, but now I need some answers. Why did you come looking for Callie Westfield?"

"She was only a lead." He quickly told the sheriff about the three cases he'd found and the photos from the crime scenes.

"So how is she connected?"

"I don't know yet."

"You don't know or you don't want to believe it?" Frank eyed him. "I know your SUV was parked outside her apartment all night. But one of you left in her pickup. Four sets of vehicle tracks were found in the snow at the murder scene. One set belonged to Carson, another to his sister, Destry, when she found him this morning. We are trying to ID the other two sets, but my deputy is pretty sure one of them is from Callie Westfield's pickup. We are securing a warrant to take impressions of her truck's tread as we speak."

"Why would you think Callie was there?" Rourke asked, and then he realized he'd practically handed her to the sheriff as the killer. He swore under his breath. "She's not your killer."

Frank raised a brow. "What makes you so sure of that? Were you with her last night?"

"Not all night." Rourke hated admitting it. "But there's more to this than meets the eye. I don't know where to begin."

The sheriff leaned back in his chair. "I'm all ears."

When Rourke finished, Frank let out a low whistle. "Have you heard from your P.I. yet?"

"No, as a matter of fact, I've been waiting for his call. I'm hoping he's found Gladys McCormick's daughters."

The sheriff nodded. "But that still doesn't explain why Callie was at the murder scenes. It would appear, just as you suspected, that she is somehow involved."

"I haven't had a chance to question her yet." He met Frank's gaze. "She trusts me. I know I'm close to solving this. Just give me twenty-four hours, and I will have the killer."

The sheriff shook his head. "I think it is more likely that you will get yourself killed. Let's not forget, you also have no jurisdiction here, especially under the circumstances. No, I'm sorry, Rourke, but given your... relationship with your suspect, I am more apt to consider you just another one of *my* suspects."

CHAPTER TWENTY-TWO

NETTIE WOKE WITH a start and looked at the clock. She was going to be late opening the store. She swung her legs over the side of the bed, but before her feet touched the floor, she remembered.

There was no Beartooth General Store to open. It had burned down, and when some fool corporation had offered to buy the lot the store had sat on for more than a hundred years and her house up on the mountain behind it, she'd taken the money and not looked back.

Now she sat on the edge of the bed, feeling lost. The store had been her identity. But it was more than that. She missed having something to do. She wasn't old enough to retire even though she was close to retirement age. What in the devil was she going to do with the rest of her life?

Marry Frank had been her answer. Now married to him, she had to ask, what next?

Nettie knew she should be happy. No, deliriously ecstatic after her near-death experience last spring. She could have easily died in the store fire. Wasn't a near-death experience supposed to bring you some sort of clarity?

Worse, she was no more near figuring out who was behind the Beartooth restoration. Someone with money. Someone with a stake in the community. Someone crazy.

Suddenly it was like a lightbulb coming on. As she quickly showered and dressed, she was more excited than she had been in weeks—other than when becoming Frank's wife.

If she was right… If she wasn't, well, then, all she would have wasted was her time, the gas it took to drive into Big Timber and probably the last of her sanity, since this was definitely a long shot.

But if she *was* right, she would have found the Beartooth Benefactor and put an end to the mystery. She felt like her old self, the woman who left no stone unturned when she wanted to get to the bottom of something.

True, that determination had almost gotten her killed.

She just hoped the person she was about to visit didn't prove as deadly as the last one she'd crossed.

ROURKE SWORE. OF COURSE the sheriff had called the U.S. Marshals' office and talked to his boss. Brent Ryan would have told him about what had happened six months ago. He would have told him that Rourke Kincaid was a loose cannon. Rourke was in even more trouble, not that it was a huge concern right now.

Not that he could blame the sheriff for making the call. He would have done the same thing under the circumstances.

Callie didn't have an alibi. If the tracks found proved to be hers…

"You said there was a fourth set of tracks at the murder scene?" Rourke asked.

The sheriff nodded. "It's believed that they might belong to Johnny Franks. He worked with Carson."

Rourke knew who he was. "He came to Beartooth about the same time as Callie, I understand. He could be your killer."

"Could be," the sheriff said, nodding. "Were you with Callie last night between midnight and four?" Frank asked.

"No. She said she went for a drive."

The sheriff seemed to chew on that for a while. "Your boss said you are one hell of an investigator."

I was, Rourke thought. Now…well, he wasn't so sure.

"You still think she's innocent of this crime." Frank raised a brow. "Even though you have no idea where she went last night?"

"I suspect she went out to the murder scene—but not for the reason you're thinking."

The sheriff chuckled. "I can't wait to hear your theory."

"Callie has what I call second sight. I think she knows about the murders, but she doesn't know who the killer is. At least not consciously."

The sheriff studied him for a moment. "You're that sure that the tire tracks will be hers?"

"I'm hoping to hell I'm wrong, but yeah, I'm that sure." He shook his head. "She didn't do it, and I'm going to prove it."

"Unless I lock you up for interfering in my investigation."

KATE, SEEING HOW badly her waitress took the news, had led Callie over to one of the empty booths and made her sit down. "You don't look well."

Callie fought the urge to cry in the woman's arms. "I'm okay. I can work."

"No, it's that headache again, isn't it?" her boss demanded.

The headache was gone. Just as it always was after the "bad thing" was over. Callie felt hollow inside. Broken. She looked up into Kate's concerned face and reached for her hand.

"You're the best friend I ever—"

"Oh, stop," Kate said, as if embarrassed. "I want you to go up to your apartment and get some rest." She smiled. "I saw that SUV parked out there this morning. You can't fool me." She sobered. "This murder has a lot of people on edge today. I don't want everyone asking you a bunch of questions. Too many of them know how relentless Carson was chasing you."

Callie nodded, wishing she didn't see the sliver of doubt begin to work itself into Kate's thoughts. Had she seen the sheriff on his way to her place, as well? "Maybe I *will* go up to my apartment."

"Good." Kate squeezed her hand and then let go. "Get some rest. I'm sure the sheriff will catch whoever did this. Meanwhile…" The bell over the front door tinkled. Kate rose and then turned back to Callie. "Take care of yourself, okay?"

Callie nodded. She'd been taking care of herself for as long as she could remember. It wasn't as if she hadn't been here before. She knew exactly what to do.

Rourke found Callie in her apartment packing. "What do you think you're doing?" he demanded when she opened the door, and he saw the suitcases.

"What I always do—run. Only this time, because of you, I have the law after me. Unless that's why you're here. Have you come to arrest me?"

He stepped into the apartment and closed the door behind him. "Listen to me. You can't run. It will only make you look more guilty."

She let out a bitter laugh. "I look guilty enough. The sheriff called and wants me to come by his office."

"You can't run. We'll get you a good lawyer. If you let me help, we can figure this out. You have to trust me."

"Why would I trust *you?* You lied about who you are and what you're doing here. Admit it. You came to Beartooth looking for me."

He held her gaze. "I came here looking for a serial killer."

She nodded, anger sparking in her dark eyes. "And you thought it was me." She frowned as she searched his face. "You still aren't sure, are you?" Her smile could have cut steel. "And yet you slept with me. Or was that part of your plan? How do I know *you* didn't kill Carson?"

"Because last night I was in *your* bed. My vehicle never left from the time we returned from dinner until you came back in the wee hours of the morning." He stepped to her, aching to touch her. "Also, you *know* me."

She shook her head. Her hair was down, a mass of dark curls that he yearned to bury his fingers in again. "I don't know you at all."

"Last night was more than just sex. I know you felt it, too." He didn't know that at all, but he hoped it was true. Had he awakened to find her in the bed next to him and not just coming home, he wouldn't have had any doubts.

Could he trust his instincts, let alone his heart? He grabbed her and dragged her to him, kissing her hard. She came into his arms, embracing him around his waist. She hung on as if she'd found herself in a strong gale.

Callie ended the kiss abruptly, shoving him back as she met his gaze. "Are you all that sure you didn't just kiss a serial killer?" She nodded. "That's what I thought."

As she turned away from him, he spotted the desserts where she'd left them and was reminded of last night, the memory bittersweet. "Now that you mention it, why don't we start with why you brought me back to your apartment last night. Was I your alibi? I should have warned you that I'm a light sleeper."

She turned back to look at him, her expression one of pain. "Isn't it possible I wanted you as much as you pretended to want me?"

"There was no pretending."

They stood glaring hard at each other. Rourke could feel the sexual tension sparking between them. He suspected Callie could, as well. "Then tell me where you went last night."

"I told you."

"I don't believe you." He pulled off his Stetson and raked a hand through his hair in obvious frustration. "Look, I don't want to believe you killed Carson or anyone else. But I can't help you unless you start telling me the truth. I know you drove out to Carson's cabin last night."

All the fight seemed to go out of her. When she spoke, her voice was small, scared. "I didn't kill him."

"But you know who did."

Callie slowly shook her head. "I don't know."

He took her arm and led her over to the couch, pulling her down beside him. She couldn't keep lying, not to him, not to herself.

"You know who murdered Carson Grant. You saw the killer when you were a child at Westfield. Did you see the killer again last night?"

CALLIE FELT HER heart drop as she stared into his dark eyes. "How did you—"

"I know all about Westfield Manor." He proceeded to tell her everything he'd learned about her.

She listened in shock. She'd suspected he'd come here looking for her. She'd never dreamed that he'd hired a P.I. to track her down. Not just track *her* down, but dig up her past.

"Cops take photos of the people who line up on the other side of the crime-scene tape. There's a theory that the killer returns to the scene of the crime."

Cold seeped into her as if the winter storm had blown in again. Now she understood. He *had* been stalking her. He had photos of her and had been watching her apartment, watching her. He'd been waiting for another murder, waiting to pin it on her.

She looked toward her suitcases. She had to get out of here. She had to run. She had no choice.

Rourke grabbed her arm as she started to get up from the couch. "Damn it, Callie, your photo was in all three of the crime-scene photos taken of the crowd. Why is that?"

She jerked free of his hold, angry and scared, but she didn't try to rise from the couch again. She'd known this would happen one day. Eventually someone would put it together. She just wished it hadn't been Rourke Kincaid.

"What do you *think* I was doing there?"

He frowned. "You tell me, but I don't believe you killed those men."

"How can you be so sure?"

He couldn't, and she saw that small doubt he fought so hard to extinguish and moved farther away from him on the couch.

"Callie." Rourke groaned. "Tell me what you were doing at those crime scenes and why in God's name you would drive out to Carson's cabin last night."

She saw pain in his dark eyes. It mirrored her own. "I didn't kill him. I didn't even know he was the one who was going to die until last night."

Rourke stared at her. "You 'saw' it?"

She nodded. "It woke me up."

"Why didn't you wake *me?*" Rourke demanded. "I was lying there right beside you. You should have known you could trust me."

"And involve you in this? I thought you were just some cowboy. I had no idea that you were a U.S. marshal."

"You have to tell the sheriff about your gift."

"Are you serious? You're not that sure you believe me as it is. If I told you I 'saw' the murder and thought this time I might get there in time to see the killer…" She let out an angry breath.

"If you have nothing to do with any of this, then why are you the one seeing these murders?"

"Don't you think that I've asked myself the same thing?" she demanded.

"Tell me how it works."

Callie took a breath and let it out. She could run, but she wouldn't get far. Hadn't she known that was the case? This man was her only hope. She almost laughed at that thought. Last night she'd admitted to herself that she was falling in love with him. Now...

"I told you how I get these flashes of information when I'm near anyone. Usually, it is what they're thinking at that moment, but I often get a 'feel' for them, what kind of person they are, that kind of thing, and, like I told you, sometimes I can see the future."

"What did you see about Carson?"

She sighed. "He is just one of those men who flirts and wants to take you out. Once he gets what he wants, he moves on. I saw that right away. I saw other things, a weakness not just for booze or drugs, but a flaw that would eventually destroy him."

"You didn't 'see' that he was going to be killed?"

She shook her head. "When last October passed without anything bad happening, I thought maybe it was over. I hadn't gotten one of my bad headaches that signaled someone was going to be killed. Then you showed up. I thought you were the one who was going to die, especially when I couldn't pick up anything from you."

He raised a brow at that. "Why would you think that?"

"Because the headaches started the day you came to town."

Rourke seemed to consider that. "Who knows about this psychic ability?"

"I haven't told anyone since I was a kid. But some people figure it out." She gave him a look. "Like you."

He stared at her. "Callie, this ability you have to know about the murders… Did it start that night in Westfield Manor when you witnessed the first murder?"

Her eyes filled with tears in answer. He pulled her to him, and she melted into his arms. "Did you see the murderer that night at Westfield Manor?"

"If I did, I don't remember. I keep thinking that if I get to the murder quickly enough, I will *see* the killer. Last night was the closest I've ever come."

He shuddered as if feeling a chill. "Are you telling me—"

She pulled back from him. "I saw her."

"You saw *her?*" She heard the shock—and the fear—in Rourke's voice. "Who is—"

"I didn't see her face. It was snowing too hard, and she passed me too quickly…. I just saw that it was a woman."

He stared at her. "Callie, if you saw the killer, then she saw you."

"Don't you think she already knows who I am?" she said with a humorless laugh. "She wanted me there last night. Just as she has wanted me at each of the murders when we were in the same city."

"What are you saying?" he asked, sounding afraid of where she was going with this.

"The headaches. She's calling me—maybe the way she did the first time. Maybe at the first one, she hoped I would stop her. Now…she wants me to know that she's killed again."

"For what reason?"

She met his gaze. "I think she plans to kill me. She *wanted* me to see her last night. Either she hopes to frame me…or she wants to end this."

CHAPTER TWENTY-THREE

LAURA SAT IN the dark room, the curtains drawn, waiting for Rourke to call. Her stomach roiled with anxiety. She'd hoped he would call first thing this morning. Instead it was a colleague of hers who used to work with Rourke. The colleague had an in with the U.S. Marshals' office.

A man named Carson Grant was dead in a town called Beartooth, Montana. Murdered. Murdered in the same fashion as a serial killer that Rourke had been told not to chase.

Apparently, the sheriff in Big Timber had called the U.S. Marshals' office. Rourke was caught. His boss, Brent Ryan, was furious.

Laura tried to feel some sympathy for him. Hadn't she warned him? But he could get his job back, if he wanted it. Rourke was too good. He would have to conform, though. He could do it if he wanted the job badly enough.

What she feared he couldn't do was walk away from Caligrace Westfield. When Callie was arrested, well, it would break Rourke's heart. He loved justice so much, she thought bitterly, now he would be getting some of his own.

Callie should have been arrested by now. Laura's

heart pounded harder at the thought. No one would care that Rourke thought Callie was innocent.

Once they looked at Caligrace Westfield's background... Well, it was there in black and white. If Laura had any hope of being one of the top profilers in the country, then she couldn't be wrong about Caligrace Westfield. Callie was the killer. It was all there in her profile. The woman had all the characteristics, including the early trauma. It would be enough to convict her. She looked guilty as hell. Any stories she told...well, that's all they would be...the lies of a killer.

Maybe Callie had confessed. Which would mean this was over. Rourke would go back to his job as U.S. marshal. Laura would return to being a freelance profiler. She and Rourke might have many more opportunities to work together, if she had anything to do with it.

He would be brokenhearted about Callie, but he'd get over it, and when he did, Laura would be there to pick up the pieces.

She glanced at her watch. Rourke should be calling soon. After all, she'd bared her soul to him. He would be feeling guilty even in the middle of all this turmoil. She knew this man. He would call.

CALLIE WENT INTO the bathroom to take a shower and get ready. Rourke had promised that he would go with her to talk to the sheriff. He hoped he'd convinced her that she needed to tell Frank Curry everything— especially about her second sight.

Still, he was worried. If she was right, then he had to find the killer before the killer came for Callie. He started to try Edwin's cell phone, when he realized he needed to call Laura. She'd been at the back of his mind since yesterday evening, when she'd made her confession. He wished he had handled it better, but he'd been too shocked.

Now he called her, glad when she answered on the second ring.

"How did your interview go?" he asked after inquiring about her flight, the weather in Seattle and her general well-being.

"The interview went great," she said. "I think there's a good chance I'll be offered the job. But I kind of like being a freelancer, so we'll see. How are things there? I heard about Carson Grant. I'm sorry, Rourke. I know how badly you wanted to believe Callie was innocent."

He shouldn't have been surprised. He knew she still had contacts in the law-enforcement community and news traveled fast. Once Sheriff Frank Curry had called his boss…

When he said nothing, she asked, "How is Callie?"

"Okay, considering. She went out to the crime scene last night. She *saw* the killer."

Silence, then, "Has there been an arrest?"

"No, she didn't get a good look. All she knows is that it was a woman leaving Carson Grant's last night. I'm hoping to hear from my private detective this morning to see if he's found Gladys McCormick's daughters."

"You're still convinced it's one of them?"

He wasn't convinced of anything. He was only praying for a break in this case and soon. "I think she's afraid to remember who she saw that night when she was five."

"Have you given any more thought to taking her to the original scene of the crime?" Laura asked. "Like you said, if the killings are a manifestation of that earlier trauma, then maybe in the place it happened, she would remember the killer."

LAURA WISHED THERE was some way to stop Rourke from making the worst mistake of his life. But she feared he'd already made it. He'd set the wheels in motion and now there was no way to stop the outcome, as if it had long ago been written in the stars.

"Of course, there is no way to know what reliving that trauma might do to her," Laura said as she had before. "If you can talk her into going up there with you, the truth might come out. But it might not end the way you want it to."

"She isn't the killer, Laura. But she knows who is."

"Once she coughs that up, you can get back to Seattle, where you belong." The silence told her more than she wanted to know. "You didn't say how the date went."

"It was fine."

Laura smiled to herself. She would imagine Carson's murder had put a damper on it. "I'm sure you've asked yourself this, but how is it that Callie turns up at the murder scenes if she and this alleged killer aren't in it together?"

"I know this sounds crazy, but she has some psychic connection to the killer."

"They're both psychic? This is what she told you?"

"No, I've seen it for myself. She has second sight."

Laura tried not to laugh. "If that were true, then wouldn't she have known who you were the first time she met you?"

"She says she can't read me."

"That's handy."

"I know you're skeptical."

"Why aren't *you?*"

She heard a change in Rourke's breathing and knew he was no longer alone.

"Well, I'm glad your interview went well," he said. "You'll have to let me know what you hear from them."

"Yes, and you'll have to let me know what happens in Westfield, if you decide to go."

"I think it's the only option now," Rourke said.

"Really? Well, good luck, then. I assume you'll want to go right away."

"Today," he said, as if he'd just made up his mind.

"Oh, I meant to ask—what did you hear from your P.I.?"

"Nothing yet. I've been calling him. It goes straight to voice mail. You take care of yourself." He was trying to get her off the line. "I'll call you soon."

"I'm sure we'll be seeing each other soon, once you finish up this case and get back to Seattle," she amended.

"Right." He didn't sound happy about the prospect. If she'd had any doubt about how far his relationship had gone with Callie, she didn't anymore.

Tears burned her eyes. "I'd say be careful, but I'm afraid it is too late for that. Goodbye, Rourke." Just as she'd feared, he was going to die.

"NETTIE!" CHARLOTTE WESTFALL Abrahams exclaimed as she opened the door. "I thought I might be seeing you again, and here you are."

"You remember me?" The last time she'd been there, Charlotte was so out of it that she'd thought the woman suffered from dementia, even though the two of them were close in age. Now, though…

"Please, come in," Charlotte said. "Best wishes are in order for your recent nuptials, I believe," she continued, ushering her into the house. "I always hoped you and the sheriff would get together."

Nettie couldn't help but stare. This Charlotte was so different from the last one. This one wasn't all made up to look like a silent-movie star. "I…I…"

"Nettie Benton Curry at a loss for words." The woman laughed. "Why don't I make us both a drink and we can talk about Beartooth?"

"You know why I'm here?" Nettie asked, unable to get over one surprise after another. Even the house looked different. The huge painting of Charlotte from that short time she'd spent in Hollywood was gone. The house no longer looked like a movie set. "I'm confused."

"I can see that, but I find it hard to believe. Nettie, I thought if anyone was onto me, it would be you." She laughed again as she went to the bar and made them each a drink. "And everyone said I couldn't act."

"You mean all that before was—"

"Just a little fun to get back at my brother. He's the one who talked me into letting that awful Pam Chandler stay with me. You know she stole my money?"

"Yes, but if you were only playacting—"

"I wasn't worried. I knew I would get every cent back, and I did, thanks to your husband." She handed Nettie her drink and lifted hers. "To more fun times." They clinked the fine crystal, and Nettie took a drink.

"It's just lemonade!"

"Nettie, dear, it is way too early in the morning to

be drinking, especially when we have much to discuss about bringing Beartooth back to its glory days."

"I was beginning to think you were perfectly sane until you said that," Nettie commented as she took the chair Charlotte offered her.

The woman smiled broadly. She really had been beautiful and now had a regal elegance about her. "I have the money, and I wanted to do something good for that community. You'll see. More young people are moving back to the ranches. Beartooth can survive as long as it has the store. So, are you willing to come back to work there, possibly part-time? I'm sure your husband isn't planning to retire just yet. What do you say, Nettie?"

For the second time that day, she was speechless.

"I knew you'd figure out who was behind the restoration, and I was hoping it was soon because I want you to help me make that store even better. Well? Are you in?"

CALLIE CAME OUT of the bathroom wearing nothing but a towel. "Is everything all right?" she asked as he pocketed his cell phone.

"I was talking to a friend of mine. Laura Fuller, my former partner at the Seattle P.D."

"Is something wrong?"

He met her gaze, not sure how to broach the subject of Westfield. It was a long shot. Worse, he wasn't sure how Callie would react. Not just to the idea. But to reliving the initial trauma. "She's worried about me."

"Really?"

"She's afraid I'm falling for you."

"Are you?"

He smiled. "You can't tell? I need to talk to you about Westfield. I think we should go there."

All the color suddenly drained from Callie's face. Rourke thought for a moment that she was going to faint. He rushed to her, taking her in his arms.

Her dark eyes were wide with alarm. She shook her head, tears spilling down her cheeks.

"You felt something." He hated that it sounded like an accusation.

She cried harder.

"Callie, tell me. You have to tell me."

"I...I...did see something."

He knew she meant she'd seen it psychically. Was she suddenly able to "read" him? And if so, what had caused that to happen? He knew how skeptical Laura would have been. *Suddenly, she can read you? Really, Rourke, are you that gullible?*

"It's all right," he said, hating that he, too, was doubting her psychic ability right now.

"It was *you*. I had this sudden flash. You were bound on a bed." She covered her face with her hands. "What if the person you're after *is* me?"

He grabbed her and pulled her to him. "It's not, Callie. I know it's not you." He could feel her trembling, feel her terror. He felt a shudder of his own.

"What if I'm going to kill you?" she said between sobs as she tried to push him away.

"I don't believe that. I will never believe that."

She pushed harder at his chest with the palms of her hands, breaking his hold on her. "You need to get away from me. Get as far away from me as you can."

He met her dark gaze. "I'm not going anywhere without you." *Handy that now she wants nothing to do with you.* Laura's voice in his head. *You mention going to Westfield, and she decides she is bad for you.*

Ignoring his owns doubts, he pushed ahead. "You are somehow the key to these murders because you saw the killer. I believe it is the same killer from when you were five. I need to know everything about Westfield that you remember."

He stepped to her and took her ice-cold hands in his. Tears welled in her eyes as he led her back over to the couch. "You probably know more about my life than I do."

As he sat her down, he said, "I know your mother died there. What I don't know, but I believe you do, is whether or not your mother killed the man who was murdered there."

Callie recoiled at his words. "My *mother?* No, of course not."

"But you were in the room when it happened, weren't you?" He waited, afraid.

Her eyes seemed to lose focus. She seemed so small, so vulnerable. She couldn't kill anyone, he kept telling himself.

"Tell me."

Her gaze slowly focused again on him. "I was there. I was told that I saw everything, but I don't remember." She looked into his eyes. "I've tried to remember. It was dark in the room. I could smell the blood. I could hear…things." She shuddered. "There was a figure by the bed, but when I try to remember, the person is…faceless."

He didn't need Laura to tell him that the reason Callie couldn't remember could very well be because the killer *was* her mother. Or at the very least, someone she knew.

"It's the first time I remember *knowing* something. I suppose that is what made me go to the man's room that night. I was *called* there, just as I was the other murders."

Rourke nodded, but he was thinking that she could have followed her mother to that room that night just as easily.

"You took the name Westfield. Did you not know your mother's last name?"

She shook her head. "She said it wasn't hers anymore. That she wasn't that person. She wanted nothing to do with her family, and apparently they wanted nothing to do with her."

"She gave you her name, Caligrace?"

"She said she wanted me to have something of hers." Her voice broke. "I think she knew she was never going to leave that place."

Was it possible her mother also had the sight? "Callie, the murders are connected to that murder at Westfield Manor. It's the only thing that makes sense. We have to go there."

CHAPTER TWENTY-FOUR

CALLIE FELT A sliver of ice work its way up her spine at his suggestion.

"Have you been back to Westfield Manor since you were five?" Rourke asked.

"No."

"The place is abandoned, but if there is some chance that it jogs your memory…" He stopped to look at her. "Are you afraid to go back?"

Terrified. "I'm afraid of what I might…discover there."

"I'll be with you."

She smiled. "Not your best plan. What if I realize that I'm the real killer?"

"You won't."

"I hope you're right."

He looked at her with such caring in his expression. He wanted so badly to believe that she was innocent. Or was this more about solving his case? She didn't need to remind herself that he'd lied to her about who he was, why he was in Beartooth and why he was so interested in her.

"You saw the killer last night as you were going to Carson's," he said. "You passed her as she was leaving. If you really think she 'called' you there…"

Callie nodded. Was he trying to save her? Or his

case? She wanted to be angry with him for deceiving her. But it was too late for that. She cared too much about him. That was why she was afraid for him. What if he was wrong about her? What if she saw the vision of him on the bed because she was the one who'd tied him up there?

She looked into his handsome face, wondering when it was that she'd fallen for him. The night at the lake when she'd pulled the gun on him? How foolish, she thought. She didn't know this man any more than he knew her. Hadn't she known getting close to him could be dangerous?

"Do you trust me?" he asked, as if he was the one who could see her thoughts.

She looked into his eyes. "Yes." For that reason, he had to know everything.

"I kept going last night after I saw her come out of the road into Carson's cabin. The front door was wide open."

"You didn't go in?" It sounded like a plea more than a question.

"I couldn't stop myself. I told myself that she wanted me to see. But did she want me to see because she'd killed him or because I'd been there earlier and—"

"You're talking crazy," Rourke said, reaching for her.

She stepped back, determined to get this out. "When I stepped in, I realized something. I'd been to the cabin before."

He groaned. "Tell me you didn't touch anything."

She shook her head.

"*Had* you been there before? Or had you seen it because of your second sight?" She could hear the hope in his voice. He didn't want to believe that she'd had anything to do with Carson Grant before he'd come to town.

"I don't know." Callie felt her voice break. "Everything was familiar. I saw the small kitchen, the missing knife, the drawer where he kept the duct tape—"

Rourke grabbed her and pulled her to him. "It's your second sight. She's making you see these things. She wants you to believe you're the killer."

"It's working."

"ROURKE KINCAID?"

"Yes?" he said warily as he turned away from Callie and walked into another room to take the call. The man on the other end of the line sounded like a cop. A cop with bad news. His first thought was Laura. Had something happened to her? The moment he thought it, he'd expected such a call. He braced himself for the worst, waiting for the cop to tell him that Laura had committed suicide. That he would expect such a thing meant he'd been thinking it for some time.

"This is Officer Alex Knauber with the Billings Police Department. Do you know a man by the name of Edwin Sharp?"

He frowned, thrown off balance. "Yes, he's a private investigator in my employ."

"I'm trying to reach his next of kin."

"Next of kin?"

"I'm afraid I have some bad news. Mr. Sharp was found dead in his hotel room."

"Dead?" His mind raced. "What was it, a heart attack?"

"I really can't say. It appears he drowned in the hotel bathtub."

"Drowned?" Rourke felt the hair on the back of his neck stand up. "There isn't any chance that he was murdered, is there?"

"Why would you ask that?"

Rourke had spoken without thinking. "The case he was working on for me... It involves a serial killer."

"This serial killer—"

"Kills with a knife, so I'm sure it is probably just what it appears." He felt sick about Edwin. The man was older but seemed to be in the prime of his life. "I'm sorry. I don't know about next of kin, but if there is anything I can do..." Rourke had a thought. "I do have a question. Was a notebook found in his hotel room? Edwin had called me yesterday to say he had found out something in the case he was working on for me."

"No notebook was found."

"Not in his car either? Edwin was old school. He took everything down in a spiral stenographer notebook. He wouldn't have let it out of his sight."

"I'm afraid no notebook was found. We got your name and number from his cell phone."

Rourke felt sick. "Officer Knauber, I'd suggest you treat Edwin Sharp's death as a homicide, then."

"What's happened?" Callie asked as he walked back into the room.

"The private investigator I hired," Rourke said. "He's been looking for Gladys McCormick's daughters, and now he's dead and the information he'd obtained is missing."

"You think someone killed him?"

"If his notebook doesn't turn up, then, yes, I do."

She stared at him wide-eyed. "Was he—"

"He allegedly drowned in a hotel bathtub." Rourke moved to the window, all his instincts telling him they needed to get out of Beartooth. Now. "Edwin is dead and so is Carson. If it is the same killer, then she had a busy night."

"You still believe it's a woman?"

He nodded. "Edwin said he'd found one of Gladys McCormick's daughters. When he'd left me the message, he'd sounded…upset. The daughter must have realized how close he was to the truth. I had no idea what I was getting the man into. If I had— Come on. We're getting out of here now."

"But what about the sheriff? I told him I would come in and talk to him this afternoon."

"I'll call him once we are far enough away he can't stop us." He hustled her out to the SUV and threw the suitcases she'd packed earlier in the backseat.

"You can't blame yourself," she said as he slid behind the wheel. "This is what the private investigator did for a living, right? His job was dangerous. He knew that."

What she was saying was true, but he still felt responsible. He'd dragged them all into this. He had to get to the bottom of the murders before someone else died. Before the killer came for Callie.

Rourke scrubbed a hand over his face as he drove out of town and headed north. All of this seemed to begin with Callie and Westfield Manor. He hated to think how it would end.

"There's something you should know," Callie said

in the seat next to him. "I've got another one of my headaches." She shot him a look. "The killer kind."

NETTIE WAS SURPRISED to see her husband come into the café. She saw him glance around and wondered whom he was looking for. Kate came out, and he asked if Callie was working.

"She's taking the day off," Kate said. "She should be upstairs."

"Yes, she should be," Frank agreed before turning to walk toward Nettie's booth. When he reached her, he pulled off his Stetson and gave her a quick kiss before sliding into the seat across from her.

She saw the lines around his eyes. They seemed deeper. He looked as if he had the weight of the world on his shoulders. Nettie desperately wanted to take some of it off. "What's wrong?"

"The whole community is up in arms over Carson Grant's murder—that's what's wrong," Frank said. "Not that I blame them. People are scared."

The murder had shaken the community to its core. The fact that it was Carson Grant, and a gruesome murder at that, made it much worse. It wasn't that long ago that the town had turned against Carson, most people believing he had killed his high school girlfriend.

But since he'd been cleared and had come back and gone to work for his sister, Destry, whom he'd reconciled with, folks had started to give him the benefit of the doubt.

"People have started locking their doors," Frank said. "There's talk of devil worshippers and alien beings. It's turned crazier than it already was. Everyone is outraged and demanding the killer be caught."

"I'm sure the talk is worse than the actual crime," Nettie said.

His look confirmed what she'd heard through the grapevine—that this time, the crime was horrendous beyond even the local gossips' imaginations.

"You'll catch him," she assured her husband. She had faith in Frank Curry. He was her hero.

He met her gaze and smiled. "The worst part is," he said, lowering his voice even though the café was nearly empty, "two of my key suspects seemed to have skipped town. One of them left me a message to say he'd be checking back in within twenty-four hours." Frank raked a hand through his hair. "I wish I'd thrown him in jail when I'd had the chance."

"Well, I have some news," Nettie said. "I found the Beartooth Benefactor. It was just as you said. Someone with a lot of money. Someone with a tie to the community. Someone who had to be crazy. Mrs. Archibald Abrahams."

"Who?"

"Charlotte, formerly Charlotte Westfall."

Frank laughed. "That's what you've been up to?"

"I went to visit her and she admitted it, and guess what. She doesn't have dementia at all. She was just proving that she was a better actress than people thought, especially her brother, Bull, rest his soul."

"Nice work, Lynette." Frank reached over and took her hands in his. "I should hire you for this case." As he saw her sudden excitement at the idea, he quickly added, "I was just kidding. I'm glad you got to the bottom of it. That must give you peace of mind to know who's behind rebuilding the store."

"There is one other thing. Charlotte wants me to

help make the store even better than it was. She's also offered me a job a few days a week. Would you mind if I worked at least until you retired?"

"I just want you to be happy. That's all I've ever wanted. So, of course I don't mind."

She smiled and squeezed his hands.

"Just as long as Charlotte will let you off so we can have a proper honeymoon. I haven't given up on Hawaii."

"Neither have I. Once you solve this murder…"

He let go of her hands, looking worried again. "I just hope we can catch the killer before there's another murder."

THE NIGHTMARE WAS always the same. The blood. The smell, the silky feel of it, the stain spreading across the bedsheets.

She couldn't breathe, couldn't move. The heavy, hot, sweating man holding her down. The agonizing pain, her screams muffled by the pillow he pressed to her face. The agonizing pain of her blood spilling out of her as her body tore.

"This is all your fault."

"No," she screamed as she stood, staring at the blood her mother tried frantically to wash out of the bedding. "It wasn't my fault. It was my sister. She—"

The slap was such a surprise, she didn't even cry out.

"Because of you, that busybody deputy will be coming by."

Not her fault. Her sister's. The man's. He was the one who had hurt her. One of the girls had found her barefoot, half-naked, bleeding and wandering the halls, crying.

"You want me to call the deputy?" the girl said when she took her to her mother.

"No," her mother snapped. "We'll handle this ourselves." And pushed the other girl out, warning her what would happen if she talked.

Her mother told her to clean herself up, told her she was now a woman and that this was her future. She stopped crying and didn't cry again until her mother told her she had a baby inside her and that it had to come out.

CHAPTER TWENTY-FIVE

ROURKE DROVE THE TWO-LANE north through miles of snowy rolling foothills. The Crazy Mountains stayed with them for so long that Callie thought the mountain range was never ending.

She'd been watching the side mirror, half expecting the law to come after them. Rourke had left a message with the sheriff that they would be back in twenty-four hours. Still, she felt as if they were being followed.

This is going to come to a bad end.

"So, you're sure about going back there?" Rourke asked, breaking the long silence.

Callie looked over at him. She still couldn't read him, but she could tell he was as anxious as she was. He was counting on her remembering the killer. He was convinced it would be the same killer she'd witnessed that night at Westfield.

If only this trip would end the headaches and the killings. Her fear was how it would end, though. There had to be a reason she never saw the killer's face. She prayed it wasn't because the face was her own.

"I'm not sure if I remember the place or if I just heard other girls from the home talking about it," she said, turning away from his handsome face to watch the white landscape blur past.

"Do you remember Gladys McCormick?" he asked, sounding anxious.

"My memories are…fuzzy. They are more like feelings. My mother at the center of them."

"So you don't remember the murder?"

"I only know what I've been told."

"Edwin said that you didn't talk for a long time after. You'd gone…mute."

She nodded and nervously smoothed her palms down the leg of her jeans. "But we don't know why. Was I too traumatized to speak because of the murder or knowing my mother was dying or realizing I could hear other people's thoughts?"

"I'm sorry," he said and reached over and took her hand, squeezing it gently. "Why *did* you choose Westfield as your last name?" he asked, as it had been something that had been bothering him.

"One of my foster parents called me that. I just assumed it was my last name."

ROURKE STARED AT the open highway ahead, worried that this was a mistake. He couldn't predict what Callie's reaction was going to be once they reached Westfield. He kept thinking about what Laura had said.

But he didn't turn the SUV around. Instead, like Callie, he kept watching the traffic behind them. He couldn't shake the feeling that they were being followed, that he'd been followed since he'd arrived here.

Edwin was dead. So was Carson Grant. Callie had seen the killer last night. He could feel everything coming to a head. What scared him most was the worry that he wouldn't be able to protect Callie. The killer had called her to all the murders. What if she called her to her death?

He glanced over to find Callie with her eyes closed. He didn't think she was sleeping, though. Ahead, he saw the turnoff to Flat Rock and slowed.

"How much farther?" Callie asked, without opening her eyes.

Rourke could see a grain tower in the distance. As he came around a curve, he saw a large three-story building sitting off by itself to the west of town.

"We're here."

CALLIE OPENED HER eyes and sat up. As what she knew must be Westfield Manor came into view, she felt dread move like sludge through her veins. She swallowed and tried to still her pounding heart as Rourke turned down a weed-choked dirt road that ended in front of the hulking structure.

"This is it?" she asked, her voice breaking.

"Does it look familiar?"

She shook her head. On the drive, she'd tried to remember her first five years of life. All she'd managed were a few fleeting memories, mostly of her mother. They were worn from years of pulling them out and looking at them. She couldn't even be sure any of them were real anymore or just fantasies that she'd made up of her mother.

Rourke killed the engine and the two of them merely sat for a few moments without speaking. Wind buffeted the SUV. In the distance a tumbleweed bounced along over the tops of the weeds to disappear behind the building.

"I need some time alone inside the building," Callie said.

"I don't think that's—"

"Please. If you want me to remember, then you need to let me do it my way." She could tell it was the last thing he wanted to do.

"An old building like that could be dangerous—"

She laughed. "That building is the least of our worries. I'll be fine. I'll call if I need you." She met his gaze. "Give me this, Rourke."

"I never knew you were so stubborn."

Callie smiled. "Wait until you actually get to know me. Stubbornness is my best quality." She opened her door and got out. The wind lashed her hair about her face as she walked toward the open front door. She half expected to hear Rourke open his car door and come after her. Or at least argue that he couldn't let her go in there alone.

To his credit, he did neither.

Callie took a deep breath, let it out and stepped inside.

ROURKE WATCHED CALLIE disappear into the blackness of the building. He started to reach for his door handle. No way could he let her face that alone. He jumped at the sound of his cell phone and then swore as he looked toward Westfield again and couldn't see Callie.

Torn between ignoring Callie's request and following her and answering Laura's call, he punched the button and said, "Laura."

"Where are you?" she said, sounding upset.

"Why? What's happened?"

"Rourke, I just heard about Edwin Sharp. I can't believe it. Tell me you didn't go to Westfield. The more I've thought about it…"

"We're here now. Callie has gone into the building. I can't talk. I have to go."

Laura said something he didn't catch, something that sounded like "my sister." Her sister must have been in Seattle visiting. He frowned as he disconnected. No, she'd said "warn you about my sister."

He shook his head. Whatever it had been, it didn't matter right now. He let that moment of concern blow away like a cobweb in a wind as he got out of the SUV and ran toward the darkness of Westfield's gaping doorway.

No matter what Callie wanted, he couldn't let her do it alone.

THE INTERIOR OF WESTFIELD looked like any other abandoned old building. It disappointed Callie that she felt nothing as she stepped inside the lower floor.

The place was a mess, charred in one corner, with the remains of parties in another. She'd thought it would be scary, but as she moved more deeply into the building, it only made her feel sad.

Had she and her mother really lived here for almost six years? It seemed inconceivable. From what she'd been told, she'd been five when her mother had died and she'd been taken away.

She tried to draw up even one of the so-called memories she had. None of them seemed to fit now. Tears welled in her eyes, filling her with an even deeper sadness. The memories were all she had of her mother, and if they weren't true…

Callie stopped at the bottom of the stairs and looked

up. Her heart leaped. She almost laughed. She remembered the stairway.

As she started to climb, she began to feel the building. More memories, tiny flashes of her and her mother here. She climbed faster, anxious now, even though she wasn't completely sure where she was headed.

Another set of stairs. She practically ran them, climbing higher and higher. She could feel the wind whistling through the broken glass. A song came to mind, something from her childhood. It hung just out of reach, teasing her with the faint memory as she reached the third floor.

She felt as if her feet knew the way. She didn't question it as she walked down the hallway past empty rooms strewn with old bed frames and mattress stuffing. At the end of the hall, she turned and stopped in the doorway of the last room at the front of the building.

The glass in the window was gone. A cold breeze blew in to stir some trash into one corner. Callie looked past it to the open window and the town beyond.

This is where it will end, she thought as she stepped toward the yawning opening three stories above the ground.

ROURKE FINALLY FOUND her standing at the third-floor window. "Callie?" he inquired tentatively from the doorway.

She turned to look at him. To his surprise she was smiling through her tears. He'd thought bringing her here would be painful. Worse, traumatic.

"You have good memories here," he said in surprise.

Still smiling, she wiped at the tears. "My mother

is here. I remember her. She loved me so much. She used to tell me stories. She loved to talk about my father, what a sweet, loving man he was and how someday the two of them would be together. He died in a car wreck before they could get married."

"Even with what happened here…" That was when he knew, without a doubt, that she wasn't the killer. She'd had a loving mother, a father who had wanted them both.

It was the killer who couldn't let go of this place—and what had happened here. Not Callie.

He stepped to her and took her in his arms. Holding her, he saw that something here had freed Callie. At least from part of the past.

But she was still bound to this place by the killer and the night of violence she'd witnessed. If he could find some way for her to either break that bond or go back to that night…

"I didn't find the answers you'd hoped I would," she said. "I'm sorry. If there was any way I could…"

"You found something more valuable in this horrible old place," he said, glancing around in disbelief. "You remembered that you were loved here."

"I did." She stepped from his arms to move to the window. "Look."

He stepped closer to see the carved name in the wood that Edwin had emailed him a photo of. Caligrace.

"She left our mark here. She wasn't ashamed of being pregnant with me. She loved me and my father."

He put his arm around her and looked out toward what consisted of the town of Flat Rock. "It's late. I should find us a place to stay. I thought I saw a motel just before we turned. I'll get adjoining rooms in case..." He hated to take it for granted that she would want to sleep with him again.

Callie didn't seem to be listening. "You said there is a stone on my mother's grave?" He'd told her about it when he'd explained everything the private investigator had found on her and her mother.

He nodded, thinking how brave she was to come here. He was sure that she hadn't known what her reaction was going to be any more than he had. Her strength awed him.

"I'd like to see it."

They walked out to the cemetery together along a grown-over path through tall dead weeds. This part of the country got chinooks that blew in and melted the snow, leaving the countryside bare. Everything was a dull dirty brown. He couldn't wait to get out of here.

Rourke turned his attention from the landscape. The late-afternoon sun shone on Callie's face as she looked down at the crude writing on the concrete headstone. She appeared so calm, so at peace. He was sure she saw the good and the bad of people because of her psychic ability. She'd accepted all of it, apparently, at a young age, including the lesson that people died, sometimes brutally.

"Someone else loved my mother," Callie said as she bent down and traced the letters. "That person must have made her this."

"I think it was the man who was the deputy at the time," Rourke said. "From what Edwin told me, the man had cared very much for your mother. But he had his own family, so he wasn't able to help the two of you as much as he would have liked."

"I'd like to meet him sometime," she said, rising to her feet. "Would you mind if I stayed here for a while?"

He looked around, seeing nothing but open country and a dying small town. There was no one on the streets. Only an occasional semi roared past on the highway in the distance.

Still, he didn't like leaving her alone. "You have the gun in your purse? It's loaded, right?"

Callie smiled. "I'll be fine. I can see the motel from here. I'll meet you there. It's a nice day for a walk." She touched his arm. "I'm sorry I didn't remember."

This place made him uneasy, as if the ghosts of the girls still inhabited it. But Callie didn't seem to feel them. Or if she did, they didn't bother her.

He stood for a moment, understanding that she needed to be alone, but also not sure he could leave her. This place scared him because he feared this was where it had begun, where a serial killer was made and still lurked in the shadows.

"Rourke, I'll be fine. I have my gun. You said you wanted to talk to the former deputy. Go."

"Promise you'll meet me at the motel before it gets dark?"

"Promise."

CALLIE DIDN'T REALIZE how long she'd been sitting in the cemetery. The sun had gone down. This time of year this far north, darkness came on quickly. She'd promised she would meet Rourke at the motel before it got dark. She would have to hurry to keep that promise. Her stomach growled. Rourke would be worried and probably as starved as she realized she was.

She followed the path through the weeds back toward the girls' home. A dust devil suddenly whirled up in front of her. She ducked her head against the dirt and rubbish that pelted her. The wind moved on to whistle in the gables of the building. Nearby, an old windmill, now nearly blade-less, gave a rusty groan.

Closer she heard another sound, this one even more haunting—and familiar. At first she thought she'd only imagined it. The voice singing had a childlike quality that drew her as much as the familiar tune. Someone was inside the building, singing a song she hadn't heard in twenty-five years.

She stepped through the main door. Deep cold shadows had filled the space since she'd been in earlier. The sweet voice singing was coming from upstairs.

Callie hesitated at the bottom of the steps, but only for a moment as the singing became fainter. The song was one her mother used to sing to her. She tried to catch the lyrics, needing to hear the rest of the song but realizing what she needed more was to see who was singing it. The song and those long-awaited answers beckoned her. She checked the gun in her purse and started up the stairs.

CHAPTER TWENTY-SIX

ROURKE HAD BOOKED adjoining rooms at the motel before he'd called the deputy Edwin Sharp had interviewed. He wasn't sure the man would have any more to offer, but he had to try.

"I can't imagine what more I could tell you," Burt Denton had said on the phone, but told Rourke to stop on by and gave him the address.

Before heading over there, he'd checked on Callie. He'd seen her small form moving around the tall weeds of the cemetery. The landscape, while winter dreary, had been open. No sign of anyone else around, so he'd driven over to the deputy's house, planning to make it quick.

The sun hadn't yet gone down as he'd parked in front of the house. But he'd seen it getting darker earlier each day he'd been in Montana.

Burt Denton had surprised him. He'd expected a younger man. The house felt empty as Burt ushered him in. He remembered what Edwin had said about the relationship with Callie's mother destroying the man's marriage.

"I figured after the last time I talked to the private detective, you had your case solved," Burt said, after they were seated in the kitchen.

"Really," he said in surprise. "Why would you say that?"

"He'd found one of Gladys McCormick's daughters."

Rourke couldn't believe his ears. "When was the last time you talked to Edwin Sharp?"

Burt frowned. "Two evenings ago. He'd called to let me know that I'd had the names wrong, but he'd still been able to track down the twins' births through their mother to get their names. I was surprised when he told me what he'd found out."

"I'm afraid I never got to speak with Edwin," Rourke said carefully. "He was murdered in his hotel room before he could tell me what he found out."

The deputy's eyes widened in shock. *"Murdered?"* A cold darkness seemed to fill the kitchen.

"What did Edwin tell you?" Rourke asked, realizing that whatever the P.I. had found out must have gotten him killed.

Burt rubbed a hand over his face, clearly shaken by the news. "Give me a minute to recall it all." He let out a breath. "He said the wild one, the one I told him about, Kathy, was actually named Catherine Ann. He hadn't had any luck finding *her.* But the nice one, she'd turned out okay, I guess. You just never know, do you?"

"The nice one?" Rourke asked.

"Lee. At least that's what I thought her name had been, since that's what I'd heard her sister calling her. I guess her name was really Laura. Laura McCormick— that was until she got married to a fellow by the name of Mike Fuller and became a cop out in Seattle."

IT WASN'T UNTIL she reached the third floor that Callie realized the song had stopped. At the same second, she sensed a presence. She froze at the malevolence she felt.

"You remembered the song."

She turned slowly and blinked, not sure she could trust what she was seeing. A dark-haired woman stood only feet away, holding a gun that was now pointed at Callie's heart.

She stared in surprise. The face was familiar. So was the look in the woman's eyes. *"Catherine?"* Her hand moved slowly to her shoulder bag, the weight of the gun reassuring her.

The laugh was familiar and frightening. "You remember me. Wow, you look just like your mother," Catherine said, taking a step toward her. "The photos really didn't do you justice."

"Photos?"

"The crime-scene ones. Surely Rourke showed them to you or at least told you about them. Seriously, I can't get over how adorable you are. No wonder Rourke is so enchanted by you. You were cute as a kid, but you're a knockout all grown up."

Callie frowned, confused. "You *know* Rourke?"

"I thought he would have told you. My sister, Laura, and Rourke were cops together on the Seattle Police Department. He didn't mention that?" She grimaced, as if tasting something bitter in her mouth. "He probably also didn't mention that Laura's been working with him on your case."

Callie felt sick. *"My* case? Laura and Rourke?"

Catherine's smile had a bite to it. "Oh, you didn't know. Laura and Rourke weren't only fellow cops. They're lovers. He has never loved anyone the way he does Laura. Last year she almost died when they were working together on a case. Now he's so protective…." She frowned. "You really don't know what's going on, do you? Rourke put his job as a U.S. marshal on the line to solve these murders. He would do *anything* to catch his killer." She raised a brow. "And now he has. That's the real reason he brought you here."

"Where is Laura?" Callie asked, her voice breaking as she looked past Catherine. "I want to talk to her."

Catherine gave her a pitying look. "She and Rourke are probably at the motel together right now. They left you to me."

"I don't believe you," Callie said. "You were the one who liked hurting people. Laura was the good twin."

"Are you trying to hurt my feelings? I know dear, sweet Laura used to always come to the defense of you and your mother. My sister kept me from picking on you, didn't she? Well, she's not here now, is she?"

Callie knew better than to try to turn and run back down the stairs. She knew her only hope was to go for her gun. "You're the one who killed those men. But why involve me?"

"You involved yourself that first night when you came into the room when I was…" Catherine stopped. "You saw me kill that man, but you never talked. Why?"

After all these years, Callie saw it. The room, herself as a child of five watching as the girl stabbed the man in the bed with the bloody knife in her hand. She now felt the confusion, the fear and ultimately her own pain as she saw the girl doing the killing. "Because you didn't kill him. Laura did."

Catherine laughed. "Laura? Not dear, sweet Laura. How could you think such a thing?"

"Because it's true. Laura killed him. She killed him because of you."

"ENOUGH OF THIS," Catherine snapped. "Clearly, you don't know what you're talking about. It's probably the shock of coming back here. It can do strange things to you, can't it?"

"I know all of it," Callie said, her hand resting on her shoulder bag. She'd managed to unzip a small opening. If she was quick enough, if she could find the gun and get it in her hand fast enough, if—

She knew there were too many ifs. Catherine was holding a gun on her, and there was no doubt in Callie's mind that the woman would use it.

"You're responsible for all the pain Laura has suffered. You flirted with that man. He thought you wanted him. Maybe *you* did."

Catherine shook her dark head of hair. "You couldn't possibly know. You were too young to—"

"The man grabbed the wrong twin. Laura tried to tell him, but he thought you were just playing hard to get...."

Tears welled in Catherine's eyes, but she quickly wiped them away with her free hand. "Enough of this. *You* are the problem. You've always been the problem. You just had to come down to that room, didn't you? Laura said you think you're psychic?" She laughed, but the sound died quickly on her lips. "If you're psychic, then tell me what I'm thinking right now."

"Rourke will never believe that I killed myself."

Catherine looked surprised. "So, it's true. You can

read my mind. Then you must know that Rourke will believe whatever Laura tells him to believe. Come on. Let's go visit your old room." She motioned with the gun.

Callie had no choice but to turn down the hall. She kept her hand on the top of her shoulder bag, but she could feel Catherine's intensity. *Wait,* she warned herself. *Wait.*

"Rourke will be so distraught for bringing you here when he finds out what you've done," Catherine said as she shoved Callie into the room.

The wind whipped through the hole where the window had been. It kicked up dust on the floor and sent some of the mattress stuffing skittering out into the hallway.

Rourke. He wasn't with Laura. He'd gone to talk to the deputy. When he returned to the motel and she wasn't there, he would come looking for her. Callie worried that it would be too late, though.

Catherine motioned to the windowless opening three floors above the hard, cold ground below. "So sad, but then again, you couldn't live with yourself. Too bad you can't leave a suicide note and confess to the murders. But this will have to do."

"He won't believe that I killed myself. I have good memories here and he knows it. I don't feel the way you do about this place."

"How do you know how I…?" Her eyes narrowed. "You really do know how I feel. Mother always said she thought there was something weird about you. That must be how you knew I planned to kill you after you witnessed the murder. That's why you were hiding in the stairwell that day when you overheard Laura and

I arguing. You were the one who told your mother that I had killed my sister."

Callie shook her head. "You didn't push Laura down the stairs. She pushed you. She wouldn't let you hurt me because there was goodness in her."

Catherine laughed. "Goodness? She and Rourke plan to frame you for all these murders. That doesn't sound like goodness to me."

"She's protecting you. She's protected you all these years."

"Out of guilt." Catherine's voice broke. "Who pushes her twin sister down a flight of stairs? Who stabs a man to death? You're wrong about Laura. We're co-killers. If you were really psychic, you would know that."

"I know Laura wants this to stop."

Catherine nodded. "That's why you have to die. Climb up on the windowsill."

"You aren't going to kill me, and I'm not going to jump out that window," Callie said with more bravado than she felt as she turned enough that Catherine couldn't see her slip her hand into her bag. Her fingers touched something cold and hard. The gun. She found the grip—and the trigger.

"I guess you aren't as psychic as you thought if you think I'm not going to kill you."

"There is only one way this can end. You have to turn yourself in."

Catherine laughed. "Laura might want to, but I will never let her. She's weak. I was always stronger. That's why Mother loved me more. She saw Laura's weakness and hated it. Just as I hate it."

The woman raised the gun. Callie looked into her eyes and knew Catherine would kill her. There wasn't time to pull the gun out of her purse. She turned the barrel toward Catherine.

"Climb up on the windowsill now," Catherine ordered. "Otherwise I will shoot you. I'll put the gun in your hand. Either way, you're going to die."

Callie pulled the trigger.

So did Catherine.

CHAPTER TWENTY-SEVEN

ROURKE LEFT THE deputy's house running scared. Laura. He couldn't believe it. Not the Laura he knew. He thought back to the restaurant that day in Seattle when her behavior had surprised him. Had she recognized Callie even then?

He shuddered. No, it couldn't be true. She would have said something. She would have…mentioned that her mother lived in Montana? Hell, that her mother was even dead? Laura had kept a whole lot more from him, including that she was one of the twin daughters of Gladys McCormick.

Rourke looked toward Westfield Manor as he walked to his SUV. It was nothing more than a hulking dark outline against the waning light. Laura had to have known from that first day. The deeper he'd gotten into the case… He groaned. He'd told her *everything,* even things she would have already known.

He'd even told her his theory, that one of the twins was the killer.

Hadn't Burt said the other twin's name was Catherine? That much Laura had admitted. She had a sister named Catherine. She'd said they weren't close. Just as she wasn't close to her mother.

Knowing the circumstances, Rourke could understand why she kept her mother secret. She'd apparently been afraid to tell him—even when she could see him getting closer and closer to the truth.

He swore as he tried to make sense of this. The temperature had dropped as the day gave way to the coming night, but he hardly felt the cold. Laura had to be covering for her sister. That would explain why she'd been so adamant about Callie being the killer. Had she just hoped that was the case? Or was she ready to send an innocent woman to prison for multiple murders?

Rourke told himself there had to be another explanation. He *knew* Laura. And yet, the profile she'd done of the killer had not only fit Callie, but Laura and her sister. Had she been trying to tell him something, and he just hadn't been listening?

He couldn't think clearly; his head was spinning.

If Laura *was* covering for her sister, then where was Catherine? Didn't she usually come out to visit Laura this time of year in Seattle? Yes, in…*October*.

His heart began to pound harder. Catherine always visited in October.

He felt an urgent rush of fear as he hurriedly climbed behind the wheel. What was it that Laura had been trying to tell him earlier on the phone? Something about her sister. Something her sister was going to do? Or something she'd already done?

"Oh, God." Edwin. What would Catherine have done to keep him from finding out the truth?

Rourke put the key in the ignition, and then he remembered. It had been Laura's suggestion that he bring Callie here. He thought of the women serial killers, the "co-killers." How about one who was a cop and one… What was Catherine? Simply a psychopath?

Are you so sure it isn't Catherine and your pre-

cious Callie? Laura's voice in his head. She'd been so adamant that the killer was Callie. To protect her sister? Or herself?

Even though his mind rebelled against the path his thoughts had taken, he couldn't wait to get to Callie. Starting the engine, he quickly backed out and headed down the main drag. Surely Callie wasn't still at Westfield. She'd promised she would get to the motel before dark. It was almost dark now.

As he neared the motel ahead, he prayed she was safe in the room. He'd left a key for her at the desk. She would know to—

His phone made a familiar sound as he got a text. He grabbed it and quickly checked. Callie. It read: I'm at the motel waiting for you.

His relief made him suddenly weak. As he turned in, he saw that the light was on in the adjoining motel room, the curtains closed. She'd kept her promise. He let out the breath he'd been holding as he parked in front of the unit and got out.

All he could think about was getting to Callie and making sure she was safe as he unlocked the motel-room door. Stepping in, he heard the sound of the shower running and, filled with even more relief, locked the door behind him.

SHE HEARD HIM come into the motel room and turned her face up to the warm spray of the shower. Rourke was here now. Everything was going to be fine.

After what had happened at Westfield... She tried not to think about that. She knew she wasn't thinking clearly, but then, who would be under the circumstances? She had thought about calling Rourke and telling him what had happened at Westfield, but she knew it would be better in person. All she could think about was washing off the blood.

"Glad you're back," Rourke called through the closed bathroom door. "You had me worried."

She made a demurring sound, the water probably too loud for him to make it out. But she knew he would come to her. He loved her. He would open the bathroom door. He would take the sound as an invitation. He would imagine the hot water, the thought of his naked lover waiting for him, slick and smelling of soap.

The bathroom door opened, just as she knew it would. She could hear him stripping off his clothes and catch movement through the steam and frosted glass of the shower stall. She waited, longing to feel his arms around her, making her feel safe. Loved. She needed him now more than ever.

She caught alluring glimpses of flesh through the steamed-up shower door a moment before she heard him ask, "Mind if I join you?"

She'd read somewhere that a vampire couldn't come into your house unless they asked. Once you said "yes"... Where had that crazy thought come from?

She answered with a soft, seductive chuckle, and he did what she knew he would, what she'd prayed he would. He opened the shower door. As she moved to one side, turning her back to him, he stepped in.

CHAPTER TWENTY-EIGHT

As ROURKE STEPPED into the shower, all he saw through the steam was bare, wet soapy skin—and long dark hair. He'd been so happy to find her here, waiting for him. He knew he'd disappointed her. He'd lied to her. He'd even thought she was a killer at those moments when he'd had his doubts.

Callie didn't think that they knew each other, let alone could love each other after such a short time. Especially after the lies.

He just wanted the opportunity to get to know her. All his feelings for her came in such a rush that if she hadn't turned around, he would have told her that he loved her.

His eyes widened in alarm. He tried to step back, but she had already grabbed his arm, had already jabbed the syringe into him.

CALLIE OPENED HER EYES. Blood ran down into her right eye. She blinked and tried to sit up. The room spun wildly, forcing her back down. She closed her eyes and lay on the worn wooden floor of the room she and her mother had shared as she tried to sort out what had happened.

She remembered the voices—two of them standing over her, arguing—didn't she?

"*Catherine, oh, my God, what have you done now?*" *Laura's voice, sounding close to tears.* "*Look what you've done now.*"

"*Stop crying like a baby,*" *her sister snapped.* "*You knew this had to end. Isn't that why you got me here? You needed someone to do your dirty work. Help me lift her. We'll throw her out the window.*"

"*No! I can't do this anymore. I want you out of my life.*"

Callie had felt someone touch her temple, but when she opened her eyes all she saw was darkness for a moment.

"*She's not dead. I just grazed her,*" *Catherine said with a curse.* "*We have to finish her.*"

"*Oh, no, look, there is a puddle of blood in the dark shape of a halo around her head.*" *Laura cried harder.*

Callie heard the sound of a hard slap and Laura's cry of pain.

"*Laura, are you serious?*" *Catherine demanded.* "*Callie is no angel. Remember, she tried to take Rourke away from you.*"

"*She was such a sweet little girl. Is that why you hated her so much, Catherine? Did you know I used to pretend she was my little sister? My only sister.*"

"*Snap out of it, Laura. You have to finish her off. Now. We don't have much time. Either shoot her or help me throw her out the window. I have to do everything for you, don't I?*" *Catherine yelled at her, their voices echoing through the old building.*

Callie blinked up at the dark image standing over her.

That was where the memory blurred and dissolved. Callie opened her eyes again. The smell of the blood filled her nostrils. She forced herself to sit up. Her hand slipped in the blood on the floor. Her blood.

She picked up her cloth shoulder bag, feeling by the weight of it that the gun was gone. So was her cell phone. She pressed the cloth to the wound on her head to stanch the bleeding as dark spots tried to blot out her vision. Closing her eyes again, she fought to stay conscious.

Over the pounding in her head, another memory of the two arguing surfaced, this one old and yet as familiar. She saw Laura and Catherine standing at the top of the third-floor stairwell.

"I have to do everything for you, don't I?" Catherine yelled at her twin, their voices echoing through the old building.

"No, I never asked you to hurt anyone."

Catherine's laugh. "Hurt? That little brat saw you kill that man, Laura. She has to be dealt with. She'll tell if I don't shut her up."

"She won't. I'll talk to her—"

"You're so weak. You make me sick." Catherine's slap and Laura's sudden cry echoed through the back stairwell as Callie watched from her hiding place. "Either you take care of her or I will. Only I will make the little brat pay for spying on us."

Catherine started to turn away, to go back through the door to the third floor. She was looking for Callie. That was why Callie was hiding in the stairwell. Now Catherine would go to her room, where her mother was too sick to protect her.

Laura reached for her twin. She didn't mean to push her. She meant to grab her arm, to try to reason with her. Callie knew this, but she didn't know how.

Catherine lost her footing. Her arms flailed, her eyes widening. "Help me!"

Laura lunged for her sister, but at the last minute, she pulled her hand back. Catherine fell, tumbling down to finally come to a stop in the space at the base of the stairwell.

Callie had run, terrified of what she'd seen. Terrified even more because she'd known the truth. She'd run back to the room and tried to tell her mother what had happened. But she hadn't been able to speak.

Now, opening her eyes, she pushed herself to her feet and looked around the room, remembering all of it, including the horrible secret that had been locked away all these years.

Why wasn't she dead? Why had she been spared? As she staggered toward the door, head banging like a war drum, she knew who the real killer was. She had to get to Rourke.

CHAPTER TWENTY-NINE

ROURKE KINCAID WOKE tied to the motel bed. His wrists and ankles were bound, his mouth gagged, and a blindfold had been tied over his eyes. Something had been thrown over him, but he could feel that he was naked beneath it.

He'd seen enough of the crime-scene photos to know what happened next. He could hear someone in the room with him, but for a moment, he couldn't remember how he'd gotten there. It came back slowly. He saw himself entering the motel room after getting what he thought was Callie's text, hearing the shower, stripping down and stepping in, only to find—

"Laura." He tried to say it around the gag in his mouth, suddenly acutely aware of how her victims had felt. They'd been panicked at finding themselves helpless. But they hadn't known until it was too late that they were at the mercy of a woman who enjoyed torturing and killing men.

Rourke knew.

Sweat beaded his forehead and upper lip in the darkness of the blindfold. He tried to simply breathe, but as the drug wore off, he could feel places on his body where he hurt.

Vaguely he remembered fighting her in the shower before the drug knocked him out. That thought made him feel a little better. He was glad he hadn't gone down without a fight. Had Edwin fought, as well?

"Laura?" The word came out unintelligibly again. "Laura."

He heard her move to the side of his bed. As she stepped closer, he caught a scent of perfume that he would never have associated with Laura Fuller. But then again, he'd never known the woman, had he?

She removed the blindfold first.

He blinked up at her, surprised again by her dark hair. Even her blond hair had been a lie, he realized. No wonder he'd mentally questioned her being a blonde that day at the restaurant in Seattle. Her coloring was that of a brunette. He suspected this was her natural color, dark brown. Had she changed it back to its natural color in the past few days or was this a wig?

She stared at him for a moment before she reached to remove the gag, but stopped. "I'm going to take your gag out. I'd prefer you didn't make a lot of noise, not that it will do you any good because there is no one around to hear."

The motel clerk had given him the two rooms at the end away from the office. Hadn't he said business was slow? Rourke had laughed at that since the entire town was dead as a graveyard.

"Promise to be quiet?" she asked.

Rourke nodded and flinched when she touched his cheek as she removed the gag. Her blue-eyed gaze met his again. A chill ran the length of him at what he saw in her eyes.

"Laura—"

"I'm not Laura. I'm her sister, Catherine."

"Where is she?" he asked, his voice hoarse. "Is she with Callie?"

"Don't worry, Rourke. Callie isn't going to be a problem anymore."

His heart sank. He was the one who'd brought Callie here at Laura's suggestion. He'd played right into her and her sister's hands.

"Everything is going to be all right now. Laura's going to take care of you." Catherine turned then toward the open doorway between the adjoining rooms. He could hear water running next door. "Laura," she called. "He's awake and all yours."

Catherine patted his cheek. "You're lucky it will be Laura and not me." She left then, disappearing into the other room.

He heard the water shut off in the adjacent room and the sisters talking in low voices. They sounded as if they were arguing. Callie. What had they done to her? Was she tied up in the next room?

Rourke fought to free himself from the duct tape on his wrists and ankles, thinking again of the other men who had tried to escape and failed. He knew how this ended, and yet if there was even a slim chance of saving Callie...

He heard the shower come on in the next room and looked up to find a blonde Laura standing over him. "Hi, Rourke."

"Laura." It came out a plea. He told himself that his only chance was to convince her not to do this. They'd once been best friends. But even as he thought it, he was reminded of her confession of love for him. He'd hurt her. Now she was a woman scorned.

It was an unforgiving woman who stepped to the

side of the bed—not the homicide detective who'd been his partner.

He desperately wanted to ask where Callie was and what they'd done with her, but he held his tongue. Just the mention of Callie again would make things worse, he thought. If he had any hope of reaching the old Laura…

"What's going on, Laura?"

She gave him a rueful smile. "I didn't want it to end like this, Rourke. I did everything I could to keep this from happening, but if you're anything, you're relentless when you get on a case."

"Why didn't you tell me about Westfield, about your mother, about…Catherine?" he asked, dropping his voice as he glanced at the open doorway to the adjoining room.

"How could I tell you about my family, my past?" Laura moved around the room. She could feel Rourke's eyes on her. She had his undivided attention now, she thought ruefully. "The first time I saw her photograph, I thought I'd seen her before. Even her name sounded… familiar. I didn't remember Westfield at first, at least not by name. My mother moved us around every few years. We lived in all kinds of weird, awful places. I was just a kid. I'm not sure I ever knew the names of the places where we lived, or cared."

He watched her pace up and down at the end of the bed and wondered if he could trust anything she said.

"When you told me about the connection to Westfield Manor…I couldn't believe it. I didn't *want* to believe it. I never thought I would have to tell you about my past. Never thought I'd ever have to tell *anyone*. I thought I'd buried it."

She stopped moving to look at him. Catherine had only given him enough of the drug to get him into the bed without him fighting her. She'd underestimated him. He'd fought her until the drug had taken effect.

Normally, Catherine preferred doing this somewhere more private than a motel room. But in a town like Flat Rock, the motel was empty except for the rooms Rourke had rented, and fortunately, they were at the end of the row. They had lots of privacy and no one to interrupt them.

"Laura, you don't want to do this."

"Shh," she quieted him as she pulled up a chair next to his bed. "You want to know the real me, Rourke? I'm the daughter of Gladys McCormick, the identical twin daughter, the one my mother never liked." She laughed. "Identical but so different. Catherine is…" She glanced toward the open doorway. "She was the special one. As far back as I can remember, she flirted with any male, no matter how old he was."

"Laura—"

"Let me finish my story, Rourke. Catherine and I were twelve that year when things got really bad. Twelve, but Catherine acted like she was sixteen. I saw her flirting with that awful young man who worked for our mother. Some might say she was asking for it."

His eyes widened. "No one asks to be raped. Edwin said it was one of you."

"Your P.I. got that right. One of the twins *was* raped. But it wasn't Catherine. I…" She hated that, even after all these years, saying it made her voice break. "I was the one that horrible man raped. He thought I was

Catherine. I kept telling him…" She swallowed back the bile that rose in her throat. "He…hurt me."

"Laura, I'm so sorry."

She brushed at her tears. "I'm not telling you for your pity—"

"It's not pity."

Laura couldn't bear to look at him for a moment. She cleared her throat and continued. "The rape was bad enough, but my mother and my sister…" She shook her head. "They acted like I was to blame for what happened. But it wasn't me. Don't you see? It was Catherine."

"Callie saw you."

"Yes. I loved Callie. I used to pretend she was my sister and not Catherine. I kept Catherine from hurting her."

"That's why she couldn't remember. She was protecting you."

CHAPTER THIRTY

PRESSING THE CLOTH of her shoulder bag to her head, Callie worked her way down the stairs. At the bottom she had to stop for a moment to grip the rail, too dizzy almost to stand.

She could see the motel sign across the field. As she started through the tall dried weeds, she spotted a piece of metal pipe. Picking it up, she used it like a crutch. All she could think about was getting to Rourke. She prayed that it wouldn't be too late.

Her head ached. There was a dullness that she'd never felt before. Her only worry was making it to the motel. She tried not to think about what Catherine had said. Rourke in alliance with Laura, his former partner at the Seattle P.D.? That couldn't be true.

As she neared the motel, she saw Rourke's SUV parked in front of the last room in the row. She wanted to run down there and make sure he was safe, but in her heart, she knew he wasn't. She had to get help. She didn't know how much longer she could stay on her feet. Weak from loss of blood and her pounding head, she headed for the motel office.

When she reached it, she caught her reflection in the glass. Her face and clothes were covered in blood. She would scare the motel manager to death. But once he saw her he would call for help.

As she started to reach for the knob of the door that led into the office, she saw the crude note taped to the small window. *Be back in fifteen.*

She had no idea how long the manager had been gone, but she didn't see a vehicle anywhere around—except for Rourke's SUV. She tried the bell next to the door. It rang inside, but no one came.

For a moment, she hesitated. Then she lifted the pipe still in her hand and put the end of it through the window in the door. The glass shattered, sounding like a gun had gone off. Callie looked down the row of motel rooms toward the one with Rourke's SUV parked in front.

She had to lean against the door for a moment to keep from passing out. Then she broke out the rest of the glass, reached inside and opened the door. She went straight to the phone and dialed 911.

"What's your emergency?" an operator asked after the first ring.

"I need an ambulance and the police." She read the name of the motel off the sign.

"You're in Flat Rock?"

"Yes. Hurry."

"Can you tell me the nature of your emergency?"

"I've been shot and there is a killer—" She couldn't talk any longer and dropped the phone. Behind her, on the board where the room keys were hung, she saw that two were missing, one from each of the adjoining rooms. She snatched one of the extra keys from the board and headed for the door.

ROURKE FLINCHED AT the cold hatred in her eyes as Laura talked about her sister, Catherine.

"I killed him, but Catherine... She found me in the man's room. She saw Callie and knew that she'd witnessed all of it. Callie seemed to be in shock. Catherine told me to get out of there...."

He could see that something had happened after that between her and her sister. "She covered for you?" There was more; he could sense it. "And your mother covered for you?"

"Yes, we were told never to say anything. The deputy couldn't prove anything.... Catherine said I owed her." Laura's chuckle held no humor. "She turned everything around. She told Mother that she'd killed him."

Rourke saw that she looked confused for a moment.

"Catherine was afraid Callie would tell someone," she said in a small, quiet voice. "I loved Callie so much. We would sing this song her mother taught her."

"Laura, why in God's name didn't you tell me this?" But he knew the reason. He thought of the photographs from the crime scene. The photos that Laura hadn't put in the homicide file. She'd hidden the photos because she'd been covering for her sister. The other two murders in Seattle. Had she tampered with evidence on those cases, as well?

He could see that she was afraid of her sister. But to cover for her, knowing what her sister had been doing for years? Laura was a cop!

"How can you let her go on killing, Laura?"

"I...I didn't know at first. We lived in so many places. I never knew the names. I was just a kid, shuttled around, from one horrible girls' home to the next. You have no idea what it was like. The girls were all mean to us, and the men..."

He saw her eyes glass over as if she was back there

in that awful place, just a child herself. "What was your sister going to do to Callie?" he asked as he recalled what Edwin had told him about one of the twins pushing the other one down a flight of stairs.

Laura met his gaze. "I pleaded with her not to hurt Callie. We were standing on the landing in the third-floor stairwell. Callie hadn't said a word since…that night. I told Catherine that I would talk to her, that she wouldn't tell anyone if I asked her not to, that we were friends. But…" Her voice dropped to a whisper. "Catherine was jealous. She just wanted to hurt Callie because I loved her." Laura began to cry.

"Laura, no one should have had to go through what you did," Rourke said. "Please. Untie me. Let me hold you."

She looked at him through her tears. He saw her weaken, and then something changed in her. She shook her head and rose from the chair to pace again at the end of the bed.

Past her, he watched the open doorway to the other room, afraid Catherine would return too soon. "Laura."

When she looked at him, he motioned with his head for her to come back to the side of the bed.

"You told me that you trusted me with your life," he said. "Trust me now."

"My sister, Catherine…" Her voice broke, and she looked toward the open doorway between the rooms again as if she'd heard her sister. "She's dangerous. You don't know what she'll do."

"Laura, let me help you," he whispered.

Her eyes filled again. "It's too late."

"It's not. If you untie me, I can handle your sister. We'll get her help."

"But they will blame me."

"No one will blame you."

"I didn't stop her. I was afraid—"

"Laura, I can see that you're afraid of her. Please, let me help you. Remember when you and I were a team? We were unstoppable. We can be again."

He saw her weaken even more. She glanced toward the doorway to the other room, then reached behind her and picked up a knife.

For a moment, he thought he'd failed. He felt his stomach drop. But with more relief than he'd ever felt, he watched her cut the duct tape binding his left wrist to the bed frame.

She had cut almost all the way through the tape, when she suddenly stopped. He saw the change come over her.

"Catherine," she said in a hoarse whisper. "I can't. Catherine—"

"Laura, hurry. Cut—"

But she cocked her head to the side as if she had heard something in the next room. She hurriedly laid down the knife on the bedside table and began to move away.

"No, Laura—"

She turned back, picked up the gag and stuffed it into his mouth hard. The look in her eyes told him that when she came back, it would be with her sister, Catherine. Whatever hope he'd felt was gone.

CHAPTER THIRTY-ONE

CALLIE FUMBLED AS she tried to put the key into the motel-room lock. Her vision doubled for a moment. Finally the key went in. She couldn't hear anything inside the room at first as she unlocked the door as quietly as possible and pushed it open.

The room was dark, the curtains drawn. She blinked, trying to focus. It appeared empty, but she could hear water running. Someone was in the shower? Rourke?

Could it possibly be true about Rourke and Laura? Was she a worse fool than even she thought? She was trying to make sense of all of it as she stepped in and closed the door behind her. Catherine thought she was dead. Did Rourke think the same thing? Were he and Laura in the shower together?

Callie didn't think a heart really broke. At least she didn't before that moment. She felt a sob rise up in her chest. Until that moment, she hadn't admitted the truth about her feelings for Rourke.

What if Rourke and Laura really were lovers and they had planned this whole thing to frame her? Rourke hadn't told her that he and his friend Laura had been homicide investigators together on the Seattle police force. Nor had he told her that he was working with Laura on this case.

Wasn't it possible he kept even more from her?

She almost turned and left, telling herself she couldn't bear it if Catherine had been telling her the truth. She looked down, surprised to see that she still had the piece of pipe in one of her hands and the room key in the other. Moving toward the bed, she started to lay both down. What she really wanted was to lie down on the bed and curl up in a ball and sleep. She didn't know how much longer she could keep standing.

The sound of voices in the adjoining room startled her. She recognized Laura's, then Rourke's. But something was wrong. They didn't sound like lovers. And if they were in the other room, then who was in the shower in this room beyond the closed bathroom door?

Picking up the pipe again, Callie moved toward the door to the adjoining room.

ROURKE KNEW THAT once Catherine came back into the room, he wouldn't stand a chance. He tried to spit out the gag, but had no luck. Just as he knew there was no reason to try to call Laura back even if he could.

For a moment, he'd thought he'd reached the old Laura. But one sound from the other room and her twin had Laura under her control again.

Laura was moving slowly toward the open door to the next room as if she'd heard something. He suspected she'd only imagined it since he could still hear the shower running.

Hurriedly he looked around, knowing he had one chance. Once Laura returned with Catherine—

Laura had left the knife just out of his reach on the bedside table. Before she'd stopped, she'd cut through most of the duct tape on his left wrist. He pulled as hard as he could and felt it give. Just a little more.

His left wrist broke free as he heard Laura say, "Callie? What are you doing here?"

His heart lodged in his throat. Callie was in the other room? Fear froze him, but for only a second. He pulled the gag from his mouth. Every instinct in him told him not to call out to Callie as he reached for the knife on the bedside table and hurriedly began to saw at the duct tape binding his right wrist.

"I WANT TO see Rourke," Callie said as she started toward the open doorway. She was glad she hadn't put down the pipe.

Laura stepped in front of her, blocking her way. "It's over between the two of you. He doesn't want to see you."

"That's too bad, because I want to see him."

"You don't look well, Callie. You look as if a gust of wind could knock you over."

"I'm okay," she lied, lifting the length of metal pipe. "Move out of the way, Laura. I don't want to hurt you."

"You're wasting your time. Rourke and I share something the two of you will never share. He's a lawman. He gets on a case and nothing stops him." She smiled. "He does whatever he has to, even seducing a suspect, to find the killer. He might have told you he loved you…. Like I said, he'll even lie. That's how much he loves his work. But if you really want to see him…" She stepped aside. "He used you, Callie. Go to him. But you will never have him. No woman ever will. His work will always come first."

Callie kept her eye on Laura as she moved to the open doorway and quickly stepped through. For a mo-

ment, she was so shocked to see Rourke on the bed
that she froze.

"Shut the door and lock it," he cried.

Just seeing him bound to the bed… The room swam.
She heard the shower shut off in the room behind her
as she tried to stay on her feet. Her head seemed to
buzz as she tried to make sense of what was happening. Rourke had a knife. He was sawing through duct
tape that had his ankles bound to the bed frame.

"Callie, she's right behind you!"

She hadn't heard anyone behind her—hadn't sensed
anyone. With a start, she realized that she hadn't picked
up anything from Laura. No psychic flashes at all from
the moment she'd been shot.

It was why she turned too late. Suddenly Laura was
beside her, a gun in her hand. Only the barrel wasn't
pointed at her—but at Rourke.

Callie swung the pipe. She heard it connect with
Laura's arm, the sound a sickening crack. Laura's
scream of pain was lost in the sound of the gunshot.

Running on nothing but sheer will, Callie swung
the pipe again, knocking the gun from Laura's hand.
It skittered across the floor, and Laura dived for it.

Rourke still had one ankle bound to the frame, but
he managed to catapult himself over the side of the
bed and grab up the gun from the floor. "Stop, Laura!"
he cried, aiming the weapon at her. "Don't make me
kill you."

Laura laughed, grabbed the knife up from where
he'd dropped it at the foot of the bed and launched
herself at him.

Callie saw the expression on Rourke's face and realized in that split second that he wouldn't be able to pull the trigger and kill his former partner. She swung the pipe, this time catching Laura in the side of the head. The woman fell onto the bed next to Rourke, the knife sticking in the mattress just inches from his heart.

His face was pale, the white sheet wrapped around him splattered with blood from where he'd caught a bullet in the shoulder. His gaze widened as he motioned to the door behind her. "Catherine—"

Callie turned, but the doorway was empty—just as she realized it would be. Callie thought of the angel out in the field, away from the others buried in the West-field cemetery that she'd walked out to see, and the name on it. But it was another memory, along with the one in which Laura and Catherine were arguing and Catherine tumbled down the stairs to land, her neck broken, her eyes open, seeing nothing.

Earlier, as she'd lain bleeding on the floor, when she'd opened her eyes there had been only one sister standing over her.

"Catherine can't hurt anyone," she said to Rourke. "She's dead. She's been dead since she was twelve. Laura killed her, and her mother forced her to become both herself and Catherine so no one would ever know."

Callie heard the wail of sirens in the distance. The room began to swim. She saw Rourke reach for her. The last thing she remembered was dropping the pipe as he caught her before she hit the floor.

CHAPTER THIRTY-TWO

CALLIE OPENED HER EYES, and for a moment, all she saw was white. White walls, white sheets, white light coming in through the window.

Then a dark shape stepped in front of the window. The dark silhouette moved toward her. A scream rose in her throat but quickly died as the shape spoke.

"Callie." The word came out on a relieved breath as Rourke took her hand. "Thank God," he said as he lowered himself into the chair next to her bed. "I was so worried about you."

She stared at him, praying that she wasn't hallucinating from some drug Laura had given her. Or worse, dreaming. For all she knew, she and Rourke could be dead.

"Rourke?"

He smiled, his eyes bright with unshed tears. "You're safe. We're all safe. Callie, there's something I have to tell you. Callie?"

She squeezed his hand and closed her eyes.

When she woke again, the room was dark.

"Ms. Westfield?" A doctor materialized from the dim light of the hallway. He turned on a lamp next to her bed. "How are you feeling?"

She reached up to touch her temple. It was covered with a thick bandage.

"Let's see how you're doing, okay? Follow my finger. That's right. Good. Now this way." He produced a small light and shone it in one eye and then the other, before pocketing it again. "Good."

Callie stared at him, at first not understanding what was wrong. "Am I…?"

"You're fine. You're in the Havre hospital. You were brought in from Flat Rock after being shot. But you were lucky. The bullet only grazed your head. You have a concussion and you've lost a lot of blood, but you're going to be just fine. I want you to rest now—"

"Rourke?"

"He's down the hall, resting, as well. We operated on his shoulder. He's doing fine." The doctor turned out the lamp. "You've been through a lot. Rest is the best thing for you now."

She watched him go, realizing that she hadn't picked up even the smallest of flashes. By the time a series of nurses came and went, Callie knew it really was gone. She heard no one's thoughts. It was as if she'd gone deaf. Her second sight was gone, just as quickly as it had come.

It left her with a strange feeling of both sadness and relief. The world had gone silent. She would get used to it. Just as she would get used to everyone she met being a mystery. But how would she know whom to trust?

She thought of Rourke. Look what had happened when she hadn't been able to read him. Just the thought of him made her heart ache. She told herself that she couldn't believe anything Laura had said, and yet, she knew at least some of it was true.

Would Rourke have pulled the trigger and killed Laura? Callie hadn't thought so. She still didn't. Laura hadn't thought he could either. She was right about that, just as she was right about Rourke being a lawman first and foremost. He'd come to Beartooth to catch a killer, and he'd done it. Now he would be going back to Seattle.

Her life… Callie had no idea where her life would take her now, just that she had to move on as she always had. Even with the past no longer chasing her, she had no reason to stay in any one place too long.

Callie closed her eyes. She was safe. Rourke was alive. So, why did she feel so empty inside?

"HOW'S YOUR SHOULDER?"

Rourke looked up to find Sheriff Frank Curry standing in his hospital-room doorway. "I've had worse."

Frank nodded and smiled at that. "Mind if I come in?"

Rourke waved the sheriff into the room.

"I was worried when I heard that both you and Callie had gotten shot. Good thing she has a hard head," Frank said, as he pulled up a chair.

"Fortunately." He'd spent time with Laura at the shooting range. She was a crack shot. If she had wanted to kill Callie, she could have on the first shot. Why hadn't she?

Rourke had more questions than he did answers. He told Frank what Callie had told him about Laura's mother forcing her to become both herself and her twin to keep the authorities from finding out that she'd killed Catherine.

"What kind of mother would do that to a child?" the sheriff demanded.

"Gladys McCormick was sick. Apparently, her own

mother had spent most of her life institutionalized, I've now found out." Edwin Sharp's notebook had been found in Laura's vehicle. The local authorities had brought it to him. "She must have had her own problems and passed a lot of them on to her twin girls."

Frank shook his head. "That's why I like crows."

"In Laura's mind, all the awful things happened to Catherine, and yet, she believed Catherine to be her mother's favorite."

"So it was like a split personality," the sheriff said.

"Somewhat, except she believed Catherine existed as another person, a living evil sister who did terrible things." Rourke thought about when Laura had been putting the profile together. "She was describing herself when she told me about the serial killer."

"She would know that person better than any profiler ever could," Frank agreed.

"To make matters worse, I was telling her everything I was learning." Rourke shook his head. "I got Edwin killed. By the time she killed Carson, she knew she had to frame Callie. That's why she suggested I bring her to Westfield."

"It could have been a last-ditch attempt to clear the Catherine side of her," Frank said. "She probably told herself she wouldn't kill again."

"I think she wanted to get caught," Rourke said. "She could have killed Callie. She could have killed me, as well. I'm not sure she wouldn't have if Callie hadn't arrived when she did, though."

The sheriff studied him for a moment. "You were both lucky."

"She couldn't hide who she really was anymore.

Worse, she'd told me she was in love with me. I was so surprised, I didn't handle it well."

"You never loved her?"

Rourke shook his head. "Not that way." He thought about that moment with her coming at him with the knife. Had it been her? Or Catherine? Would he have shot her? He would never know.

Callie didn't believe he could have killed Laura. Callie had saved him from finding out.

"Laura knew she would never have you…" the sheriff was saying. "She must have thought you were in love with Callie."

"I *am* in love with her."

"Does she know it?" the sheriff asked.

"I've tried to tell her." He shook his head. "I lied to her from the moment I met her. It's hard to build a relationship with someone after that."

"I still believe that love conquers all," Frank said, picking up his Stetson and getting to his feet. "Well, congratulations. You solved your case. I'm sorry I had to call your boss. But I'm sure after this, you don't have to worry about your job."

Rourke nodded. His job was the least of his worries. Nor did he feel any of the elation he usually did after solving a case.

After the sheriff left, the doctor came in to tell him he was going to be released.

"What about Callie?"

"She's already left. I thought you knew. The sheriff came to pick her up."

CHAPTER THIRTY-THREE

"I WAS SO worried about you," Kate said as she pulled Callie into a hug. Her gaze went to the bandage on Callie's temple. "How is your head?"

"Fine," she said, touched by Kate's concern. "I'll have a scar, but it is one I can see. I think those are the best because sometimes we need a reminder of what we've been through."

Kate shook her head. "I love your attitude. You've been through so much."

"So have you, and look how it's turned out," Callie said, smiling. "I heard you went to see the doctor."

Kate broke into a huge grin, but quickly tempered it. "It's still early, and I hate to get my hopes up again, but—"

"You're pregnant. I'm so happy for you." Callie took her friend's hand. "I never told you, but I used to have this…ability. I could see other people's lives, even some of their futures. I lost that ability when I was shot, and I'm not sorry it's gone."

Kate stared at her wide-eyed. "Are you going to tell me you were a fortune-teller?" she asked with a laugh.

Callie explained the flashes she'd gotten since she was five.

"That's how you knew about the murders?" Kate asked when she'd finished.

Callie nodded. "Laura McCormick drew me to the murders—just as she had the first one. A part of her must have wanted me to stop her." Callie shook off the memory of how close she'd come to being killed. How close Rourke had.

"But I'm glad I saw your future, Kate, before I lost that ability. You are going to have a healthy baby..." She stopped. "Do you want to know the sex?"

"Are you serious?" There were tears in Kate's eyes. "Tell me."

Callie felt her own tears. "You're going to have a beautiful baby girl."

Kate began to cry as she pulled Callie into another hug. But as the hug ended and Kate spotted the suitcases, she said, "Don't tell me you're leaving."

"I've never been able to stay in one place long," Callie said, unable to admit even to herself how much this was tearing her up inside.

"No, I can't bear losing you as a friend," Kate said. "I need you more than ever to help me through this pregnancy."

"You are going to breeze through it. All systems go. Don't worry."

"I won't worry if you're here."

"I can help you find a new waitress—"

"It isn't a new waitress I need. I've never felt as close to anyone as I have you, and trust me, I used to move a lot myself, and so I've never had a close friend. Please, stay."

Callie looked to the mountains out the apartment window. The Crazies glistened white against the deep blue sky. She had loved it here, had felt at home for

the first time in her life. But after falling in love with
Rourke...

"I'll come back when the baby is born," she promised. "I wouldn't miss that for the world."

"You're just trying to get me to name her after you,
aren't you?" Kate joked. "Seriously, I understand if you
have to leave for a little while. I could tell how you felt
about...that cowboy. But, please, come back. Soon."

ROURKE CAUGHT CALLIE loading her suitcases into her
pickup. "You left the hospital without saying goodbye."

Callie leaned against her truck. She was still pale,
but not as much as she'd been that first morning at the
hospital. He'd been so afraid for her.

"You were going to leave without saying goodbye?"
he asked.

"I hate goodbyes."

He could feel the warm October sun on his back. All
the snow had melted off, but it would be back. Winter
had taken hold of the peaks in the Crazies, blanketing
them in a cover of white that would stay until spring.

"Don't we even get to talk about this?"

"What is there to say? You're a U.S. marshal who
solved his case. I'm a waitress who can't stay in one
place. That kind of sizes it up."

"I don't think so."

"Rourke, you were just doing your job."

"It was more than that, and you know it. What are
you so afraid of, Callie?"

"I've pretty much faced all my fears, wouldn't you
say?" She shook her head. "Laura said a lot of things,
but there is at least one that I believe. You live to catch

bad guys. I could have been the killer, and yet look at the lengths you went to, trying to get close to me."

"I got too involved. I lost sight of everything except for one thing. I wanted you."

She looked away. "You and Laura. Were you ever…?"

"We were never more than homicide partners and friends."

Callie's gaze came back to his. "She was in love with you."

"I didn't…know."

He could see that she didn't believe that. "How could you not?"

It was a question he'd asked himself for days. How could he not have realized a lot of things? He'd been so busy building his career that he hadn't paid any attention to the woman he'd once trusted with his life.

"Callie, you have to know how I feel about you."

"Please don't, Rourke. I'm not sure anymore what is real and what isn't. All of it feels like a lie. I don't know who you are, and you sure as the devil don't know me."

"I was the one I was lying to. I told myself I was doing what I did because you were a suspect and I needed to get to the truth. But the truth is…I fell for you."

"True or not, after we made love, you weren't sure you hadn't just slept with a serial killer."

Any man in his right mind would have had his doubts when he woke up to that empty bed that night. But if he had been doing his job like he should have, he wouldn't have climbed into that bed to begin with. "I'm sorry. I wish I could start all over with you, no secrets between us."

She said nothing, her arms crossed over her chest, her eyes bright with unshed tears.

"I have to take care of some things," he said, hating that he had to leave and yet seeing that staying probably wasn't the answer either, since Callie was cutting out of Beartooth herself. "I have to go back to Seattle for a while."

"Your life is in Seattle."

It certainly didn't feel that way. Leaving here, leaving Callie, was the last thing he wanted to do. "What about you?" he asked. "What will you do?"

She shook her head.

"You're free of the past. Free of Westfield."

"Am I?"

He hesitated, fearing he might make things worse between them if he tried to convince her right now how much he loved her. "I have something for you. It's actually from the private investigator I hired. Before his death, he found your grandparents. It was in his notebook that the police found in Laura's possession. I thought…" He pulled the envelope from his jacket pocket and held it out to her.

She stared at it but didn't take it.

"My *mother's* family? The one who banished her because she was pregnant?"

"Their names and address are here, but also your grandparents on your father's side of the family. Apparently, both sets of family members have been looking for you and your mother for years."

He saw her swallow and, as if bracing herself, take the envelope. But she didn't open it. In fact, he wasn't sure she ever would.

"If you don't want to meet them alone…" He knew better than to say more.

She folded the envelope and stuffed it into the back pocket of her jeans before she met his gaze. "Goodbye, Rourke."

ROURKE'S MEETING WITH his boss at the U.S. Marshals' office went pretty much as he'd thought it would. He still had a job.

But if he wanted to keep his job, he had to stop playing cowboy. He actually laughed, because he'd realized that was really all he'd ever been: a cowboy, born and raised.

As he turned in his badge and his gun and walked away, he'd never felt freer. He'd chased a career for so many years, believing he could make the job fit him and his free spirit.

"What will you do now?" It was Laura's voice in his head as he left the U.S. Marshals' office. She would have never understood how he could give it up after working so hard to get where he was.

"What will I do? Whatever I want," he said aloud as he climbed behind the wheel of his pickup. "Whatever I want."

When the Realtor in Big Timber, Montana, called to tell him she had another ranch listing he might be interested in, he smiled at the timing.

"Give me a couple of days," he told her.

It surprised him how little it took to pack up everything he owned, load it into the back of his SUV and walk away from the big city where he'd lived.

He was looking forward to the road trip to Montana. He had a lot to think about. He'd succeeded, and yet he'd failed the people closest to him. Maybe if he had been paying more attention…

He knew he had to put the past behind him. He'd seen what it had done to Laura. Callie had survived her past and been freed at least from the murder part of it. Where was she now, though? Still running?

Rourke thought about trying to find her. It made him think of the story Sheriff Frank Curry had told about the crows. They'd been hurt, one of them killed, but eventually, they had come back home to a place where in their hearts they'd known they would be safe and loved.

He had to believe that Callie would come back one day. She loved Montana. He thought, even with everything that had happened, maybe she had a special place in her heart for Beartooth. Maybe even a little piece of her heart for him.

There was only one more thing he had to do before he could move on. He had to see Laura. Her injuries had been minor, a slight concussion and a broken arm. After her arrest, she'd been sent to the state hospital for evaluation, then allowed to return to a hospital closer to her doctor in Seattle.

He'd been relieved when her psychiatrist called to say that he could see her. Apparently, she'd been asking for him, saying he was the only "family" she had left.

The visit took place in a small room with the doctor present.

"How are you doing?" Rourke asked as he took the chair the doctor offered him across from Laura. She had a bandage on her head, and her arm was in a cast from being broken when Callie had hit her with the pipe. Other than that, she looked fine.

The blond wig was gone. Her naturally dark hair hung around her shoulders. She really was a very attractive woman, not to mention smart and capable. It was hard for him not to see the woman he'd thought he'd known for years.

"I'm doing great, all things considered," she said, smiling. Her blue eyes were bright. She looked at him with humor in her expression, as if he was the only one who wasn't getting the joke being played on him.

No wonder he hadn't seen the other Laura, he told himself. "Do you know what happened?"

She laughed. "Seriously? I got hit in the head, but not that *hard*. Rourke, I need you to find Catherine for me. They actually think I killed those men."

Rourke's heart broke for her. Laura had been his homicide partner. He'd trusted her with his life. How could he have not seen the Catherine side of her?

Because she'd seemed so normal, like she did now—and because he hadn't looked closely. He'd been too busy catching bad guys.

Laura met his gaze, hers steady and blue and pleading. "Rourke, you have to believe me. I didn't know Catherine was committing the murders. I didn't even remember Westfield. Rourke, I honestly believed the killer was Caligrace. She fit the *profile*."

He didn't know what to say.

She took his silence for agreement. "I have some ideas where you might be able to find Catherine," Laura continued, sounding like the cop she used to be. He thought about the night she'd been shot, when he'd held her hand while they'd waited for the ambulance. He recalled her words. They gave him a chill now.

Her mother's body had been exhumed and an autopsy had been performed. Gladys McCormick had died from suffocation—not the cancer that had been slowly killing her.

As if he needed more convincing as to what Laura was capable of doing. She was a cold-blooded killer and had been since the age of twelve. He hated to think how many men she'd murdered, but someone else was chasing those cases now.

"Catherine usually shows up this time of the year, but I can't depend on that happening now," she was saying. "That's why I need your help. Once you bring Catherine in— Rourke, are you listening to me?"

He nodded, thinking of her with that knife in her hand, her eyes wild with blood thirst.

She scoffed and looked to the doctor. "You see what the problem is?" she demanded of the doctor. "No one will help me find my sister. *She* killed those men. Catherine said she did it for me, but she enjoyed it." She looked from the doctor to Rourke and back again, getting more agitated. "You have to believe me. She's the one who is sick. Once Catherine is locked up—"

"Laura, your sister, Catherine, is dead. She died when she was twelve from a fall down the stairs," the doctor said, not unkindly.

She stared at him. "No, that's a lie."

"You pushed her down the stairs at Westfield. The fall broke her neck."

Laura was shaking her head, clearly agitated now. "No, Catherine—"

"Don't you remember helping your mother bury her? You buried her in the field beyond the cemetery, away from the others. Your mother bought a ceramic angel and put it on her grave."

"You can't believe anything my mother tells you."

"You told me yourself just yesterday," the doctor said. "Don't you remember?"

She picked at invisible lint on her mental-institution jumpsuit and began to cry.

Rourke couldn't bear to see her like this. He started to rise to his feet, needing to get out of this room before he broke down.

Suddenly Laura looked up. At first he thought she was looking at him. But her gaze seemed blank, as if she was seeing something else entirely. When she spoke, she sounded like a little girl.

"No, Mother, I can't. Please."

The voice changed again, becoming harsh and grating. "You did this, Laura. You did this terrible thing. You have no choice. You must pretend sometimes to be Catherine."

She drew back, cringing. "You're hurting me."

"You have to be both Catherine and Laura, do you hear me? If you don't, they will find out what you've done. They will take you away and put you in prison or in some mental hospital where they will do horrible things to you like they did to your grandmother."

"I can't be Catherine, please, Mother."

"You will be or the sheriff will come for you. Now stop crying and show me how you can be Catherine."

A change came over Laura. She sat up, her expression suddenly cold and calculating. She turned slowly to look at the doctor.

"Hello, Catherine," he said and motioned that it was all right for Rourke to leave. "We need to talk about your sister, Laura."

CHAPTER THIRTY-FOUR

"Do you hear that?" Sheriff Frank Curry asked from out on the lanai.

Nettie joined him to look out at the ocean. There was nothing but turquoise water as far as the eye could see. Waves rolled up onto the white sandy beach in a soothing roar as the trade winds rustled the nearby palm fronds.

"I hear it," she said as her husband put an arm around her and pulled her close.

"Have I told you yet today how much I love you?"

Nettie laughed. "Only a half dozen times. I think this tropical air is good for you."

"We made it, Lynette. We finally did it." Frank looked down at her, his blue eyes bright. "Did you ever think it would really happen, Mrs. Curry?"

"I never doubted it," she said as she snuggled closer.

He laughed. "I suppose we should go down and get one of those umbrella drinks on the beach."

"I suppose. Or we could stay right here and watch the sunset from that king-size bed over there."

Frank chuckled softly as he leaned down to kiss her. "I signed you up for hula lessons tomorrow while I try my hand at surfing."

"You did not!"

He laughed as he drew her back into their room.

Outside, the waves washed to the shore while the wind whispered secrets in the palms. Inside, Frank swept his wife up in his arms and carried her back to bed.

EPILOGUE

HAWAII HAD BEEN a dream come true. Nettie felt as if she was floating on a cloud for the months since they'd been home. She couldn't help smiling whenever she thought about that week on the beach with Frank.

But she was glad to be back home. Frank had told her he would build her a house, but she'd insisted she would be just fine in his old farmhouse. It needed a good cleaning, and she would put her mark on it as the new lady of the house, though.

She was working a few days a week at the store now, helping to get it stocked. She'd been afraid she would be sorry the store wasn't hers. Instead, she felt relieved when she left each day.

As she was almost finished putting away some of her favorite things in the farmhouse kitchen, Nettie pulled out the junk drawer and froze at the sight of the unopened manila envelope as she saw the return address. The state DNA lab.

For a moment, she couldn't remember what she'd been looking for. The old Nettie Benton would have snatched up that envelope in a heartbeat, steamed it open and read it without even a twinge of guilt.

But after almost being killed, she'd tried to change her snooping, gossipy ways. She'd tried even harder now that she was married to Frank. Still…

She picked up the envelope and turned it in her fingers. It wasn't as if she didn't know what was inside. The state had run a paternity test on Tiffany after she'd been arrested to see if she really was the daughter of Pam and Frank Curry.

Frank, being Frank, had never opened it. "She's my daughter." He'd taken responsibility for Tiffany because Tiffany believed he was her father. She'd been raised to hate him. Worse, raised to try to kill him. Pam had poisoned that poor child against Frank, then walked away.

But what if Pam had lied not just to Tiffany, but to Frank? Nettie wouldn't put it past the woman.

The answer was in this envelope.

Nettie stared at it. Would knowing Tiffany's true paternity make it any easier on Frank? She doubted it. But if she was right, maybe one day...

Moving toward the kettle on the stove, Nettie began to steam the envelope open. She wasn't sure she even wanted to know the truth. What did it matter now?

The glue began to loosen. She slowly pried the envelope open, then lifted out the report.

It took Rourke a few weeks to finish up things in Seattle and get back to Beartooth. The ranch the Realtor showed him was too small. He had changed his mind about what he was looking for.

After a few days of searching, they found the perfect one. He didn't hesitate, even though his future was up in the air right now. As he walked around the property, he told himself that Callie would come back one day.

In the meantime, he would have to build a house,

one that faced the Crazy Mountains, but the size and location of the ranch were exactly what he wanted and needed. Until he got the house built, he could live in the cabin that was already on the land.

Thanks to his parents, he had plenty of money to return to the cowboy he'd been. Come spring, he would plant hay and alfalfa. He would start off running a couple hundred head of cattle and see how it went.

Once the paperwork was all signed, he finally drove into Beartooth to the Branding Iron Café. He hadn't been in since his return. He'd needed time to adjust to Callie being gone.

He hoped that Kate had heard from her, though. He'd told himself to forget her, but it was impossible. Callie had changed his life. He wasn't the same man. He'd fallen in love, and it had made him see everything differently.

Instead of Callie's old pickup, there was a newer-model SUV parked next to the apartment stairs at the back. Not that he was surprised. She'd been leaving the last time he'd seen her. By now she could be anywhere.

The bell tinkled, and Kate called from the kitchen, "Have a seat. I'll be right with you."

Rourke took his usual table. He thought of the first time he'd sat here. Like today, all he'd wanted was to see Caligrace Westfield. At the sound of footfalls, he looked up to see her come out of the café kitchen.

His heart leaped to his throat. He couldn't breathe. She hadn't left? Or she'd left and come back? It didn't matter; he'd never been so happy to see anyone in his life. He realized that must be her SUV parked outside.

He was hit again with the same blindsided feeling

he'd had the first time he'd seen her. What was it about this woman? It was all he could do not to jump up and take her in his arms.

CALLIE WALKED TOWARD Rourke's table, remembering the first time she'd seen him sitting there. She'd felt wary, as if she'd known even then that he was dangerous. She just hadn't known how dangerous.

The cowboy had stolen her heart.

She set down a glass of ice water, handed him a menu and began to pour his coffee without a word.

"Hi," he said, sounding nervous. "I'm Rourke Kincaid. I just bought a ranch to the east of here. I'm going to be running a few hundred head of cattle for starters. Need to build a house. I was wondering if you could tell me where I could get some good Thai food around here."

Callie met his gaze. "Rourke Kincaid, huh." She couldn't help but smile.

"Want me to tell you what else I'm thinking about?" he asked.

She shook her head. "You're thinking about going to Saddlestring Lake tonight since it might be the last time before winter sets in. You're thinking of bringing a couple of cold beers—no glasses—and a blanket."

He cocked his head and grinned. "A blanket? You're amazing. That was exactly what I was thinking. I don't know what *you're* thinking, though, but I never make love on the first date."

"Then we'd better get those first two dates over with before tonight."

"Whatever you say." Rourke pulled her down into his lap.

Callie closed her eyes as he kissed her, reveling in the sensation of finally feeling as if she'd found where she should be always.

"I thought you were a U.S. marshal," she said when the kiss ended and he let her go.

"I don't know where you heard that." He grinned. "I've always been a cowboy."

Callie looked into his dark eyes. He was the most handsome man she'd ever known. "In that case, welcome to Beartooth, cowboy."

"It's good to be back."

She stared into the future, seeing nothing and yet seeing everything. She and Rourke. A wedding. Children. A ranch with a view of the Crazy Mountains. She'd never dreamed it was for her, but now realized she'd never wanted anything more.

All of it would be a surprise. Her second sight hadn't come back, not that she could ever read Rourke anyway. She would have the rest of her life to get to know the man she'd fallen in love with. She couldn't wait.

* * * * *

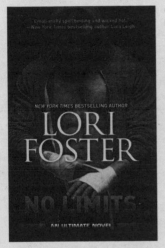

New York Times bestselling author

JEANIENE FROST

brings you into a world of shadows, where anything is possible. Except escaping your fate.

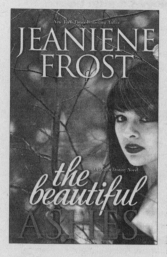

Ever since she was a child, Ivy has been gripped by visions of strange realms just beyond her own. But when her sister goes missing, Ivy discovers the truth is far worse—her hallucinations are real, and her sister is trapped in a parallel realm. And the one person who believes her is the dangerously attractive guy who's bound by an ancient legacy to betray her.

Adrian might have turned his back on those who raised him, but that doesn't mean he can change his fate…no matter how strong a pull he feels toward Ivy. Together they search for the powerful relic that can save her sister, but Adrian knows what Ivy doesn't: that every step brings Ivy closer to the truth about her own destiny and a war that could doom the world. Sooner or later, it will be Ivy on one side and Adrian on the other. And nothing but ashes in between…

Available now wherever books are sold!

Be sure to connect with us at:

Harlequin.com/Newsletters
Facebook.com/HarlequinBooks
Twitter.com/HarlequinBooks

www.Harlequin.com

PHJF905

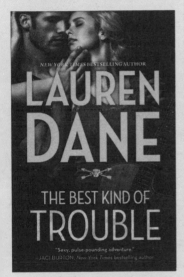

SARA ARDEN

In Glory, Kansas, the best bakery in three counties may not only bring together ingredients for sweet treats, but be the place where a wounded hero can forge a forever kind of love...

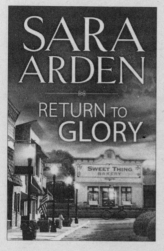

Jack McConnell's back in the hometown he left behind five years ago, battle-scarred and feeling like half a man. But Betsy Lewis only sees the hero who saved her life and set her heart on fire. Now she's burning to save his life in return. She'll use every trick she's got up her sleeve, from her generous natural assets to her talent for baking, to coax Jack out from the bottom of his whiskey bottle.

At first, Jack responds to Betsy like any red-blooded man would. He's always denied his attraction to the innocent girl he used to know, but he's returned to find Betsy's grown into a full-on woman with strength enough for both of them. Until Jack realizes the only way to conquer his demons and be worthy of the hero's mantle she's pinned to his shoulders is to save Betsy one last time—from himself.

Available now wherever books are sold!

Be sure to connect with us at:

Harlequin.com/Newsletters

Facebook.com/HarlequinBooks

Twitter.com/HarlequinBooks

REQUEST YOUR FREE BOOKS!

2 FREE NOVELS
FROM THE SUSPENSE COLLECTION
PLUS 2 FREE GIFTS!

YES! Please send me 2 FREE novels from the Suspense Collection and my 2 FREE gifts (gifts are worth about $10). After receiving them, if I don't wish to receive any more books, I can return the shipping statement marked "cancel." If I don't cancel, I will receive 4 brand-new novels every month and be billed just $6.24 per book in the U.S. or $6.74 per book in Canada. That's a savings of at least 22% off the cover price. It's quite a bargain! Shipping and handling is just 50¢ per book in the U.S. and 75¢ per book in Canada.* I understand that accepting the 2 free books and gifts places me under no obligation to buy anything. I can always return a shipment and cancel at any time. Even if I never buy another book, the two free books and gifts are mine to keep forever.

191/391 MDN F4XN

Name _____ (PLEASE PRINT) _____

Address _____ Apt. # _____

City _____ State/Prov. _____ Zip/Postal Code _____

Signature (if under 18, a parent or guardian must sign) _____

Mail to the Harlequin® Reader Service:
IN U.S.A.: P.O. Box 1867, Buffalo, NY 14240-1867
IN CANADA: P.O. Box 609, Fort Erie, Ontario L2A 5X3

Want to try two free books from another line?
Call 1-800-873-8635 or visit www.ReaderService.com.

* Terms and prices subject to change without notice. Prices do not include applicable taxes. Sales tax applicable in N.Y. Canadian residents will be charged applicable taxes. Offer not valid in Quebec. This offer is limited to one order per household. Not valid for current subscribers to the Suspense Collection or the Romance/Suspense Collection. All orders subject to credit approval. Credit or debit balances in a customer's account(s) may be offset by any other outstanding balance owed by or to the customer. Please allow 4 to 6 weeks for delivery. Offer available while quantities last.

Your Privacy—The Harlequin® Reader Service is committed to protecting your privacy. Our Privacy Policy is available online at www.ReaderService.com or upon request from the Harlequin Reader Service.

We make a portion of our mailing list available to reputable third parties that offer products we believe may interest you. If you prefer that we not exchange your name with third parties, or if you wish to clarify or modify your communication preferences, please visit us at www.ReaderService.com/consumerschoice or write to us at Harlequin Reader Service Preference Service, P.O. Box 9062, Buffalo, NY 14269. Include your complete name and address.

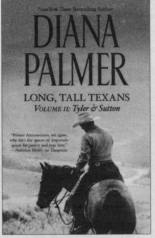

B.J. DANIELS

77846 ATONEMENT	___ $7.99 U.S.	___ $8.99 CAN.
77757 REDEMPTION	___ $7.99 U.S.	___ $9.99 CAN.
77673 UNFORGIVEN	___ $7.99 U.S.	___ $9.99 CAN.

(limited quantities available)

TOTAL AMOUNT	$ _____
POSTAGE & HANDLING	$ _____
($1.00 FOR 1 BOOK, 50¢ for each additional)	
APPLICABLE TAXES*	$ _____
TOTAL PAYABLE	$ _____

(check or money order—please do not send cash)

To order, complete this form and send it, along with a check or money order for the total above, payable to Harlequin HQN, to: **In the U.S.:** 3010 Walden Avenue, P.O. Box 9077, Buffalo, NY 14269-9077; **In Canada:** P.O. Box 636, Fort Erie, Ontario, L2A 5X3.

Name: _____

Address: _____ City: _____

State/Prov.: _____ Zip/Postal Code: _____

Account Number (if applicable): _____

075 CSAS

*New York residents remit applicable sales taxes.
*Canadian residents remit applicable GST and provincial taxes.

H HARLEQUIN®HQN™
™ www.Harlequin.com

PHBJD0914BL